KISS OF NOIR

Visit us at www.boldstrokesbooks.com

By the Author

Femme Noir

Kiss of Noir

KISS OF NOIR

by

Clara Nipper

2010

ISBN 10: 1-60282-161-5
ISBN 13: 978-1-60282-161-3

THIS TRADE PAPERBACK ORIGINAL IS PUBLISHED BY
BOLD STROKES BOOKS, INC.
P.O. BOX 249
VALLEY FALLS, NY 12185

FIRST EDITION: AUGUST 2010

CREDITS

EDITORS: CINDY CRESAP AND STACIA SEAMAN
PRODUCTION DESIGN: STACIA SEAMAN
COVER DESIGN BY SHERI (GRAPHICARTIST2020@HOTMAIL.COM)

Dedication

To my spark, Kristopher Kris

PROLOGUE

I was thirty-six when I left the big city for the Big Easy. They say New Orleans is like a woman—beautiful, deceitful, and deadly. All I know is, I had to leave Los Angeles on the run and the Crescent City beckoned like a broad on her back.

CHAPTER ONE

L ying on my belly, I tried to move, but it was too great an effort. I opened one eye. The other was gummed shut. Blurry streetlights shone in the dark distance. Sirens wailed over someone else's problems. Echoing traffic noise told me I was in an alley.

"Jesus," I muttered through my swollen lips. I tasted the dark iron of my own blood. The asphalt was wet and gritty under my cheek. Garbage smells—rotten bananas, dog shit, bad fish—assaulted me further. For a second, I thought I would vomit, but I willed it back. I tried breathing deeply and decided I had at least one broken rib. A large shadow darted. A cat or a cockroach. I grimly tried to smile.

Little by little, I turned myself on to my back. "Aaaahhh!" I groaned as I lay there, staring up through the buildings at the stars, so far away and indifferent.

I fumbled in my pockets until I found my cigarettes and a wooden match. After my adventure in Tulsa, I had resigned myself to buying cigarettes on the regular. All foolishness of quitting was gone. I flicked my thumbnail across the head of the match and it exploded into tiny fire. I lit my cigarette and inhaled shallow. My crotch felt cold and wet so I touched my pants.

"Lord God, I done pissed myself!" I whispered, shaking my head, my shaved skull rolling back and forth on the ground. Cleo murdered; I'm unemployed and homeless; life is right on track.

And there, laid out on my back in the French Quarter, I started laughing. It started out small and grew to a ripe richness, floating out to mix with the traffic noise.

CHAPTER TWO

Nine months ago

They lost! My hands hung like dead birds between my knees. I stared, hollow-eyed, at the scoreboard. One of my players lay on her back on the court. The rest of them straggled back to the bench amid the tumultuous applause for the other team. A few of my girls were crying and fighting it.

My mind was stuck. I couldn't move. This couldn't be true! This *did not* just happen! Even the tiny buzz I had received from sipping gin-spiked water had evaporated. My team surrounded me. The awkward silence thickened. The happy noise from the winners was terrible. Some of my team stared at their shoes. The cheering continued, fans pouring onto the court to embrace the victors, who were leaping and doing cartwheels. I tasted aloe and tiny green apples. I glanced at the scoreboard, shook my head, and looked at the opposing coach, who was smirking at me.

This roused me. I glared a look of dignified royalty to my nemesis, who was fake blond and fake chipper and utterly detestable. I stood, stretched my arms to take my team into a group hug. Like lost, grieving lambs, they obeyed. I murmured encouragements I had memorized, hoping my team believed them. I didn't. Not tonight.

"The important thing is that we played our best. We gave it our hearts and souls. In order to be winners, we must also sometimes be losers." Blah, blah, blah, blah.

The teams lined up parallel to congratulate and console each other. The insincere mumbling and hand slapping drew us, two enemy coaches, closer and closer together.

I remember you, Camille. My thoughts like dirty knives chopped infection into my mind. We went to college together, played ball together. You were the baddest perky white bitch I ever saw. You got away with more shit in school and in play than anybody because of your bouncy bleached hair, big innocent eyes, and toothy grin that nobody but me saw as the polar freeze that it was. You fouled against your own teammates and you never even got your dainty wrist slapped. I bet you don't even remember that bad ankle sprain you caused me, and I lost play in three games just because you had to lunge for the ball.

We were slowly approaching each other.

And you weren't very good, either. My stomach boiled as I sent Coach Camille waves of hate. I don't know how you *ever* made coach, you fraud. And you're just as big a pussy lover as I am, but you wear makeup and do your hair and wear skirts that show your legs. You're a lesbian coward. My lip curled into a sneer.

I should've buried you tonight, you sorry-ass cracker. I am better than you as a player and as a coach and damn sure as a dyke. I'm braver, bolder, blacker, better, buffer, butcher, and bitchier than you on your best day. I stood up straight, extending my body its full six-foot height and expanding my chest as I drew close to Camille.

"Hey, girl, long time no see!" Camille grinned, her eyes twinkling.

"Yeah, you haven't changed a bit." I stood, full of venom.

"Oh, Nora." Camille pulled a mock sad face. "You just have sour grapes." She shrugged, dimpling. "Nothing new there."

We still clasped hands, each trying to crush the other.

"No, no, it was a good game. Let me just point out that my team is new. Your seniors almost didn't beat my *freshmen*." I laughed, looking at the scoreboard again. "I ain't got nothing to be bitter about because I know for damn sure I won't see you here at the playoffs again next year."

Camille pulled me close, our hands welded together. She threw an arm over my back and whispered in my ear, "Yeah, you won't see me here next year because I got your job. It's a done deal. You're out and I'm in."

I jerked away, struggling for composure, and stared at Camille.

"Oh, they haven't told you yet?" Camille giggled, "I'm sorry."

I snorted. "That's bullshit. Somebody just promised you that while you gagged on his dick."

Camille's eyes went dark as she swung her fist at me and I dodged it easily, laughing. There was a gasp from the players and the remaining fans. I clocked Camille with a hook.

Oh, my God that felt good! I shook out my fist.

Camille hit the floor hard. I was on her, ready to punch all of my rage into Camille. We scrabbled and hit, me remaining on top. It was but a few stunned seconds before people rushed to break it up. I was pleased that I got in some respectable blows before the fight was stopped by meddling crybabies. I stood, panting and smiling, bouncing on my toes, ready for war. I didn't have a mark on me. Camille was weeping and needed help to stand.

"You hit like you play. Weak!" I spat. Camille was carried off the court, her sobs ricocheting around the stadium. The remaining fans, previously galvanized, now broke the spell and continued leaving.

I still stood on the court, breathing deeply and grinning. I felt like a hungry wolf. I was ready to force my team's victory right here, right now, with a brawl. One of my players touched my shoulder.

"It's over. Snap out of it. Come on."

I shook her off. "I'm okay. Everything's cool."

Another of my players, a loose cannon herself, ran up. "Coach D, that was awesome! *Pow!* Goddamn, that was great! You're my hero, giving that sniveling loser something she really deserved—"

"Shut up," I barked. "Everybody to the showers! Now!"

My team filed out. I remained, alone in the middle of the court, waiting. Soon the president of the university, who always attended the games, the vice president, and my own assistant coach appeared out of the wings and approached me. They looked too solemn for me not to know what this meant. I shook my head, tasting blood. I lifted a weary hand to dismiss them. "You don't have to say anything. I'm gone."

"Miss Delaney—"

"That's *Coach*. And really, I'll just get my stuff and be out tonight. That way is easiest on all of us."

"We need a termination meeting. Papers must be signed, there are loose ends…"

I looked at them, my anger ebbing and sad acceptance filling me. "Fuck all that. What will you do, fire me?" I sighed. "I didn't do anything wrong. I'll go, no questions asked. Your problem is that you don't know that sometimes a good punch is the right answer."

No one said anything. I dug my fingers into my eyes. "It's been a great ten years." I sighed again. "I've done an excellent job, haven't I?" I asked the president. Everyone else dropped his eyes.

"Well, this past year—"

"I've been the best, haven't I?" I demanded.

The president stared at me for a moment, then softened and nodded.

"I knew it," I whispered. "Thanks, you can go." I turned and walked out, my head high.

The locker room was thick with steam. The Babel of women's voices sweetened the steamy air. Women strode around in various stages of nudity.

"Hey, everyone! Come here, I have an announcement," I shouted. The hush was sudden. My team gathered at once, one even running out of the shower, her hair still sudsy.

"Now, let's not make this a big thing," I said sternly, "but this is good-bye." A chorus of protests rang in the humid air. I held up my hands. "Shut up. That's the way it is. I've enjoyed working with all of you. Now just carry on. Remember what I've taught you and kick ass next year. I'll be watching."

I left in the shocked silence that followed.

DJ Nix, my star forward, surprised me by catching me before I leaped into my Wagoneer. "Go away, little girl," I growled. "You heard the news. Beat it."

"Coach," DJ said so tenderly that it squeezed my wounded heart. I rolled my eyes, frowned, and waited expectantly.

"Coach," DJ repeated. She reached out and held my limp wrist. DJ shrugged. "After all we've been through."

I was ten years old again, struggling not to cry. "Yeah, so?" Gruff, that was the ticket. I jerked my arm out of DJ's clasp.

DJ's face hardened. She whispered fiercely, *"You owe us more than this!"*

I stared at her as long as I could. Then I nodded, swallowed the dry baseball in my throat, wincing at the effort. I got in the vehicle, started the motor and rolled down the window. I sighed and looked at

DJ, who stood with her hands balled into her pockets, tears streaming down her face.

"I know," I said. "I know. But I can't. This is all I've got."

DJ's mouth twisted as if she'd eaten lemon. "Fine."

I sped off. I hated long good-byes. I wouldn't stand for a bunch of emotional ninnies to cry and pour out their hearts. That would be too much. They had their whole lives ahead of them. Let them work it out amongst themselves. I didn't want to be put on the rack of their grief. I had to regroup and form a new game plan, and fast. I was thirty-six now. What in the hell would I do with myself? Find another California college and start over from the bottom? I clenched my jaws. Absolutely not. The possibility that I might not even be wanted by anyone else in any capacity after this episode was a new, terrifying idea.

Well, I would just find a university on the East Coast and let my record speak for itself. There, that quick it was decided. I returned to my apartment and started packing, feeling stronger by the second.

I had turned on the television for noise company and the sports came on. I heard my name and turned, feeling stunned and boneless. There, big as life, was my fight with Camille. They replayed it, slo-moed it, and analyzed it from every direction. I grabbed the remote and switched channels. Nope, the bad news was on every single station. Some taking it as a harmless humorous prank among pros that provided much-needed excitement and some were seeing it as a racist confrontation and everything that was wrong with sports today. My blood drained from my body. I saw myself with that crazed grin on my face, ready to destroy the world. I cringed. I was so accustomed to the television cameras, I had forgotten they were there. I saw footage of the college's faculty keeping the press away from me and a reluctant interview given by my assistant coach. I hadn't even realized the administration had chased the reporters away or thrown them the bone of a dull, meaningless sound bite with the president.

My telephone started ringing. I grabbed my keys and headed for a bar.

CHAPTER THREE

I returned home hours later, sloppy and stumbling. I had gone to a dive across town that was purely for getting and staying drunk. There was no television, no pool table or dartboard, no dance floor. Just big swallows of hard liquor and pea soup smog of smoke and stale breath.

The men I sat with at the bar asked no questions. Their hands shook and their eyes were either focused inward or thousands of miles away. They were unkempt. These men obviously had no families, no sweet soft women caring for them. They had given up and no one came to see about them. The men had the sour odor of loneliness.

It made me so sad to sit among them that I drank doubles. Visions of The Redhead swam in my mind.

"Gin and tonic," I said, my sober voice cutting through the weepy slurs. "Extra large, very strong."

"Gin and tonic, huh?" The bartender grinned. "How's Bombay?"

I was puzzled and irritated and glared at him. "If that's what you've got, that's fine. I don't care," I said. One of the two men I was sitting between was close to passing out. I tapped out a cigarette and lit it with one deft movement. The bartender stood still, seeming to wait. I looked up and noticed his gaze. "Do I need to beg?"

The light in the bartender's eyes flickered and dimmed. He poured the drink and gave it to me. I laid a bill on the counter and squinted through my own smoke. "Thanks, man." My cigarette bobbed with my words.

"You're welcome." The bartender smiled again. "Haven't seen you in here before."

"No, and God willing, you never will again." I gulped my drink and looked around.

The bartender bristled. "Well, it's not the Taj Mahal, but—"

I waved my hand and smiled. "No, no, man, relax. It's perfect."

"Enough about me," he said. "So what do you do?"

"I drown my sorrows," I snapped. Then I raised my drink and gulped the rest, jingling the ice. "What do you care?"

The bartender flinched. "Just making conversation. What's your problem?"

I pushed my glass to him, nodding for a refill. "Double. And I have no problems. What makes you think I have a problem?"

"Oh, you have a problem. This is the last stop before hell." The bartender set my second drink down hard and it splashed some.

"Yeah, I've got a problem." I sighed. "But I don't want to talk about it."

The bartender shook his head and moved away to wipe a vacant counter section. I was able to drink in peace.

CHAPTER FOUR

After I stumbled into my apartment, I collapsed in bed with my shoes on. To the bar stench that clung to me, I added my own nauseating miasma: rage, sweat, tobacco, gin, and lust. I tossed and turned, my stomach churning, my head spinning, and my mind numb with shock.

I needed a friend. Somebody strong, somebody I wouldn't sleep with. I needed a brother. I staggered to my address book and looked up a name. I weaved back to bed and dialed the number. It was two hours later there.

"Who the fuck is calling me now?" Sloane's voice was gravelly.

"Sloane Weatherly! S'me, Nora Delaney. 'Member?" I closed my eyes.

"Hmm, Nora, Nora…let's see…hell yes, I remember you. You came in a hurry, left in a hurry, and Max still hasn't calmed down."

My eyes flew open. Max! Maybe I should go back to Tulsa and let Max, The Redhead, give me solace and soothe my wounds. I was too drunk and messed up to even fantasize about it. "That right?"

"What's wrong with you, Nora?"

"Nothing that a new job won't fix."

"Oh, Lord, what have you done, fool?"

"You didn't see the TV?"

"Nigga, I got a *life*. And I ain't got no job for you. What do you want?"

I sighed. "I dunno, nothing, I mean, nothing I guess."

"Don't you have any people?"

"Nah." I was wary. I wanted Sloane to know what I needed without my having to say it. "How'r you?"

"Are you drunk?"

I belched.

"Are you calling me in the middle of the night while you're all drunk and shit? Pull your sorry ass together. This ain't cool. Call me sometime when you're sober." Sloane hung up.

She was right. I frowned, feeling self-pity try to gather itself into tears. I wanted someone to tell me it was okay. I wanted someone to comfort me. I wanted someone to reassure me that I was all right. I placed the phone back in its cradle where it rested on my nightstand. I had a cell, but it lay dusty in a drawer. I still insisted on having one main landline that was an old-fashioned heavy black dial telephone with cords. It was substantial and satisfying—like I preferred my women. Big, sensual, smooth, and pleasurable to hold.

I rested, not sure what to do with myself. I felt the bed trying to pitch me off. The phone rang, startling me from the edges of a stupor. For the first time, I hoped it wasn't a woman.

"Yeah?"

"T-Bone! That you? Saw your show on ESPN. Baby, you know how to hit!"

There was only one person who called me T-bone. "Ellis!" I sat up, my head spinning. "Hambone! What are you doing up so late?" I struggled not to slur.

"Oh, you know, just watching you scandalize yourself on national TV. I've laughed my ass off all night and Sayan is mad at you for making black folk look a fool, and when I argued, she kicked me to the couch."

I rolled my eyes. Sayan was Ellis's touchy proud wife. "What did you say?"

"I said that pasty ho had it coming and you were just there to deliver. Anybody could see that. She swung first! And someone would have beat her ass eventually, you were just at the front of the line. I say you did your people *good*."

I lay back and smiled. "Oh, Hambone, you always know how to talk to your wicked cousin."

"So what's up now, you through?"

"You know it."

"You drunk?"

"You know it."

"That's my T-Bone. Girl, get your ass down here. Let my wife fatten you up and let me whup your ass in some street ball."

"You talk crazy, Ham."

"Why? What you got keeping you there?"

I sludgily processed this. "Uh-huh."

"So? Come down to the Crescent City and sponge off me for a while. You know I owe you."

"Ellis, I told you then to forget about it and I meant it. You owe me nothing."

"C'mon, I could use the company. You could be here eating pea and bone by tomorrow night."

"Aw, Ham…"

Ellis's voice was clear and firm. "I want you to come."

I nodded in the darkness. "Thanks, Hambone, I'll call from the road."

"Great."

I hung up and redialed Sloane. "Going to New Orleans to stay with my cousin." My voice was sloppy.

Sloane laughed. "Who is this?"

"Aw, Sloane, I feel so bad. Tell Max—"

"No, man," Sloane said roughly. "Tell her yourself."

I closed my eyes, my stomach churning. "Right."

"So who is this cousin?"

"Ellis Delaney. Mom's sister's son. Runs a pawn shop not far from New Orleans. Gonna take me in." My voice cracked.

"Good. You take care, N. Don't drink it all."

"You got it."

After I put down the phone, I ran to the bathroom and vomited until my belly was sore. When the heaves subsided at last, I scooted back and leaned against the wall and felt worse. My head was a little clearer but that only let me see that I was a butch who couldn't hold a job, a woman, or my own liquor. I was nothing. I began coughing. I fumbled for a cigarette and lit it with my thumbnail against a match, taking small comfort in the warm friendliness of fire. My mouth tasted nasty and the smoke helped. I began shaking and leaned over the toilet to vomit and spit again. All the while, between my first two right fingers, the cigarette smoldered steadily. I started sweating and sat back again. Only religious when convenient, I muttered prayers and rested. I drew a cup of water and rinsed my mouth. I took a tentative swallow. I curled my body back into the tiled corner, huddling on the small cushion, of rug, and spent the rest of the night dozing, waiting for sobriety to return.

At dawn, I stretched, still dizzy with poison. I brushed my teeth, squirted drops in my red eyes, showered, and ate my last six eggs. I packed, not really caring what I kept. My future beckoned; I could buy new things. I made the calls that ended my life in Los Angeles. And then I started to drive.

CHAPTER FIVE

When I reached New Orleans, I didn't know whether I was anxious or excited but I knew another taste would help. Following the directions Ellis had given me, I grew more and more antsy and therefore sipped more and more frequently until I didn't even bother to put the cap back on my bottle of gin. And instead of returning it to my backpack, which rested on the passenger seat, I just let the gin ride, open-mouthed, nestled in my crotch.

I drank a large swallow as I passed through New Orleans and continued south.

"A toast to the Big Easy." I held up the jewel-green bottle to the rearview.

Suburbs thinned and gave way to wet wilderness. My skin prickled as I spied turtles and large birds sunning themselves on fallen trees half submerged in murky swamps. Trees pressed in on me from both sides and Spanish moss dripped from their branches and swayed in the breeze as if confirming that this place was haunted. The wilderness was alien and spooky. It was as if I were seven years old and passing through a monster's territory and that monster was holding its breath, about to attack.

My windshield was already filthy, dotted with hundreds of insects that had accumulated only since crossing the state line and multiplied the farther south I traveled. So when a large bug splatted right in from of my face, I jumped and gasped, swerving the car a little. The spray of window cleaner was comforting, as if it could wash away my sudden, irrational fear of the swamps. I swigged more gin.

"I'm comin', Hambone, I'm comin'!" I cried, giggling. I punched on the radio but couldn't find any sound that didn't jar me further. I snapped it off.

Gradually, homes appeared, then neighborhoods, and then the neighborhoods expanded and merged. I pulled over to study Ellis's directions. I noticed my hands were shaking. "Might as well have a little drink. Calm me down," I muttered.

I continued driving. I was going to a wealthier neighborhood where the homes were very old and very large. The trees got thicker and bigger, the streets wider, the houses farther apart and farther from the street. I pulled into a long driveway, gaping. I sped around to the rear of the house where the three-car garage was. Suddenly, a squirrel ran across the drive and I cried out and swerved to miss it.

Doing so, I crashed into the stone wall that surrounded Ellis's back property. I was too loose and relaxed to be hurt and too nervous about being here to be upset about my old workhorse Wagoneer. I whipped my head around to see the squirrel safely mounting a neighbor's bird feeder. I sighed with relief. I opened the driver's door with difficulty and left it open as I stumbled toward the back door.

"I'm here!" I called giddily, waving the gin bottle. "I'm here, y'all! Ha, ha, I'm here!" I fell into a laughing fit.

The back door blew open. Ellis and a woman came out running. "What the hell?" Ellis roared. Then he fell on me with a big laugh. "You made it, T-Bone! So good to finally see you again!" We hugged tightly. I was moved by unexpected emotion and refused to release either Ellis or my bottle until I was ready.

"C'mon, c'mon, T, it's okay." Ellis patted my back and eased me out of the hug.

"Family jus' look so good to me now," I slurred. "Oh, Ellis, I'm sorry it has been so long."

Ellis nodded and waved me away.

"I meant to visit more...oh, you are so grown up!" I embraced him again.

"It's all right, Nora. You're here now. It's all right," Ellis said. The woman watched us, glaring.

I stepped back and started to take another drink. The woman jerked the bottle out of my hands. "Here, honey, let me take that," she snapped.

I straightened up and threw back my shoulders. "And who is this ripe, luscious peach?" I licked my lips and tried to look cowboy.

In response, the woman poured my gin onto the driveway.

"Uh...Nora, this is my wife, Sayan," Ellis stammered. Sayan's eyes were smoking, her lips poked out, and I was flirty, wanting to appease her.

"Your wife! Your wife! I remember you got married a while back. Oh, Ham, you did good!" I grinned and swooped Sayan into a bear hug, lifting her off the ground and swinging her in circles. The gin bottle flew out of Sayan's grip and exploded on the driveway.

"Put me down, you crazy heathen! Oh, Lord, you put me down *right now*!" Sayan yelled.

I let her go and stood expectantly, waiting for the warmth and welcome to come pouring out.

"Now you listen and you listen good." Sayan stuck her finger in my face. "Ellis told me about your situation and why you need to stay with us. But I don't want you here, do you understand?"

"Sayan," Ellis said.

"Just a minute, Ellis, some things need to be said," Sayan retorted.

"Yeah, Ellis, why don't you go on inside?" I said, feeling suddenly sober. "Sayan and I have business."

"Well, I don't know..." Ellis said, looking from one to the other of us.

"Go on, do what she says," Sayan said. "Pour us some iced tea." Deflated, Ellis slunk into the house.

"All right, what's your problem with me, sister?"

Sayan rolled her eyes. "I have six sisters and ain't a one of them *you*. My problem with you is you're a nasty freak, for one."

"Hold on!" I said.

Sayan's eyes flashed red. "I *know* you do *not* want to interrupt me, *do you*?"

I shook my head, glancing wistfully at my broken gin bottle. "No, ma'am."

"Humph," Sayan replied, slightly mollified. "Number two, I don't know what kind of influence you'll be around here and I need to protect my family."

"Protect!" I choked. "I *am* family!"

Sayan's head swayed like a cobra. "Now, what did I tell you about that?"

I dropped my eyes. "Yes, ma'am."

"You come down here with your sorry drunk ass, tearing up my house, looking for a handout and you're a grown woman! You too old to be acting a fool! You're gonna be somebody's auntie, you know that?"

"Ellis gonna be a daddy?" I whooped, darting a gaze cautiously at Sayan's middle, hoping not to be slapped for it.

"Yes, he sure is," Sayan answered, grinning and stroking her abdomen. "I'm only a month along, but he or she is in there."

"Oh, my, oh, my...Ellis, Ellis, Ellis. Old Hambone a father." I smiled.

"Yes, at last. We're settled and the time is right. We're finally making our family and I don't need your raggedy ole self messing things up and bringing trash into my house."

"But I won't—"

Sayan grabbed my jaw and shook it. "You and me need to get some things straight right here and now before you set one dirty foot in that door."

I pried Sayan's hand off and waited.

"First, you gonna work and you gonna work all day, every day. You're gonna keep yourself clean, and by clean, I mean you shower, use deodorant, brush your teeth, and gargle every day. And you wear clean clothes. I ain't gonna have no funk making me sick. You're gonna wash your own clothes. You can go to a Laundromat or do them here, but if you do them here, you follow my rules and you stay out of my way. I don't want you tearing up my new Neptune or leaving your ratty clothes to mold in there. You keep your room and your bathroom clean. I am damn sure not picking up after you or scrubbing your toilet and I expect it to stay clean. I am not your mama. She don't live here and I pray she raised you right. I will check it every week. All clear so far?" Sayan crossed her arms and threw one hip sideways.

I was too stunned to be offended and too dependent on Ellis right now to object, so I nodded meekly.

"Next, you will quit all this drinking if I have to lock you up or drive you to AA *myself.* And you know how mad I'd be if I had to do that. So you take yourself in hand. Use your time here to get yourself together, and that means no drinking."

"Ever?"

"Never. Not one drop. If you're still here when the baby comes, you can have carbonated grape juice to celebrate with us."

I threw up my hands.

"Then you better get back in that truck and keep on going," Sayan stated.

I looked at my wrecked car, still kissing the stone wall. I had nowhere to go. My shoulders drooped. I looked at Sayan and nodded.

"And you will help me around the house. I was not put on this earth to clean after any laid-up lowlife. You will help just like Ellis helps: washing dishes, vacuuming, and taking out the trash." Sayan held up her hand to forestall all arguments. "I have maid service but that don't excuse nothing. This is not a vacation and you should be responsible for yourself and your messes."

Miserable and full of regret, I gazed at the back door where I saw Ellis grinning at me. I smothered a matching smile and focused on Sayan.

"Furthermore, you will not smoke in my house. Never. And I have a nose like a hound. And if I even *suspect* you got reefer up in here, I will put you out. I am not playing. So if you have to smoke cigarettes, you do it outside and you'll pick up your butts. If I find *one* butt... what?"

I was feeling exhausted, overruled, tipsy, and giddy, and I got an irrational attack of giggles. I couldn't stop myself. I tried to swallow my laughter but I belched instead. "'Scuse me, ma'am." I moaned as laughter overtook me. I bent over and leaned my hands on my knees. I noticed Ellis had disappeared from the door. Sayan barking the word "butt" kept echoing in my mind. *If I find* one *butt; if I find* one *butt*, the unfunny nature of it became terribly funny.

Sayan's stone goddess face broke apart. Peals of laughter rang from her mouth. I was barely able to straighten but I patted Sayan's back and shook my head, wiping my eyes.

Sayan's eyes closed as she surrendered and laughed. Our voices mixed well like harmony and melody. Sayan leaned a little on me.

When at last we began to catch our breath, hiccupping a few more giggles, I embraced Sayan. I held her tenderly. I whispered in her ear, "Listen, Sayan, I'll be good, okay? Trust me. I respect you and all I ask in return is respect. I'm grateful to you for letting me stay here when I need it so bad. Let's try to be friends, all right?" I released her.

Sayan looked as if she might cry. I said just the right thing. Sayan nodded. "Ellis loves you so much. Welcome to our home. I am glad you're here." She stepped away, composed herself, and threw back her shoulders. "Don't make me regret it. We can talk about church another time."

"Oh, Lord." I rolled my eyes.

We walked to the house together, me frisking like a puppy. Ellis opened the door for us, his eyes round and his mouth open with amazement. "Nora?" he said.

I punched him on the arm. "It's all good, Ham. We worked it out."

"Except churchgoing and finding a man," Sayan added.

"We worked it *all out*," I stated. "What you got good to eat?"

CHAPTER SIX

After a quick meal of leftover étouffée and okra and tomatoes, Ellis cleaned up the kitchen while Sayan showed me around the house. She pointed out the custom-made wool rugs, the prints and paintings on every wall, the vases never to touch, the chandeliers that needed constant dusting, the walls covered in silk damask, the draperies of heavy velvet that closed out the harsh Louisiana sun, the antique chairs, tables, armoires, bookshelves, and cabinets in every room, and how I was to behave around each.

"Don't sit in that chair; that's a ladies' chair from the eighteenth century and it is fragile. See how it's low to the ground for a woman's smaller frame?" Sayan eyed it with love.

"Why don't you put velvet rope barriers around everything?" I asked.

Sayan pursed her lips and looked me up and down. "I may have to."

"This place is like a museum," I said, feeling oppressed by the formal, European atmosphere.

"I know, isn't it beautiful?" Sayan crowed. She ran her hand along an intricately carved side table of burled oak that shone like a mirror.

"Where did you get all this junk?" I asked, not wanting to touch any of it. I hadn't known what to expect of Ellis's house, but had hoped for a squashy leather recliner, a big stereo, and a bigger television with remotes for everything, including the lights and the ceiling fan. I had pictured myself snoozing and drooling, if not in Ellis's big daddy recliner, then on a soft, fat sectional while wrapped in a snuggly blanket, the game blaring on television, my hand still in a bag of Cheetos. This furniture was too formal, too spindly, too old, too rich, and too *white*. It looked stiff and uncomfortable. Where was I going to *live* while I was here?

"We got it from Ellis's auctions, of course," Sayan replied, fluffing a brocade pillow.

"Ellis's auctions?"

"Yes, you know, his annual dinner dance sales. Every September he rents a ballroom in New Orleans and has a black-tie dinner and a band and he auctions the best of what he bought the previous year. A lot of families use him for their estate sales. So he gets entire homes full of lovely things."

"And *you* get the first pick of everything, right?"

Sayan grinned slyly in response.

"All right, all right, I can dig it." I nodded and looked around with a fresh eye. "Old Ellis cleaning out the plantations. Good deal."

"Let me show you your room." Sayan led the way past ornate clocks, paintings of horses and dogs, and glass cases of goblets, flutes, and figurines. "Don't bump anything. Don't put your hands on the wall and don't pick that up!" She stopped dead and tapped her foot until I placed the figure of a woman back on to the shelf. "That's an art deco piece." Sayan adjusted it minutely and brushed her finger down the figure.

"She's beautiful," I said, staring hungrily at the voluptuous statue.

"Keep your mind clean," Sayan snapped, shoving me down the hall. We walked and walked until we reached the farthest room in the house. "Here's where you'll stay." She opened a door. The room was less formal than the others and had a recliner and a television. It also had a private bath.

"Mmm, very nice." I was pleased and relieved.

"Notice how it looks," Sayan said. "That's how I want it to stay."

"You think I'll ruin your house, puddin'?" I joked, pinching Sayan's chin.

Sayan's jaw tightened. "I am not your puddin'. And you better not do anything foolish. My mama raised me right and I know how to take out the garbage."

I sighed. "We've already settled this. Let's not get into it again."

I knew how to distract a woman on the warpath. "Does the baby have a room?"

Sayan lit up. "Come on, I'll show you."

We walked by the master suite. Sayan opened the door next to her and Ellis's room. It was under construction with ladders and paint buckets set on swaths of plastic sheeting. The room had a wall of windows well shaded by oaks and magnolias. There was a deep window seat in the middle. The light that filtered in was muted and comforting, creating an atmosphere of enchantment.

"The crib will be there…the rocker there…I'm going to have a chaise put there in case I can steal a nap. Over there will be bookshelves and toy boxes…the changing table is there. When the baby's older, I'll put in a desk and table with Legos and art supplies…what?" Sayan asked, her eyes shining.

I was smiling at her, paying no attention to Sayan's pointing plans. "Nothing," I said.

"Well, let's go find Ellis," Sayan said, closing the door gently as if not to wake the baby.

We returned to the kitchen and off that room was the one I had dreamed of. A big-screen television was showing a baseball game.

"Hey!" Ellis waved from a monster recliner. "Make yourselves to home!"

I ran in, jumped, and dropped like a felled tree, laughing and kicking my feet. "Now you're talking, Ham!"

"I've got work to do, so I'll leave you two alone. Crab Mornay all right for dinner tonight, baby?" Sayan leaned over Ellis. They kissed slowly and sweetly. Ellis's arm went around her back and his other hand cradled her abdomen. She relaxed in his embrace and draped her arms down his back. I concentrated on the game.

"That is just great, sugar. You know whatever you do is all right with me."

"With some fresh corn on the cob, tomato salad, and strawberry shortcake for dessert."

"Mmm, that sounds so fine," Ellis said.

"That okay with you, Nora?" Sayan asked.

I looked up, surprised at being consulted. "Sounds good to me."

"We need to put some meat on your bones," Sayan said. "Don't we, Ellis?"

"Sho 'nuff." Ellis grinned.

Sayan kissed his head and closed the door.

Ellis kept grinning but put a finger to his lips. He tossed me a bag of pork rinds and he opened a mini-fridge within arm's reach of his chair and threw me a beer.

"Oh, yeah, Ham, oh, yeah!" I stretched out, balancing my drink and the rinds on my stomach. I hadn't indulged in pork rinds since childhood.

"This is the life." Ellis flipped his chair all the way back.

"You got it." I sighed, closing my eyes in delight.

CHAPTER SEVEN

"That is it, Nora Delaney. That is my place." Ellis and I sat in his Mercedes at the drive-in barbeque and dairy bar Tassie Pie's, across the street from Delaney Pawn. We were finishing soft-serve vanilla ice cream cones. We had just eaten barbeque bologna lunches and the little cardboard boats were full of trash and sauce at my feet.

"Huh," I snorted, "don't look like nothin'." I licked my cone long.

Ellis glanced at me, his eyes wide. Then he relaxed. "T-Bone, I'll kick your ass."

"How about tonight, you and me, on the driveway?"

Ellis tipped his cone at me. "You got it."

"So that's where it all started," I said, my tone reverent.

"That's where *I* started." Ellis spoke as if in a trance as we both gazed at the shop. It took up half the block. The shop had plate glass windows with goods displayed in them and protected with bars. There were cloth awnings over each window and whiskey barrels full of bright zinnias and marigolds at the curb. Under the awnings, against the building, in the shade, were wooden benches worn smooth paired with buckets of sand for ashtrays and a garden hose curled under one bench like a snoozing snake. There were hanging pots of petunias and more whiskey barrels of flowers between benches. And over it all, near the roofline, was a neon sign: DELANEY PAWN—BEST TERMS ANYWHERE. Above the front door awning were suspended three gold balls.

"What's that mean?" I asked.

"Oh, that's the old symbol for an ethical and trustworthy pawnbroker. Dates back to the Medicis in Italy and St. Nicholas—"

"Santa Claus?"

"No, well, sort of, but St. Nick, who is the patron saint of not only children, but also murderers, the poor, bankers, pawners, poets, and prostitutes, et cetera. It is the symbol of luck and good fortune."

"How you know all that shit?"

"I watch *Jeopardy*."

"Hmm." I crunched my cone. "So it has really worked out well."

Ellis nodded after taking a big bite of ice cream. "Nora, I'm so glad you're here. I've been wanting you to see this for the longest." Ellis bumped me. "Why didn't you come down before now, huh?"

"Foolish. Foolish and thinking I was too busy. I'm sorry."

Ellis smiled. "It's all right. You're here now. And I get to show off a little. That's where *I* began," he repeated. "This neighborhood, starting my business, meeting Sayan and her family, finding a church, working hard, and here I am. All due to you."

"Stop it, Ellis. We agreed."

Ellis nodded. We finished our cones. I brushed my hands over my slacks. "So what do you want me to do?"

"First, come on in and meet the fellas." Ellis retrieved his fedora from the backseat and set it neatly on his head. "You need a hat to protect you from the sun. You got one?"

"Not yet." I smiled, feeling utterly content. I let my eyes drink in the sight of my handsome Ellis, a grown man, silhouetted against his successful business.

"Hurricane's coming," Ellis breathed.

I stiffened. "What?" I said sharply.

But Ellis didn't answer; he just walked toward the store.

I followed, glancing anxiously at the blue sky.

CHAPTER EIGHT

Inside, bells tinkled overhead and I was relieved to be out of the sun and heat. It was dim and cool in the shop. I let my eyes adjust and take in all the merchandise. Musical instruments, tools, jewelry, electronics, appliances, sporting goods, everything I could imagine.

"Just like a department store," I marveled.

Ellis grinned. We walked to the center where there was a big circle of space. Near the back of the open area was a battered old counter with an ancient cash register. Next to that was a large stained card table. Two old men sat at the table playing dominoes. When Ellis approached, they stood.

One old man smiled merrily. He was the color of molasses with a small red afro shot with white. "Ellis," he said in a graceful Haitian accent, "who you got with you, your twin?"

The other man transferred his hand-rolled cigarette to his mouth so he could extend his hand. "I'm Cleo," he said.

I shook his hand. It was a nice shake, firm but gentle. I was careful not to squeeze too hard. Cleo's knuckles were enlarged. His palm was warm and dry and felt safe. Cleo was the color of polished cherrywood. He had several freckles on each cheek and his hair looked like steel wool.

"Nora Delaney," I said, "and you could be Ellis's twin too. You his daddy?" I joked.

"I guess you just hang out with this sucker long enough, you get to look like him." Cleo smiled warmly. His eyes crinkled at their edges. I just wanted to climb into his lap.

"Yeah, I think I'm getting Ellis's bone structure," the other man said, stretching his skin over his cheeks with his fingertips.

"And this is Drew Ekalibato," Ellis said.

"Drew," I said, shaking his hand.

"My man, Ellis!" Drew cried. "What's up?"

"Let's sit," Cleo said. We all sat at the table and I studied the elaborate knot of dominoes that crept over the table. Cleo disrupted my reverie by stirring the dominoes into a messy circle and replacing them in the box with soft clicks.

"I'm loaning y'all Nora here to help out for a while," Ellis said.

"Ha, ha, you don't say!" Drew cried. "What you do, gal? What kinda trouble you in?"

"Uh…" I stammered. "I'm just on sabbatical for a while from my coaching job in LA."

Cleo froze and stared at me. Drew stood suddenly, knocking down his chair. "Jump back!" he cried. "*You* the one?"

"You're Ellis's cousin! You were on television!" Cleo said.

"Hoo, hoo," Drew sang. "You clocked that uppity bitch!" He dangled his gnarled fingers for me to touch with my own, which I did, beaming. Drew strutted around his chair, righted it and sat again.

"Ellis has it on tape," Cleo said. "We watched that a million times. You look different on TV. We didn't recognize you."

I glared at Ellis, who grinned and shrugged.

"Bam!" Drew yelled. "Lights out! Game over!"

"On sabbatical, huh?" Cleo eyed me with suspicion. "Fired is more like it."

I put my hand to my brow, wanting all this to go away. Cleo went to the counter, rummaging in its dark depths. The bells tinkled over the door. A group of men approached, fanned out, and began browsing.

"Doughboy, Rentie, Little C, JJ, Superman, Claude." Ellis recited their names with a smile, nodding at each. They smiled and mumbled back, retreating into the goods.

Cleo returned with a half-full bottle of whiskey. "Let's drink a toast to Nora, new to these parts but never too late!" He swigged and passed the bottle to Drew, who drank and passed to Ellis, who also drank and gave the bottle to me.

"I already had a beer last night and I wasn't supposed to. I promised Sayan…" I protested feebly. The men all looked at each other.

"She trained fast, no?" Drew said. "Sayana is all bark without the bite."

"She doesn't seem that way to me." I shrugged and took a long swallow.

Cleo stared into my eyes. "She ain't," he declared.

"Oh, you in trouble now!" Drew laughed, slapping the table. I winked at him and had another big drink.

"Then no point in moderation," I added.

"Ho, now," Cleo said. "Just a taste. It ain't after five yet."

I looked at Ellis. "What the hell have you gotten me into?"

Ellis shrugged again and stood. "For your own good, cuz." He slid his chair under the table. "Now make her work and you fellas report everything to me." He squeezed my shoulder. "See you at closing."

"My man!" Drew said, waving.

"Later, El." Cleo's eyes lingered on Ellis's back and as if sensing it, Ellis turned and held his gaze for a moment.

"And, Cleo, if that hurricane comes, you know what to do." He winked. Cleo nodded with a smile.

"Huh?" Drew glanced outside. "Ain't no storm—" Cleo's elbow in his ribs silenced him. Drew looked at me. "Oh." He smiled. "I get you. Sure, we'll take care of everything."

When Ellis had gone, Cleo relit his cigarette and dumped out the dominoes. "First you learn to *play*."

Six hours later, I had learned how to operate the old cash register, which consisted of hard smacks on its metal sides; I had lost all the money I had to Cleo and his devilish dominoes; from Tassie Pie's across the street, I had enjoyed a shrimp po' boy so fat with big shrimp that they dropped out of each end of the sandwich into my lap as I tried to eat it. The shrimp were so clean and fresh I worried they were still alive. I had learned how to write tickets for customers once Cleo determined the amount of the pawn, which I was not to do yet, and now Cleo had me dusting, armed with a can of polish, a rag, and a feather duster. I was offended at first, but it was only a reflex. Once I began, I thought about it. I was really enjoying myself. I was relaxed and could feel the long-buried but familiar stirrings of happiness and contentment. Ellis was my safe haven right now and I would help in every way possible. I breathed deeply, smelling lemony wax. Leaving me were the worries about managing student athletes; going was the anxiety about keeping motivation high; going was the thirst for the drinking binges before, during, and after every game; going was the killer drive that had been exhausting me; draining away was the stress about winning and staying on top; fading was the ambition for possible promotion to a larger, more prestigious college; gone was the ass-kissing I did to the faculty so I could be left alone to run my team as I saw best. Gone! I released my shoulders and smiled.

Here I was with family and allowed a long time-out. A period to take stock, to get my constitution together, to rejuvenate and discover my next direction.

I hummed while I worked. I heard the door bells and turned to look.

An old white man went to the counter and waited while Cleo finished rolling a cigarette.

"Stub, you back again!" Drew looked up from a *National Geographic*.

Stub grinned, his few remaining teeth pearly white. "Yessir," he told Drew. "I need to rely on you fellers once again."

"All right, what you need this time?" Cleo leaned on the counter and squinted through his smoke.

I approached quietly from the side.

"Lessee…lessee…" Stub stroked his grizzly chin with his left hand. "I need smoke. I need food. I sure am hungry, Mr. Cleo, sir, and I need some shine. A man can't live without a little fun, now can he?"

"Sure can't!" Drew called.

"Here, Stub." Cleo reached under the counter and held the half-finished bottle of whiskey they had used for toasting me earlier that day. "On the house. That will get you started."

"Much obliged, much obliged, Mr. Cleo, sir. You have a kind and understanding heart."

"Just walk on the side of the roads, in the ditches if you have to, all right, Stub? Don't get hit again, hear?" Cleo opened the bottle and put it into Stub's left hand.

"Yessir, I mean, nossir. I will stay to the sides." Stub gulped the liquid, his Adam's apple bobbling in his bristly, scrawny neck. My mouth watered in response. I still had the taste. I hoped it would let me be soon.

"Okay." Cleo scribbled on a ticket. "Are you having any parties?"

"Ah!" Stub sighed, set the bottle down. and wiped his mouth with the sleeve on his left hand. "Mmm, lemme see…I might be overdue for a party or two, yessir."

"My man, you rhymin'!" Drew said. Stub laughed until spit flew from his mouth. His greasy hair came unglued from his bald scalp and fell forward as he bent over, slapping his left knee.

"How's this?" Cleo handed him a slip with a figure. I studied the man. Unless he had a ring in his pocket, he didn't have anything to pawn. Stub frowned at the number. "Now, Mr. Cleo, you know I don't have much learning, is that a three?" He poked at the paper with his left index finger.

"Yep. And it wouldn't hurt you to get reading specs. Here, look at it now." Cleo removed his own glasses from his shirt pocket, unfolded them, and helped slip them on Stub's face.

Stub grimaced and pinched his eyes to slits. "Yessir! Yessir, I sure do see it now, good and clear." He glanced at me, and Stub's eyes were so magnified by the glasses, they looked like bloodshot blue ping-pong balls. Startled, I stepped back.

"That is more than generous, Mr. Cleo. That will do nicely. I sure do appreciate it."

"I know, Stub," Cleo said as he gently removed the glasses and replaced them.

"I can get the money," I said. I set my dusting tools on the counter and banged on the register. I was desperate to know what Stub was pawning.

In horror, I watched as Cleo flipped up the right sleeve of Stub's shirt, unfastened his artificial arm and removed it, putting the limb somewhere in the back. I stood at the open register, my mouth gaping.

"Look at him!" Stub pointed at me with his shoulder stump. "You sure shocked the shit out of him!"

"I'm a woman," I replied, grinning. Stub quit smiling and looked me up and down. "Sure shocked the shit out of you too, huh?"

Stub laughed. "Gimme my money. I gotta go shopping."

"How you going to pay it back this time, Stub?" Drew asked. "You're a genius for finding and stretching a penny."

"Like I always do. Sell my blood for some of it. What's it to you, old fart?" Stub shrugged the shrug of people so overloaded with big problems that every detail of life seemed miniscule and inconsequential.

"Here you go, Stub. You take good care now and we'll see you soon," Cleo said.

"Thank you, sir." Stub raised a limp salute. "Bye, y'all!" he said with a toothy smile.

"Bye," we responded.

Drew shook his head. "That's sad. That is so sad. Vietnam, you know."

Cleo dropped his eyes. "Yep. Served well and turned into a poverty-stricken, drug-addled, drunken swamp rat with more medical problems than all three of us together." Cleo snorted. "The government."

"My man," Drew sang softly, mournfully.

"That's some shit," I said, watching Stub limp down the block.

"Well, we do what we can." Cleo sighed, sitting again. "Smoke?" He held a hand-rolled cigarette to me and I accepted with relief. "Let's play." Cleo stirred the bones.

"I ain't got no scratch left!" I exclaimed, having been skillfully distracted from Stub. "You took it all."

"We'll play for nothing. Just practice," Cleo purred.

I laughed. "All right, you crafty old fart."

CHAPTER NINE

The rain was falling in heavy sheets. The store was empty. Ellis was at the other shop with an appointment.

I sat at the table with Cleo and Drew, playing dominoes. I was fussy and bored. I never won this game and the rain made me restless.

"C'mon, what you got, N?" Drew nudged me out of my petulant reverie.

"Play 'em if you got 'em, my sister, but don't show your panties all at once," Cleo muttered.

"Sweet, why you talk that smack all the time? All these years I never know what you're saying. Some voodoo?" Drew asked.

Cleo just smiled wide, his gold tooth glittering. I slapped a domino onto the end of the crooked black avenue they had already created.

"Oh, too slow, too slow." Cleo grinned. "I bump."

"My man! You won again!" Drew shook his head.

"Play without me this time," I snapped.

"How you ever going to learn if you don't play?" Cleo asked.

"I ain't learning shit but how to lose my money to you, and I could have done that without these lousy dominoes," I said.

Cleo laughed, air hissing out between his teeth. "You got that right."

"Cleo been playing forever, ain't you? Thirty years?" Drew asked.

"More than forty years. Tried poker but that ain't for me. Bones is my game and she is a hard mama."

I stretched, my spine popping. "I need a break!" I felt for my cigarettes and put one in my mouth. Good thing about Ellis, he permitted smoking in the shop. I got a wooden match and rested my thumbnail on it as I watched Cleo for the thousandth time roll his own. I never tired of seeing him take out his ancient leather tobacco pouch, remove papers, sprinkle some tobacco into the crease of a tissue-thin rolling paper, roll, and seal it quick and fluid like a magic trick.

I slammed my match and cigarette on the table as I stood. "Be right back," I said.

"Hey, Nora, where you going in this hurricane weather?" Drew called as I left.

When I returned with a paper sack, I went to the back to remove my wet shoes and shirt and to dry my head. I walked back to the table barefoot, wearing my wife-beater and jeans. I placed a pouch of tobacco and a package of papers in front of Cleo.

"Teach me something I can use," I said.

"My man!" Drew said.

Cleo laughed and nodded. "All right, all right, all right." His voice was always soft and gravelly as if he were casting spells or suspended between worlds and half his voice addressed the living and half the dead. "Sit down, girl, I'll get you going. First, that is wrong." He pointed to the tobacco. "But it'll do."

Cleo told me to watch him and he showed me over and over and I tried until we had a pile of cigarettes, his perfect, mine wilted, leaky, and lumpy. Drew witnessed all this with an amused smile.

We practiced rolling for over an hour.

"Now you're getting it," Cleo rasped. It was a companionable silence, occasionally one or the other of them murmuring whatever occurred. The rain drummed for entry. All was quiet and sleepy.

"Here comes trouble," Drew said suddenly, his voice loud with tension and disturbing the peace.

Cleo and I followed Drew's gaze. Cleo groaned.

"Who else would come out on a day like today except that fool?" he said.

I looked at the approaching man. Tall, pale, reed-thin, with lots of dark curly hair water-matted to his skull.

"What's wrong with him?" I asked.

"Nothing, nothing." Drew laughed, shaking his head and waving his hand in dismissal.

The door opened and the overhead bells rang.

"'Sup?" the man said, shaking his slicker like a dog.

"Aw, man!" Drew said, shielding his face. "Take that shit somewhere else."

"Where's Mr. El? I got something to talk over with him."

"Out," I answered. "Can I help you?"

"Who the fuck is she?" The man jerked his thumb at me.

Drew covered his eyes. Cleo shook his head. "Now, Johnny, don't do this."

I stood slowly, once again relishing my full six-foot height. "Who. The. Hell. Are. You?"

"Say, say, say, I didn't mean nothing. I'm Jonathan Fallana, but you can call me Johnny. I just need to see El real bad and I wondered where he was, that's all. He has something I *need* in the back, if you know what I mean."

"He's out." I looked down from my Amazon height into Johnny's melty green eyes. "If you got something to sell, I can help you."

"No, no, not today. Say, why don't we just chill and play some bones?"

"Sounds good to me," Cleo said, setting aside the rolled cigarettes and stirring the dominoes. "You in trouble again, Johnny?"

"Fine," I said, "you'll have to find your own chair."

"Sure, I get you. I'll just pull up this"—Johnny grunted and slid over a large black box—"speaker and sit on it. Cleo, man, you know they got me hooked on a murder? And I got the proof. I mean, Ellis has the proof, but I got to get it from him before they arrest me. But I'll catch him later. Let's have some action. What are we betting?"

"Nothing," I answered sharply.

"Just a gentleman's game," Cleo said, smiling. He winked at me.

"Skip me, I got to book," Drew said, checking his watch. The rain had not abated. The shop's windows were beginning to fog. "I got to do a little something, something."

"Don't go, Drew." I pleaded with my eyes.

"Well." Drew checked his pager. "Let me make a call." He stepped into the back.

"Say, man, sure. We'll be here," Johnny said.

"Why don't we play for lunch?" I said.

"I'd love a free lunch." Cleo grinned.

"I'm all about that," Johnny answered.

Drew sat down. "What did I miss?"

"Johnny is buying us lunch. Either him or Nora," Cleo said.

"Got her taken care of?" I asked Drew.

"You know it," Drew stretched out his palm to me and I slid my hand across his.

"I never understand how an old man like you gets all those PYTs. What are you, double Cleo's age?" Johnny said.

"I am old enough to know what women want," Drew answered pointedly.

"Drew got to keep the females happy," Cleo said.

"Ladies?" Johnny wolf-whistled. "They better keep me happy is all I got to say."

"That right?" Cleo said, watching the dominoes reveal themselves. "Mild and careful, that's what she says."

"Hell, yeah, I'm the one with the dinero." He rubbed his fingers together.

"Quit woolgathering, your turn," Cleo snapped.

The dominoes' clicking voices were the only sound for a while. I knocked. Then to Johnny, "You have money?" I was incredulous.

"I got a little income." Johnny smiled.

"Nickel for Drew, two dimes for Cleo," Cleo said, recording the points in the curious hieroglyphics of dominoes.

"We did agree that the winner buys lunch, right?" I asked.

Cleo glanced up, his brows thunderous. "Hell no, we agreed that the woman buys lunch."

"No, loser buys lunch." Drew looked hard at Johnny, who was studying his hand.

"Oh, right." I smiled.

"That ain't me," Johnny said, laying down a tile.

"Dime for Johnny," Cleo said.

"So what gives you this income?" I couldn't let it go. I slid a domino to one end.

"Hmm?" Johnny was observing the game.

"Zip for Nora, zip for Drew," Cleo said.

"She wants to know how you get your lucre, man," Drew said.

"My money makes money, that's all," Johnny answered.

"Oh! You're a trust fund baby, then," I said, full of contempt.

"Naw, I wouldn't put it that way," Johnny said.

"Meemaw and Peepaw still pay your bills, that's cool," Drew said with a nod.

"Are we gonna play or not?" Johnny was flushed, his eyes flashing.

"Play then, it's your move," Cleo said, perching a cigarette on his lip. Johnny clacked a domino onto the table and watched Cleo record no points earned. "Lotta money out there," he whispered, "lotta money out there. Give me some of that, sweetheart."

"Nope, can't, old man, 'cause it's all mine." I grinned as I placed my domino on the edge of the angular path, closing the points.

Cleo whistled. Drew smacked the table. "My man!" he exclaimed.

"Say, that is rotten. That sure is rotten," Johnny said, frowning at the game.

"Game is not over yet," Cleo said. "Plenty more money on the other end. Let's go."

"I sure am getting hungry," Drew said, licking his lips.

"Dime for Drew. Now, shut your legs, honey, hold on to that," Cleo said.

The play progressed quietly until Drew knocked. Then Johnny. Then me.

"Hee, hee, hee, it's down to me, I guess. Domino!" Cleo rasped.

"You sucker!" Johnny whined.

"My man!" Drew smiled.

"Let's count the points," I said.

Cleo obliged. "Uh-oh, Johnny, this is really gonna cost your folks."

"That's all right, that's all right. Say, what's everybody want?" Johnny stood and put on his rain slicker.

"Barbeque," we three said in unison.

"From Tassie Pie's," Cleo said, his eyes resting on the joint directly across the street from the pawn. Too many times to count, hungry customers came in to pawn something small, like a watch or a tool; something that would bring them just enough money to go to Tassie's and have a feast.

"Just what, ribs, baloney, pork?" Johnny asked.

"Some potato salad," Drew said.

"And some coleslaw," I added.

"And chips and pickles and peppers and bread," Cleo said.

"And cold drinks," Drew said.

"All right, let me go." Johnny dashed into the pouring rain to cross the flooded street.

"I'll say one thing, he's a good sport," Cleo said.

"You fixed it, didn't you?" I asked.

Cleo laughed. "Now why would you think that?"

"Thought so."

"My man!" Drew boomed.

While Johnny was gone, silence settled back into the room. I resumed rolling cigarettes, Drew stared at the rain, Cleo trimmed his nails with a knife.

"Sure is quiet," Drew murmured.

"Don't nobody need money on a stormy day," Cleo answered.

"There! Look at that!" I held up a perfect cylinder.

"I'll take that." Cleo put it in his mouth. "See how she smokes. Now you just got to do it fast."

"When will Ellis be back?" Drew asked.

I shrugged. "Miss him?"

Drew flushed. "No, just seem like he's been gone too long."

"Worried about him?" I asked.

"Shut up."

I grinned at him. "I'm sorry, you're old enough to be my daddy. I guess I should show more respect."

Drew turned to Cleo. "Did I just get an apology and an insult?"

Cleo nodded, smiling. "Little brother is feeling fine today."

The phone rang, startling all of us.

"Pawn," I barked into the phone. I grimaced and held the receiver away from my ear. "But...yes, ma'am...I'll tell him...right away." I hung up.

"Who was that?" Drew asked.

"Cindy," Cleo said without looking up from his hands, beneath which was a pile of curly nail parings.

"How did you know?" I asked.

"Who is Cindy?" Drew said.

"Johnny's girlfriend," I answered. "Seems like he is in trouble."

"Oh, she's always like that," Cleo said.

"What did she want?" Drew asked.

"For Johnny to come home and explain himself. He moved out again," Cleo told them.

"What's that mean? Again?" I said.

"Well, Johnny and Cindy have this on-again off-again thing, you know? And they're all the time either perfect love birds or he is breaking her heart leaving. Cindy has settled on him, but he ain't settled on her. And she is one determined white bitch. She means to keep that man if it harelips the South. But see, he comes in here and he is for real. He tells it that he doesn't love her and she just takes him back, no questions asked, and lets him walk all over her, so of course he goes back whenever he's bored between affairs. He is in love with his own self and he has no trouble getting cute things to line up and love him for his looks and his easy money that he ain't earned. But Cindy is convinced that it's true love and nothing he does will wise her up. So he hooks up with her, does what he wants, breaks up, does what he wants, gets with her again, and so forth." Cleo finished talking, ground out his butt and brushed his clippings into the trash.

"He must come around when I ain't here because I don't know all this. And ain't that some shit?" Drew said.

"Aw, you ain't seen nothing yet. Jonathan Fallana is a piece of work."

"Or maybe a piece of shit," I said. They all laughed. The rain streaked down the windows in heavy rivulets. A dark form ran for the door and shoved it open. The bells tinkled.

"I'm a drowned rat!" Johnny shouted, holding sodden steaming bags of food. Cleo and Drew and I all exchanged glances and laughed again.

"Give me some help!" Johnny said, dripping a puddle on the floor.

"Sure, man, sure thing." Drew jumped up and took half of the water-spotted sacks. He held a greasy one up to his nose. "Mmm, this one's mine."

"Like hell," Cleo said. I cleared the card table.

We sorted out the food and each settled into lunch and silence. It was blissfully quiet. When there was nothing but trash and bones, Cleo and I smoked our hand-rolled joints.

"Yeah, nothing like that first taste of smoke to cleanse the palate and settle the belly," Cleo said.

"Now all I need is a cushy woman to nap on," I said. Murmurs of assent. "By the way, Cindy wants you to call."

Johnny shrugged. "Was she crying?"

"No, she was yelling."

"I'll wait until she's crying." Johnny smiled, his eyes gleaming.

"You are wicked," Drew said, shaking his head.

"That woman is going to beat your ass one day," Cleo said.

"That's a lie. She's too hung up on me to do anything. I got her right here." Johnny wiggled his pinkie. "Anybody else call?"

"No. But why don't you introduce me to Cindy? Sounds like she could use a friend," I said casually.

Drew and Cleo watched in shock.

"What? You gonna be her friend? Sure." Johnny leaned back on the speaker, a toothpick perched jauntily between his teeth.

"Cool, when?" I said, smooth as a shark.

"Wait, man, Johnny, don't you know—" Drew began.

"Nora and Cindy will be friends, ain't that sweet?" Cleo interrupted.

"Oh, my man. I got you. Sweet, yeah. Just don't be sweet to my baby's mama," Drew said.

"I still can't believe an old man your age made a baby with a twenty-year-old girl. You're a fossil like me. Why don't you marry her already?" Cleo asked Drew, who ignored him, instead focusing on Johnny and me, winking and grinning.

"Huh? What's up? What you all talking about?" Johnny said.

"Nothing, nothing, just be cool. I'll just do Cindy a favor, that's all," I answered.

"Yeah? Like what?"

"Like wise her up," I said.

Johnny laughed. "Better women than you have tried that. Look at me." He stood. "Look at my face. Look at this cleft chin. Look at my profile. Look at my hair." Johnny ruffled his damp black curls. "Look into my eyes." Johnny stared at me with his big green soulful eyes. "Look at my hot bod." Johnny raised his shirt to a chorus of groans from Cleo and Drew. "Feel my muscles." Johnny flexed his bicep and thrust it in my face and I obligingly pinched it. "Look at this ass." Johnny turned around and bent over. Cleo and Drew left the table in disgust. "And best of all, look at this." Johnny fumbled in his pants.

"You're not goin' to show me your dick, are you?" I said.

"No, something the ladies like even better." Johnny removed his wallet and split it wide to reveal a thick wad of green bills.

"You are such a pig!" I said.

Johnny shrugged, his eyes twinkling. "Don't matter. Don't you get it? All this buys my laundry done and pressed, my shoes shined, my house cleaned, my food cooked, my regular poon, and all the strange I want. It buys me a play-wife and my freedom all at once. Hell, it will even buy my car washed if I want. Am I right, brothers?"

Drew threw the lunch garbage away, not answering. Cleo sat down, sucking on a toothpick.

"Brothers, am I right?" Johnny said to Cleo, whose eyes sharpened and he removed his toothpick and pointed it at Johnny.

"No, man, we ain't brothers. We ain't nothing alike. I am a *man* and you are a foolish *boy*. I respected my mama and when I found someone, I respected that woman enough to marry her and treat her right and stay married 'til the day she died. I didn't play around and she didn't either. That ain't cool, what you doing, Johnny. When you mess with the female and treat her like trash, you make bad voodoo for yourself. Just don't be near us when it all comes down." Cleo replaced the toothpick. Johnny sighed and shrugged, stunned by Cleo's words but trying to act unfazed. I cleared my throat, feeling uncomfortable about my own female messes that might rain hell down on me.

"Well, I got a good situation and I like it just as it is. Cindy ain't going nowhere because she's on the payroll." Johnny cupped his crotch. "Know what I'm saying?"

I sat forward. "No, fuck all that, pretty boy. What I would do is," I dropped my voice to a whisper, "wise her up." Then I licked my lips.

Johnny jumped away from me, sneering. "Oh, you nasty bulldyke! You crazy! You'd get nowhere, believe me. Cindy don't play that way."

"They never do until they meet me," I said.

"Sure. Well, you can try if you've got your panties in a twist, but it's a dead end. *I know.*"

"I can seduce *anyone*," I said, feeling my fangs. "And she is a woman in need."

"Hold up, hold up," Drew said. "Johnny, man, you don't *care* if Nora makes a move on Cindy?"

"That's cold, Johnny," Cleo said.

"What the fuck, we ain't *married*," Johnny said.

"But she's living in your house, sleeping in your bed, washing your skidmarked drawers, and cooking your supper," Drew said.

"She's free and I'm free," Johnny said, his voice stern. "I don't ask her to do none of those things. She do them because she thinks it will keep me. Well, look, it don't."

"You're a pure-D bastard," I said.

"Like I said, it don't matter. I still get all the bj's I want."

"Johnny, you talk too damn much, but that Q was good," Cleo said, closing the subject.

"Yeah, man, that was some fine shit," Drew added.

"It was okay. I've had better," I said, thinking of Tulsa.

Johnny snorted. "Sure."

"Let's play bones," Cleo said.

"All right, I'm in," Johnny said.

"When is Ellis getting back?" Drew asked. I rolled my eyes.

The rain poured down, flooding into torrents at the curbs. Trash was swept toward the drain gutters, washing the town clean.

Chapter Ten

"Mrs. Clyde, may I present Nora Delaney, my cousin and apprentice? Nora, this is Mrs. Clyde, a well-established long-term client and dear friend. Nora, behave," Ellis said.

"Oh, Ellis honey, how many times have I *implored* you to call me Julia?" she said, batting her eyes and raising her hand to my chin. I cupped the hand with a caress and kissed the air above her skin. I held the hand a few seconds too long, appraising the woman and assessing the possibilities. From the ground up: expensive and edgy. Older woman, mid forties, but very sexy. Muscular, meaty legs with a fine, round, fiery fanny perched on top. Luscious belly pouch, sweet, curvy waist, breasts like the prow of a great ship draped with a vulgar excess of jewelry like a dime store Christmas tree. Succulent pale neck and a pouty, sulky face. All blond in the head. Her eyes were huge, navy blue, and slightly crossed like a Siamese cat's.

"Me yow," I drawled.

"I beg your pardon?" Julia asked, withdrawing her hand and staring at Ellis.

"Nora, what did I tell you? I'm sorry, Julia, my cousin doesn't have any raising. Please excuse her. Nora, apologize to Mrs. Clyde. She is a lady—"

"That she is." I grinned.

"Nora, go get my briefcase out of the car. *Now.*" Ellis pushed the keys into my hand and shoved me toward the door. "I am truly sorry, Julia," Ellis repeated as I slouched to the exit. "I had hoped for Nora to assist me with your account, but now that is out of the question. Please accept my apology."

"Accepted, Ellis. We go back too far for anything to come between us. But do keep that horrible person out of my affairs," Julia said.

"You have my word," Ellis said. "Now, shall it be the same terms for these items?"

I looked back at the two of them before I left. Julia turned her head and met my glance. Pure hatred glittered in the woman's crossed cat eyes. I blew her a kiss and closed the door behind me.

In the car, I realized Ellis never left his briefcase in the car. It was with him at all times, as if handcuffed to his wrist. So I just sat and waited, feeling like a chump. I smoked but got no pleasure from it. I knew Julia better than Ellis, and I knew what that woman wanted and how she wanted it. After all these years, I didn't make mistakes about sizing women up. Ellis was just too polite and married and that made him blind. Julia's wealth gave her a screen of propriety, but that wasn't her. I knew it. I may have lost my coaching career and some of my dignity, but not that. Never that.

After some minutes, Julia emerged from the anonymous storefront. She saw me sitting in the car, waiting like a lapdog, and she sneered. Julia approached the car slowly, pulling gloves on like a reverse striptease. I licked my lips and stared at her, waiting.

"Your cousin," Julia said, frigid with contempt, "will be out shortly. We have concluded our business for today."

I continued to stare, feeling the power of my own silence.

"Well, good day." Julia smacked sunglasses on to her face.

I remained quiet. All eyes.

"I said good day!" Julia repeated, getting shrill.

I said nothing. I didn't blink.

"What is the matter with you?" Julia charged the door and punched it with her gloved fist. I didn't flinch. "Ellis knows the proper way to treat me, someone of my class and stature," Julia continued harshly, hoping to prod some shame from me. "He is courteous and professional!" Julia shrieked. "He has race manners!" she added acidly, in desperation.

I allowed a tiny smile to curve the edges of my mouth. I did not speak. I looked away from Julia and stared front, cutting Julia dead.

"Why, you…you *beast!*" Julia exclaimed. She fumbled in her pocketbook for her keys and dropped the whole thing. Femme supplies clattered everywhere. Lipstick, compact, tissues, lotion, wallet, coins, gum, perfume, business cards, and a rabbit's foot scattered all over the concrete. I watched all this and extracted another cigarette and thumbed a match. I blew out the match and tossed it into the handbag mess on the sidewalk. When the match landed next to her compact, Julia gasped. "You are abominable! Incorrigible! You should be flogged! Have you no shred of decency? Respect? Kindness! I'm going to march in there and tell Ellis all about you, you creep!"

I enjoyed this smoke immensely. It was perhaps the finest of my life. Julia was scrambling, trying to gather her things with gloved hands.

I smoked, still silent and staring off into the distance.

"Oh, help me," Julia cried, slumping to the sidewalk in her skirt and pumps. "Please help. I must go. I have an appointment. Can't you give me a hand with this?"

I raised my eyebrows and squinted my answer. I liked Julia just where she was. A snotty dignified woman looking perfectly ridiculous sitting on the sidewalk and grappling at her belongings like a soft-shell crab.

"If you don't help, I shall cry!" Julia said, her mouth drawn and ready for tears.

I scratched my jaw, wondering what was keeping Ellis. I watched Julia on the ground. A moment passed. I finished my cigarette and tossed the tiny butt out the window where it landed near Julia, who whipped off her gloves and threw everything back in her purse triple-quick. Her jewelry rattled and clanked with her movements. "All right, then," she said, "I see." She snapped her bag closed. The fury was gripped as tightly as her pantyhose gripped her thighs. "So that's what you are." All blond ice. She stood, towering over me in a well-groomed rage. She smoothed her suit over her big curves. She flipped two fingers toward me with a beautiful embossed business card clamped between them. "My number."

I took the card and put it in my pocket without looking at it. I stared up at Julia, who sniffed, turned, and clicked away, her caboose switching with anger that just made me want to hit that thing.

Ellis emerged at last, his briefcase in tow. He locked the shop and started the car. He couldn't lecture me because I laughed all the way home.

CHAPTER ELEVEN

The sun was sharp and pointy, cutting the skin and blinding the eyes of anyone unfortunate enough to go outside.

The bell above the door rang. Johnny came in, accompanied by a tall, thin, swivelly woman with brown sugar bed hair. I thought at first glance that she was a pretty young man, but then recognized the hips and jawline as female. I ran a hand over my stubbly skull and smelled my breath. I regretted getting so comfortable and therefore lazy with my grooming, just as Sayan had feared. I straightened my collar and tucked in my shirt. No one else was even paying attention to the visitors.

"Nora, what's your name?" Johnny asked.

"Delaney. Nora Delaney." I puffed up, trying to loom large. "Of LA," I added and held out my hand.

The butch smiled sourly and clamped her hand onto mine. "Payne Phillips of Bayou La Belle D'eau."

"Pain, you say?" I asked with emphasis.

Payne spelled her first name. "Old family tradition. It's my mother's maiden."

"Well, that is darling," I said. "Here, let me offer you my chair."

"No, thanks, I'll sit here." Payne boosted herself onto the counter.

"Yeah, everyone? This is my bud from the old neighborhood, Payne Phillips. Payne, you've met Nora, this is Cleo Sweetleaf and Drew Ekalibato," Johnny said.

"I'm of New Orleans and he's of Haiti," Cleo said.

"Pleased to meet you all." Payne followed her statement with a dazzling smile.

Cleo grunted and Drew shook her hand.

"What are you talking about, old neighborhood, Johnny? You live in your mama's house just down the street. You ain't moved a foot since you was born. Good thing she passed and left you a place to live, eh?" Cleo said.

"I live here because I like it. I could live anywhere I please," Johnny said.

"Can I get the little lady something to drink?" I asked.

Payne burst into laughter. "Are you talking about me? Miss Delaney, you can relax. Johnny brought me in because he thought we could be friends. I'm not gonna step on any toes. Come on now."

"Sure thing," I said. I looked into Payne's eyes and they were sweet around the edges and smoldering in the centers. "Let me get you that drink. Would you like some strawberry milk? Or a fruit soda?"

Payne scowled. "I'll take whatever you're drinking."

"Say, say, me too," Johnny added.

"Get it yourself," I called from the back. I brought Payne a beer. "Here, let me open it for you."

"Give me that." Payne grabbed the bottle, snapped off the cap, and flung it at the trash. It went in pretty as you please. Payne smiled and drank.

"I like a peaceful pawn. Don't you two go turning this place into a harem," Cleo said.

"I won't if she won't." Payne grinned and lit up the room. I rolled my eyes.

"You know dominoes, Payne?" Drew asked. Johnny had gotten himself a beer and sat on a speaker. Cleo, rolling a cigarette, stopped to listen. I leaned against the counter, my arms locked across my chest, wishing I had better shoes and a fresh shirt.

"Sure I do! I grew up around here, didn't I? What do you play?"

"St. Mary's," Cleo answered.

"Do you know Memphis Twist or Ragtime?" Payne asked, leaning forward in eagerness.

"Sure." Cleo smiled warmly, his eyes twinkling. "Do you know Crown Jewels or Midnight Special?"

"I know Crown Jewels," Payne replied. "What do you want to play?"

"Well, these here," Cleo indicated Drew and Johnny and me, "only know what I've taught them, and that's St. Mary's."

"Fine with me. What's the pot?" Payne asked, rubbing the faded, aged dominoes with reverence. They were soft and blurry with use.

"Nothing. But sometimes Little John buys us lunch."

"Mmm-hmm, some good shit too, huh, my man?" Drew said.

Johnny sipped his beer. His phone rang.

"If that's Cindy, you better go on home, boy," Payne said.

"Oh, fuck y'all." Johnny stood and went outside to answer the call.

"Deal you in, Nora?" Cleo asked.

"Come on, my man, let's kick some ass," Drew said.

"No, I'm feeling sick," I said.

"Hope it's no one you've eaten," Payne quipped, passing dominoes. Drew laughed and Cleo giggled.

"My man!" Drew held out his hand to Payne, who slapped it.

"Oh, give me a break," I spat. "I'm getting some air!" I headed for the back door so I wouldn't run into Johnny. I heard Payne say, "Touchy, isn't she?" I stopped to listen further.

"Not usually," Cleo said. I exhaled.

"Well, you know, you can't get two of us in the same room, we'll swagger each other into oblivion."

Cleo grunted.

"Ob...obliv what?" Drew asked.

"Never mind," Payne said. Dominoes clicked.

"Slide in easy, honey," Cleo murmured. I went outside where the sun stabbed me.

When I returned, Cleo was smoking a cigarette and frowning over a gun and a wedding ring that a woman was trying to sell.

"Please, you gotta help me," she said, looking over her shoulder. "I got four kids." She glanced around again. "They've gotta eat."

"Sure, I can take them off your hands, but it won't be much."

"I'll take whatever you can give me. I don't care." The woman ran a hand through her hair. She leaned to look outside where a battered old station wagon held four quiet children, all sitting in their seats, facing forward. I got a chill seeing this.

"You want a loan or a sale?" Cleo asked.

Drew, Johnny, and Payne were all fiddling with toothpicks or cigarettes or dominoes, their eyes downcast.

"I can give you more if you sell them." Cleo had the ring on the first knuckle of his pinkie finger.

"Sell. I will *never* need these again." The woman chewed her lip.

"Well, how about that?" Cleo wrote a figure on a pad and slid it over to her.

She swallowed hard and blinked. Then nodded. "Oh…okay, if that's all you can…"

"Yep, that's the best I can do. Take it or leave it."

"No, no! I'll take it. That's fine. Thank you, sir." The woman bit her nails.

"Wait." I stepped up. "Here, take this." I handed the woman two hundred dollars. Then I slid the gun back to the woman. "And keep this. You may need it. Got any ammo we can give her, Cleo?"

Cleo glared at me but pushed a small box of bullets across the counter.

"Good. Now take this, get food and a tank of gas, and go somewhere safe far away. And no matter what, don't go near him ever again. You or your kids, got it?"

The woman began crying. "Oh, God, oh, God, bless you, bless you, bless you all. I'll pay this back, I swear I will."

I waved her away. The others watched me like a pack of coyotes hiding in the bush.

"I never thought my life would be like this, you know?" The woman sank to the floor. I gave her a hand full of tissues from the box under the register. Sometimes people cried when they pawned things. It paid to be prepared. "I thought he was nice, you know?"

I sat with her on the floor, patting her knee. Cleo handed her the cash for the wedding band. She cried for a few moments in silence. The telephone rang and the woman jerked and jumped to her feet. Cleo answered the call. The woman embraced me while babbling, "I'll never forget you. May God bless you for your kindness. I'll pay this back. I swear. I have to go. Thank you, thank you." The woman scurried out, trailing tissues.

I strutted to the table and sat with a gusty sigh. "Well, what did I miss?"

"I'm buying lunch," Payne said with a brilliant grin, "for those who played."

I looked at Cleo, who was still at the counter with paperwork. He winked.

"Yeah, I didn't want to be suckered again, so I sat out too," Johnny said.

Drew smiled. "My man beat her and I didn't do too bad."

"So what are y'all gonna eat?" Payne asked.

"Chicken," Cleo said. Drew shrugged his assent.

"Chicken for three, then." Payne stood and towered over me. "Nothing for the hero?" she said. I glanced up, my eyes narrowed. The men watched us.

"You got a problem with me?" I asked. Johnny shook his head at Payne, who glowered at him.

"Let's keep it friendly, y'all," Cleo rasped gently.

Payne said, "Cleo is right." Everyone relaxed. "But I know that woman and she's a worthless waste of skin. She—"

I stood, savoring my height. My muscles were tense. "Rather like yourself?"

Chairs scooted as the men cleared the area, going to stand by Cleo behind the counter. Cleo dropped his pen and walked to us. Payne and I were glaring at each other.

"Come on now." Cleo gripped our necks. "Snap out of it. No one has anything to prove here. If y'all can't find a way to be civil and easy, I've gotta ban Payne from the store. I can't ban Nora, so that's how it is. Be bigger than that." Cleo let go and walked back to the counter.

Payne grinned and slapped my shoulder. "Hey, sorry. Let's start over."

"Sure, it ain't no thing." I slugged Payne on the arm.

"You did a good deed," Payne said.

"Thanks."

"It was a mistake," Cleo said, sitting at the table.

"What?" I felt punched in the stomach. Drew pulled up a chair and Johnny sat cross-legged on the speaker.

"We ain't a charity," Cleo explained. "Now maybe word will get around. Can't be doing that. Everyone who comes in is a hard-luck case. Maybe they all deserve a break, but this is a business. And they understand that when they come in. Now, maybe the husband hears about this and comes after us with a shotgun. Or maybe just you."

"My man is right on," Drew said, his eyes shining as he looked at Cleo.

"We can't afford to for lots of reasons," Cleo continued. "And I *know* you can't afford to. So don't play that."

"Ha," Payne whispered.

I threw up my hands. "I can't afford *not* to! Are you all crazy? Did you see her?"

"Are you gonna save all of them?" Cleo asked. There was a hushed pause.

"No, maybe just one," I replied.

"All right then," Cleo said. "What's done is done. Let's play. Why don't you two both go for lunch?"

Payne and I stared at each other. Steel met steel.

"What the hell," I said.

"I'll drive," Payne said.

CHAPTER TWELVE

In Payne's SUV, I watched the scenery pass. Louisiana was flat and marshy, as if the whole state were hanging by a thread, ready to snap off and plunge to the ocean floor. The humidity was like Oklahoma—you needed to grow gills to breathe and somewhere on my body was always sweating. The insects had already taken over Louisiana as if it were a corpse they were eager to clean. Everything came bigger—ants the size of grapes, slugs as big as snakes, mosquitoes like little anti-human aircraft, and the cockroaches! I shuddered as I remembered Ellis's stories about them. Armored tanks they were, and big enough to be considered meat. And they *flew*. But Louisiana was also viciously green. As fecund and fertile as the valley Nile. There were oak and cypress trees with ladles of Spanish moss dripping from them, but there were also poisonous things twirling seductively around anything they could climb. And I had heard the jokes about the kudzu growing so fast that it twined around your ankles and choked off your screams as you tried to outrun it. I tried not to believe these stories. What did I know of the South? Everything in Louisiana was perpetually springing into bloom and exploding outward and upward, and the dark, dank swamps seemed like primordial soup from which life itself oozed. Anywhere there was a speck of dust, there was a seed on it bursting into life. And Bayou La Belle D'eau was mostly coastline, so to get anywhere, I had to drive past the swamps, thick with gnarled and twisted cypresses with enormous tortuous knees squatting above the placid black water. I saw millions of turtles sunning themselves and dropping nonchalantly into the water if I approached. I saw huge herons, still as statues, fishing, and flocks of pelicans basking on land bars. I heard birds I never knew existed and sometimes great crashing through the dry areas that sounded like buffalo, but I was assured it was not. Something scarier, I decided.

But twilight was the worst. That's when I imagined the terrible creatures on the hunt rising out of the steamy swamp. When I heard what I learned were owl screams, I almost jumped out of my skin. I was convinced that one evening, my headlights would pick out some enraged carnivorous beast that no one knew existed and had quietly been feasting on humans for centuries. Charles Darwin should have studied here, I thought. So I tried to travel only in daylight and I tried to stay put once I got somewhere. Once I was at Ellis's at night, I never went out again, even as a favor to run an errand. Ellis didn't press it.

"I love this area. The swamps are so beautiful," Payne said dreamily.

I grunted.

"There are lots of people who live by their wits in there to this day," Payne said, sweeping her arm toward the water.

"Really."

"Yeah, there are Cajun camps all through these swamps. They hunt and fish and almost never come to town. These wetlands go on for miles. Even experienced swamp guides can go in there and get lost forever." Payne's voice was thin.

"Yeah?"

"Uh-huh. And some people don't even have camps, they live on floats year-round."

"What's a float, another word for boat?"

"Like a houseboat. Wouldn't that be great?"

I looked at Payne sideways. "No."

"When I retire that's what I'll do." Payne's voice was determined yet soft.

"What, you'll trap and kill your own meat?" I laughed.

Payne was serious. "Sure will. I do it on weekends now. Mostly nutria, but sometimes I get bigger animals."

"What's nutria? Kelp?"

"No, like a very big rat. But good stuff." Payne smacked her lips.

"Sure, sure it is." I rolled my eyes.

"You should come with me this weekend."

I stared at her. "Thanks, but no. I have to wash my hair."

Payne glanced at my gleaming bald scalp and laughed. "Chemicals."

"Huh?" I asked.

"I'm in chemicals. Big business down here."

"Hmm."

"And you?"

I sat up straight. "I coach ball." I refused to put it in past tense.

"Oh yes." Payne nodded, her grin sparkling. "I *saw* you." Her voice was snide and she said nothing more, driving in silence.

Finally, I responded. "Ah, another fan. You follow my team pretty hard?"

"Nope."

I asked nothing more. The swamps surrounded us now as we headed for the Gulf. I couldn't place where we were going.

"Since having you skin and gut rodents this weekend didn't appeal, how about we go to the club?"

"There's a club in this tiny Catholic backwater?" For the first time, I gave Payne my complete attention.

"Sure, several." Payne turned on to a bumpy two-track dirt road. "Roll up your window, the dust will get in."

"Where are we going?"

"To Fat Mammy's, of course. Don't you know the best food is never on the main drag?"

I thought about it. Payne was right. In Los Angeles, the best authentic Mexican and the finest true Chinese were always holes in the wall down an alley or tucked into a corner without a sign. And without advertising of any kind, those places were always packed with people. People happy with food. The kind of food that was so good you didn't want to eat it in front of anyone at a table, but get it to go and have a porcine orgy with it once you got to the privacy of your own home. But the food was so tempting, it made you suck in your breath in the car and you ended up tearing through the sacks at a stoplight for a morsel to tide you over. Then, at home, you just took off your shirt and dove in, moaning like someone in a porn flick and slathering sauce or salsa or mole or curry all over yourself. Each thing you tasted was better than the last. The delicate crispness, the blend of sweet and spicy, the pungent marinade, the heavenly juice, the sticky rice, the healing soup, the buttery fish, the crunch, the silky sauces, the chiles. When finally, there was nothing left but debris, the only thing to do was shower and go to sleep. My belly grumbled at the memory of my pet places to which I would be forever loyal. The family-run shops who knew me when I came and in exchange for cash, gave me the gift of their phenomenal food. The places with real food, true food, not fussy food, not chain food, not salad, none of which satisfied anyone, but home food and while you ate it that was your home too. The tiny places know that food was a sacred love. That was their secret.

"Here we are." Payne pulled into a bare dirt parking lot riddled with deep ruts and mud berms and puddles. There were lots of cars, each parked carefully straddling a puddle or a rut and pointed in any direction. It was a bumper car jigsaw puzzle of vehicles.

The building was a one-story concrete block structure painted hot pink with a flat roof and lots of big windows. In the window next to the door was a hand-painted sign—Fat Mammy's. That was it, no slogans, no open or closed, no hours of operation, no welcome, come in! Just the surrounding forest and the crowd of cars and the splendid smell of frying chicken.

"You can stay here. I'll be right back. Can I get you something?"

"Yeah, get me some of what they do best." I held out cash.

Payne waved me away and winked. "Forget it. I can buy lunch for a hero."

I watched her, lanky and lean where I carried muscle. Payne was loose-limbed as if she were a marionette barely held aloft. I was strong and swift and hard and heavy like a panther walking upright. Payne was swively and dippy and light and utterly relaxed. I snorted. A boy, I thought.

I waited, watching people come and go. I was surprised to see it was divided equally between black and white customers. My stomach growled. I hoped there would be flaky butter-soaked biscuits, steaming fresh mashed potatoes with thick gravy, crisp, tangy coleslaw, and tender, juicy, melt-in-your-mouth chicken hidden under a scalding, crunchy crust. I rolled a cigarette, smiling and thinking of slick thighs, kinky pubic hair, big round asses, and jutting, chewy nipples. I lit up, hoping Payne didn't allow smoking in her car. I opened the glove compartment to pass the time. The gun looked to be a .38. I stared at it until I finished my cigarette and then closed the compartment as Payne sauntered out of the restaurant with several plastic bags. She put the food in the backseat and started the car.

"You know, the leprosarium is not too far from here," Payne finally said.

"No."

"Yeah, in Carville."

"Hmm."

We rode in silence most of the way. As we neared the pawn shop neighborhood, Payne, staring straight ahead, said, "The gun is for my job."

"Don't even care. I'm sure a chemical company requires you to do a lot of assassinations."

"Don't joke about it."

Payne parked in front of the pawn, but left the engine idling. "Listen, I've gotta take care of some business, so you take lunch in and tell Johnny I'll catch him later. Just leave me a sack."

I gathered the food. "Uh-huh, some new bump-bump."

"I'll pick you up tonight. Here or at Ellis's?" Payne answered.

"For what?"

"The bar. Let me buy you a drink."

I held up the bags. "It's my turn to buy."

"Sure, okay, say about ten?"

"Yeah, fine. But I'm gonna score and sharing a car won't work. I'll meet you here and follow you."

"Thought your car was in the shop."

"So? I can borrow a ride."

Payne's lip curled. "Okay, later." She sped away in a cloud of dust.

The men clamored for the food as soon as I opened the door. There were indeed biscuits and coleslaw and mashers and superb chicken and plenty of everything. Plus sweet potato pie that was as rich and creamy as candy.

After the meal, I chewed a toothpick and watched Cleo eat his pie with a knife.

"Don't you want a fork?" I asked. Cleo shook his head.

"My man." Drew groaned, stretching.

CHAPTER THIRTEEN

That night, I thought long and hard about what to wear. Not for the women I would try to pick up, but for Payne. After half an hour and my bedroom littered with all the clothes I owned, I decided on jeans and a tight white T-shirt with black boots and a black belt. I shaved my head carefully, showered, and dressed, closing the bedroom door behind me so Sayan wouldn't give me grief for the mess.

"Hey, Sayan, how you doin'?" I found her reading in the living room.

"You just saw me at supper, you know how I'm doing."

"Where's Ellis?"

"Still working, poor baby. His dinner is in the oven and I'm waiting for him. Where do you think you're goin'?"

"Uh…I'm gonna meet a friend and we're going out. Can I use your car?"

"You want to use my car to pick up perverts?"

"No, no. Pick up women." I laughed and stopped under Sayan's glare. "I'm supposed to meet Payne Phillips at the shop. Then she's gonna show me around town."

"Oh. Payne. Well, okay then. The keys are in my purse in the bedroom."

"Thanks. Say, why is it okay for Payne and not for me?"

"'Cause she's white and a fool. You're black and you're family."

"Uh-huh."

I got the keys and as I was at the front door, Sayan shouted, "Mind you fill up the tank when you're through. And deodorize it too. And don't mess with any of my stations or my mirrors. And I don't have to tell you what will happen to you if there's even one scratch or dent—"

I gently shut the door against the rest.

The car was a Lincoln and immaculate. Sayan had giddily informed me that she was going to trade it in for a station wagon in a few weeks. I would've preferred Ellis's all-black Mercedes with smoked windows and rumbling bass, but this would do.

I sat scrunched in the car and said, "Sorry, sister Sayan," as I adjusted the seat and mirrors for my six-foot frame. On the road, I gripped the steering wheel and sped by the swamps at ninety miles per hour. I drove with the headlights on high beam to reassure myself.

At the shop, it was dark. I parked in front and let myself in to get one of the beers Cleo kept in the fridge when I heard a rustling. A dark form suddenly emerged from the back room and was in silhouette from the lamp behind him. My heart raced until I recognized the fedora.

"Cleo! Goddamn, you scared me!"

"Nora?" Ellis said. "What in the hell are you doing here?"

"Oh, Ellis. That's you? You looked like Cleo in the dark."

"Now why would Cleo be here at this hour? Or you?" Ellis flipped on the light.

I breathed, my hand to my chest. "Chill. I'm meeting Payne outside for a night. I came in for refreshment." I walked to the fridge and helped myself to a couple of bottles. "Want one?"

Ellis shook his head. "I get you." He made a little dance move. "Going to the clubs?"

I grinned my response and swallowed a third of the beer. "What are you doing here so late? Sayan is waiting for you. And why are you in the dark, man?"

"Oh!" Ellis looked at his watch. "I gotta go. Just checking over accounts. No big. I had just turned everything out when I heard you. She and I have a date tonight." Our eyes met and we smiled and said "mmm-hmm" in unison.

"She's a fine woman, bro, you couldn't've done better," I said.

Ellis's face went soft. "I know." He put his hand on my head and shook it. "Lock up and set the alarm."

"I'll follow you out. I can wait in the car." I got another beer and said good night to Ellis, who had parked in back. I watched his taillights speed home to his beautiful, bounteous wife. I got a sharp pain in my chest considering that gentle home life and I cracked open my second beer to wash it away.

I heard Payne's music before I saw the car. I rolled my eyes and followed.

The bar had no name or sign on it. The building, like Fat Mammy's, was buried in the wilderness. But rows and rows of parked cars glittering in the one pole-mounted light indicated that no one from anywhere in the state had trouble finding it. I marveled at the power of the gay grapevine. Just build a bar and tell one person. By the time you open, there will be a line waiting to get in.

I parked, got cigarettes, matches, and mints and checked myself and met Payne.

"This is Marcie's," said Payne, who was sharp in a loose white button-down shirt and tight jeans and boots.

"Nice," I said, nodding. "Look, we're twins."

Payne looked at me, frowning. "Oh, for God's sake." I was surprised at her show of real anger.

"Hey, I was only joking. Let's go inside."

"No, forget it. You go in, I'll meet you in there."

I spread my arms. "What are you gonna do, go shopping? It doesn't matter. C'mon, get your sorry ass moving."

"I said I'll meet you in there. Get me a light draft beer." Payne walked off, muttering and pulling the shirt off over her head.

I pulled the door open and was assaulted by smoke and music. It was crowded but as I pushed through, I found a tiny, wobbly table in a dark corner away from the speakers but facing the dance floor.

When the waitress came, I ordered a pitcher of regular draft. Payne wouldn't know the difference.

The beer arrived with Payne, who was now clad in a black T-shirt.

"Now we're T-shirt twins," I said, pouring for her.

"Fuck off." Payne gulped her drink. "Gimme one of those." She gestured to the hand-rolled cigarettes.

"You smoke?" I passed her one.

"Only when I drink." Payne clamped it between her teeth. "Light?"

"Sure." I flicked my thumbnail across a wooden match head and held it to the fag.

"You gotta show me how you do all that." Payne squinted at me through the smoke.

"All what?" I was beginning to feel very fine.

"Roll 'em, light 'em, you know."

"Sorry, butch trade secret."

Payne laughed. She gestured around the bar. "Well, whaddya think?"

"I have been to a bar before. They're all the same." Flashback to a Tulsa Redhead.

"See anything you like?"

"Not yet, you?"

"Sure do. That little filly over there." Payne pointed to a thin woman with long, dark hair.

"Mmm," I grunted. "I guess she's better than a poke in the eye, but way too skinny."

"No, she's just right. You like the pie wagons, huh?"

I grinned. "I do hate the sticks. There's no juice. You eat the meat and leave the bones. The bones are for the vultures. It always strikes me as a bit...necrophiliac to like skinny women. I want a woman that I need a grappling hook to climb. Someone who has the fire to go all night, every night. I love the ample pulchritude that makes a woman a woman."

"Uh-huh." Payne smoked and drank. "I like tits."

"You want a skinny woman with tits? You got to be man enough to love the entire package. You got to love the real."

"I guess I'm just not man enough, then. I like 'em small and tight and athletic—"

"With big tits."

Payne shrugged. "If they've got 'em it's a plus. But the most important thing is *no fats*."

"You crackers are all mixed up and crazy like that. You've got the entire culture FUBAR. And meanwhile, you're missing the sweetest, wettest, hottest poon this side of heaven."

"FUBAR?"

"Fucked up beyond any recognition."

"Oh, ha, ha. Well, forget it. If it is no sex or sex with chubniks,

I'll pass on all of it forever. That shit is nasty. You don't know which sweaty fold to fuck."

"You've got more wrong with you than I suspected if you can't find a hot twat."

"I find all I need between the legs of women who are in shape."

"Just because a woman has curves doesn't mean she's not fit," I snapped.

"Listen, I'm not going to argue with you. You like what you like and I like what I like and we won't change each other. Between us, we can split all the women."

"So to speak."

Payne laughed. I watched her try to catch the dark-haired woman's eye. Payne tossed her hair, stared, made a big show of cigarette posturing. Finally the woman looked around, smiled, and looked away.

"Looks like I'm gonna go dance."

"Go jump those bones." I watched Payne sidle to the woman. She bought her a drink and leaned over her, forcing the woman to look up to see Payne's face. She moved her slim hips slightly toward the woman and smiled her knockout smile as she spoke to her. The woman nodded and stood up. Payne held her close and swayed, rolling her pelvis gently into the woman. Payne looked over the woman's shoulder and winked at me, and I held up my glass. When the song was finished, Payne spoke to the woman, who shook her head and walked back to her bar stool. Payne shrugged and returned to the table.

"She's very hot. I'll take that filly home tonight or I'm not Payne Phillips. See a wide load with your name on her yet?"

"Nope."

"Oh," Payne mocked sympathy, "I guess that means you *won't* be scoring tonight. Share how that makes you feel inside."

"Bite me, pedophile," I retorted. I was feeling better and better.

"What did you call me?"

I faced her. I could feel how fine I looked. I could discern my bald head gleaming, my face sitting exactly right on my chiseled bones, my T-shirt clinging in all the bulging muscular places, even my beer at the perfect level. And damn, I knew how to hold a cigarette and a woman. I knew it all showed tonight. It had been a long time since I felt all of it together. So I inhaled deeply off the pure tobacco that Cleo had showed me how to roll into an obedient cylinder and repeated, "Pedophile."

"What the fuck?" Payne was irritated, but distracted by her beer that she was drinking too fast, her cigarette that she couldn't keep lit, and the woman who kept staring at us.

"What else do you call someone who wants their sex to come in a tiny, curveless, weightless, odorless, hairless package? An entire industry of pedophiles."

"Oh, that again." Payne leaned back and sighed, unconcerned with my taunting. "What can I say? I don't like hair in my food."

I sipped my beer. Payne finished hers and refilled both our glasses. She drank half her own right away. "Listen, you think I'm so predictable?" Payne said. "You think I'm nothing but vanilla?" Her eyes sparkled with a secret.

"Go on," I said.

"Sometimes." Payne looked around the bar then leaned in close. "Sometimes I get all femmed up in drag. You know, makeup, hair, dress, shoes, purse, jewelry, the whole nine, and I go out. I find some really hot butch and I let her take me home. Then, the next night I come out as my regular self, you know, like this and I find that butch and I watch the shock spread all over her face. Then I say to her, 'yep, last night you fucked a faggot.'" Payne laughed and laughed.

I swallowed some beer and topped off both glasses. I motioned to the waitress, who nodded. "Looks like your filly is ready for another dry hump," I said to distract Payne from needing any response from that revelation. Payne dropped her cold cigarette and stood, walking with purpose to the woman.

They danced and I lost them in the crowd. I watched the people, idly wondering what their stories were. What was each of them on the misery scale? I spotted a sulky blonde at the bar reading a book. Oh, this I had to see. I drained my glass and the dancing crowd parted as I walked.

I reached the woman. Someone was on the stool next to her so I stared down the offender, jerked my thumb, and said, "Out. Mine." The offender grabbed her glass and scurried away with a frightened look. I sat on the empty bar stool. "How you doin'?" I asked my prey, tapping a cigarette on the bar.

The blonde appraised me with a scowl and returned to her book.

"What are you reading?"

The blonde sighed and showed the cover, her eyes closed in impatience.

"Stephen Hawking, are you kidding me?" I snorted.

"Why?" The blonde was beautiful. Her hair was long and curly, her face was daintily sculpted and her lips were plump, wet, and shiny with potential. She had big brown eyes, her body was nothing but curvy handrails, and all of it was hostile.

"Well, c'mon, this isn't a college class, it's a *bar*."

"I'm well aware of where I am. Anything else?" The blonde's flawless eyebrows were raised with withering politeness.

"You want a drink?"

The blonde's small hand instantly covered the top of her glass of wine. "No, thank you."

"Then how about a dance?"

"No. But again, thank you."

"Aw, come on." I placed my hand on the blonde's back where it sizzled. She jerked up straight and stared at me until I removed my hand. I motioned to the bartender. "Tank and tonic."

The blonde had resumed reading, her cheeks burning.

"Isn't ignoring me a lot of work?" I persisted.

The blonde rolled her eyes and slammed down her book. But her mouth twitched. "Yes, but it's worth it."

"Why do you come here if you don't want company?"

"That's my business." Her words were crisp and starchy.

I decided that my harmless goof approach was working best on this one. It had such honest non-threatening appeal. Then, when the blonde was relaxed, I would come out in force like a striking rattlesnake.

"You know." I paid for my drink and motioned for another glass of wine over her indignant protests. "I read a lot too."

"Is that right?" The blonde, full of sarcasm and contempt, held her eyes open only a slit to regard me.

"Yep, I've read all of Stephen King's books."

"Oh, my." Her eyes opened wide. "We're just alike!"

"Let's see…I also like dining out, sunsets, bubble baths and long walks on the beach." I surprised myself by laughing at my own joke.

"Do you also like being rejected?" She smiled for the first time.

"Love it."

"Good, then stay right here." She finished her drink and sipped from the glass I bought her. I was encouraged. I glanced out of the corner of my eye and saw Payne staring at me from the dance floor. When our eyes met, Payne turned the filly in a half-circle and buried her face in the woman's hair. I watched long enough to notice that Payne's filly was now staring at me. I turned back to the blonde.

"I'm Nora, what's your name?"

"Gwendolyn."

"It is not, what is it?"

"Penelope."

"C'mon, just tell me your name, please?"

The blonde, holding her wineglass to her lips and facing the bar, had a tiny smile on her mouth. "Jill."

"All right, forget it. I'll call you Hellion, how about that?"

The blonde turned and bored into my eyes. "That will do perfectly."

"Feel like a dance yet?"

"Not at all. Feel like giving up and leaving me alone?"

"Absolutely not."

"Then we're at an impasse." Hellion picked up her book and resumed reading.

"You know, Hell, no one's going to break into you like an armed robber. You have to invite us in."

"Like a vampire?" Hellion replied, never stopping her reading.

"Exactly."

Payne came over, nodded to me, and hugged Hellion, who was startled into reciprocating, her book crushed between them.

"Hey! How are you?" Payne grinned.

"Good. And you?" Hellion had mentally dismissed Payne and was smoothing her book on the bar.

"Just great. You're treating my bud here okay, aren't you?" Payne said.

Hellion shook her head. "Please." Her tone was unmistakable. She read again.

Leading her filly by the hand, Payne walked to my other side and squeezed in between stools to be closer. "How you doing?" she whispered.

"You know that woman?" I was incredulous.

Payne puffed with pride. "Of course I do. She comes here some. I've known her for a while."

"What's her name?"

Payne shifted uncomfortably. "Don't know," she mumbled.

"You don't know!" I laughed and swigged my drink. It felt so good to feel good.

"She's never told anybody. No one knows her name," Payne whispered.

"Well I do," I boasted.

"Yeah, right," Payne replied. Her filly wedged between them and held out her hand to me. "I'm Carol."

I took the hand, grinned at Payne, and kissed it. "So sweet to meet you, Carol."

"Thank you. I love your haircut...I mean your head...I mean..."

I nodded. "I get you. Thanks."

"Let's dance, babe." Payne dragged Carol away.

"I hope that didn't make you jealous," I said to Hellion, who was immersed in her book. When I got no response, I said, "I say, I hope that didn't make you jealous. You know you're the only one for me. It didn't mean anything. I was thinking of you the whole time. I was drunk. You've got to trust me. I've got to have some space."

After ten beats of silence, Hellion looked up. "What?"

I held her arm. "C'mon, I've got something I want to give you."

Hellion pulled away. "I don't want anything."

"You want this, I promise. C'mon outside, let me show you."

"Bring it in here."

"Will you just relax? It will take two minutes. C'mon, Professor." I pulled her toward the door. Making a move like that was always risky and when it paid off, it was sweet heaven. The woman, mute, followed me. Payne watched this with disbelief.

"What is it?" Hellion asked once we were outside in the sultry darkness. The throbbing music we left behind seemed to cause the building to pulse.

"This," I growled, pushing Hellion against the closest wall. I pressed her breathless and waited for the outraged shove. When it didn't come, I lowered my lips to Hellion's, our mouths hot with passion. I swooped and dove, eating her up, but she met me, kiss for kiss, breath for breath.

At last, I raised my mouth but still mashed her tight. "I know you," I whispered.

"Oh, yeah?" she panted, her dark eyes challenging.

"Yeah. You're hard and tough on the outside because you've been hurt so bad. But you're soft as down on the inside. You have this sassy impermeable shell and meanwhile, you're aching for someone to break through and find that out. And keep you safe. It's all just an act. And you're really lonely. You sit there and read to test everyone that comes up to you, and so far, no one has passed. But you're dying to love someone if only the right person would show up and win you."

Hellion stared at me for several seconds, her eyes soft and glowing. "I love you," she said, her voice gooey with syrup. I stepped back. "You've always been able to read me. You know me so well, you see right through me."

I was uncomfortably humbled and laughed. "All right, all right."

"You can see I'm just a frightened little girl—"

"Shut up."

"And that I have needs too. I need to be taken care of and—"

"Shut up, already!" I pulled Hellion back toward the bar. Giggles were gurgling out of her throat. I pulled her close. "Just tell me your name," I said, my lust smoldering. I felt fire rise in Hellion and meet mine. She tilted her mouth up for more deep kissing. I obliged.

"What is it? What is it?" I hissed between kisses.

"All right." She seemed carried away by my bites. "I'll tell you."

I waited.

"Mildred."

I dropped my hands from her body and shoved her toward the door. "That's fine. Get back in there and read your book."

But she turned and wrapped her arms around me. "More."

To my own astonishment, I unwound her arms. "No. No more. Nothing else from me until I have your name." I opened the door and pushed her inside.

"Louise." She grinned.

"Forget it. I'll have to see your license now." I escorted her to her stool and I picked up my own drink and tobacco pouch and returned to the wobbly table where Payne and Carol were nursing beers.

"Struck out, huh?"

I ignored this, squeezing my lime wedge into my drink and stirring it with my finger. The ice cold liquid felt good.

"She's staring at you," Carol said.

I turned around, sucking my index finger. Hellion was indeed burning me up with her gaze. I turned away.

"Why don't you go do something about that?" Payne asked.

"I have. I've told her what she has to do." I shrugged.

"Man, oh, man." Payne laughed.

"What does she have to do?" Carol asked.

"Just a little private assignment," I assured Carol, patting her arm.

"Sounds exciting," Carol said. Payne gave her the stink eye. "I love to dance," Carol said. "Do you want to dance with me?"

I looked at Payne, who appeared angry but resigned. "Sure, go ahead!" Payne laughed heartily.

I kept Carol at arm's length and kept her back to Hellion. After a few moments, there was a tug on my shoulder and a cold voice. "Mind if I cut in?"

Carol was irritated but said, "Okay, I guess not." She walked back to the anxiously waiting Payne.

I grinned, charmed by Hellion's approach. "So, we meet again. Couldn't stay away, could you?" I embraced her and kissed her neck underneath her hair.

Hellion shivered. "Shut up and dance."

"Ready to invite me in yet?"

"Never."

"Suits me. Your loss," I breathed into her shell pink ear and concentrated on my dancing. We held each other close and started only by swaying. Soon, I was lost in the hypnotic rhythm and we were both spellbound. The music, the people, the bar disappeared. There was only the two of us. I moved Hellion; Hellion moved me, our thighs and hips locked. She raised her arms and fell back; I caught her and gripped her close. We barely noticed the floor clearing. I spun her and then pressed her ample ass into my crotch. We moved, mirroring each other perfectly. I dipped and swung; Hellion matched me, turn for turn, pelvis to pelvis. She was as strong and flexible as rope. I was just sliding my hands down to her plump ass when the song ended and the spell was broken by the crowd streaming back onto the floor. I fell to my knees in front of Hellion and held my arms wide. She looked at me in horror.

"Get up, you dolt," she said.

"Oh, baby, I don't care what your name is anymore; you set me on fire," I said, breathless and happy.

"Get the fuck up." Hellion's voice was like a lash. "Go get me a drink. Now!" She sauntered off to the bathroom.

I got her another glass of wine and returned to the table with Payne and Carol. I sat and lit a cigarette, draining my melted gin and tonic.

"What the hell was that?" Payne asked.

"I have no idea," I answered with a smile, mopping sweat from my face and neck with my soggy bar napkin.

Hellion emerged from the bathroom and glared at me imperiously until I stood and took her the glass of wine.

"Thank you. That will be all for tonight," she said.

"What do you mean, baby? You can't start me up and walk away."

"I most certainly can." She looked me up and down as if she couldn't believe my cheek in objecting. She drank half her glass of wine and then removed a lipstick from her ridiculously tiny purse and refreshed her mouth. "It's good for you."

I laughed, loving this. How long it had been since I felt right? "Oh, but it's really bad for you," I answered, clasping Hellion's waist.

"No," she said airily, stepping away. "You've gotten to the gate. I can't invite you further." With melting eyes, she stared at me and added, "Not yet."

I leaned down and kissed her, long and hot and deep.

"Besides," she continued, as if I had done nothing, "you need to be ready for me." She tapped my forehead. "Up here."

"Why? I don't want a mind fuck. I'm ready where I need to be."

Hellion shook her head. I nodded, finally understanding. I lit another cigarette and sucked it hard. "You're cheating on your husband, aren't you?"

"No." She paused. "I'm cheating on my wife."

"Why isn't she here? I've asked around about you. Why hasn't anyone ever seen her?"

"Because she's in a wheelchair."

I smoothed my shocked response. "You're shitting me."

"No, I'm not. It's hard for her to get around, so she sticks to places that conform to ADA standards." Hellion's voice was brittle.

"Let me get this straight. You're two-timing a cripple? That's cold."

"Not two-timing exactly." She downed the rest of her glass and handed it to me and I flagged the bartender. "We have an open relationship."

"An open relationship. That just means you two are broken up but can't let go."

"No. No, it really works for us."

"You mean she sits home alone in a heartbroken rage while you come out and play games."

She smiled and rolled her eyes. "That shows how little you know. She does really well. You wouldn't *believe* the number of soft, sympathetic caretakers who want to scratch my eyes out and marry her."

"Phew, you two do love the drama. I like my cunts less complicated."

"Well, we thrive on it. It stimulates our passion and deepens our love."

"Sure it does. I doubt the tiny amount of outside sex you've had has been worth the enormous amount of pain, jealousy, and processing."

"Well…"

"So, forget it, honey." I caressed her face. "I don't mess with married women." I flashed on my past. "As a rule. Talk to me after you've had a clean break."

Hellion shrugged, got out her keys, and snapped her purse closed. "That's fine. There's plenty more in line just like you." She took me in her arms and whispered in my ear, "I'll be getting it good and nasty at home in less than thirty minutes, how about you?"

I shoved her away, my mouth curled. I refused to watch her leave; instead I turned and signaled the bartender for a refill.

A little ways down the counter, I nodded to a beautiful woman who stared at me. She approached me, a purposeful look in her eyes.

"Say, sistah, how you doing?" I leaned my back on the bar, slouching, and propped my elbows on the railing.

"Ubiqua." The woman held out her hand. I shook it.

"Nora. Hmm, Ubiqua, that's nice. That means big beautiful butt in Swahili, right?"

"No, it means I'll kick your sorry black ass if you disrespect me."

"Uh-huh. So, Ubiqua, how you doing?"

"Oh, I'm just fine. I am worried about you, though."

I laughed. "Don't mar your pretty face with worry about me. Why don't we dance and that will take your mind off it?"

Ubiqua held up a hand. "Don't play that shit with me. I want to talk to you."

"All right, go."

"Why do you chase white women? You know they can't do for you what a fine black sister can do. What's up with that? Do you hate your race?"

"A fine, fine, *fine* sister like you? Why don't we hook up?" I let a grin spread slowly over my face, looking the voluptuous Ubiqua up and down.

"No, I told you to cut that shit. I'm already set. I have a date. A *black* date."

"Listen." I leaned down and stared Ubiqua in the eyes. "I do not hate my race. See?" I rattled my wrist. "A bracelet from my African ancestors. I love women. And I love to lie with whoever looks good. A lot of white women look good. And a lot of black women look good. It's just easier to find white women. I don't hate *any* race. Seems like you're the one who is racist, eliminating people due to skin color."

"There are things more important than convenience. That you can't find black women to be with is the lamest excuse yet. That honky poon already steals our black men; it makes me sick that they can take our women too."

"Why don't you relax?" I sighed and sipped my fresh gin and tonic. Payne and Carol were nowhere in sight. "I've heard all this tired shit before. Quit politicizing sex. Sex is just good and I love it no matter what the color it wears."

"Nora, sex is the only politics. The oldest and original politics. Every choice we make and how we live impacts the future. I'm just trying to help you out and give you some sound advice."

"Love has no color and misery has no color either. Live and let live, right?"

"That is such a useless cliché."

"Did a white woman break your heart or steal your daddy?"

Ubiqua drew herself tall. "Neither."

"Then get lost. I'll fuck who I like."

"I told you I'd kick your raggedy ass." Ubiqua clenched her fists.

"Then why don't you? We can go outside right now and I'll let you because I'm not fighting a femme. And when it's over, I'll still fuck whatever I please."

"Just think about it." Ubiqua's manner changed to pleading. She waved to a dark woman waiting for her by the door. "Just think about it."

I sighed again. "I will if you will."

Ubiqua's eyes flashed with anger but she left without saying anything more. I saluted her masculine girlfriend before they exited.

I returned to the wobbly table, now empty. But their drinks were still there, so Payne and Carol must be around somewhere. I sat and rolled a cigarette. I tried not to think of Hellion, but of course, I did anyway.

I put Hellion on her back, nude. I stood over her, feasting upon the sight. I poured warm oil all over her. I started at her neck and drizzled it very slowly down her body. I poured over peaks and valleys, the oil hugging every curve. The oil spread shiny wetness everywhere. Her large breasts were bathed in slippery warmth, her tan nipples erect. She squirmed and moaned. I avoided her dark pubic hair, pouring the oil down each leg instead. Then I returned to her cunt and poured the rest of the oil there. "Going to have to rub it all in," I told her.

"Start here," Hellion said, swinging her legs wide.

"Don't tell me where to start." I laughed, pulling Hellion's legs closed. "I'll start here." I stripped, my flat stomach and slim, square hips flexing as I stood on the bed and then sat on Hellion's glistening middle and cradled her breasts. She closed her eyes, her chin high in surrender. I massaged oil into her chest, above and below her breasts, her rib cage, her limp arms, and her round throat.

"My breasts...please...more..." She moaned, trying to arch up to me.

"Got you just where you deserve to be," I said, ignoring the begging breasts, heavy and swaying with desire. I flicked one nipple and she gasped, trembling.

She stared up at me, and said, "God, you're hot."

"That will get you exactly nowhere."

"You know it's what you want too," she whispered fiercely.

"You have no idea what I want," I replied, stroking Hellion's sides. Even in fantasy, flashback to a Redhead.

"I do so." And with a great grunt, Hellion swung her legs up and hooked my shoulders, pulling me flat on my back. She scrambled and pinned me to the bed, grinning. "I know you want this." She stretched her arms overhead and then caressed her own breasts, moaning. "See? You do. And I know you want this too." She arched back over my legs and slid her hands down her body until she reached her cunt. I was stunned into immobility and just watched, my mouth going wet. She stroked herself, her hips pulsing, her belly shining upward. I tried to move and found my arms cleverly pinned by her feet.

"Hey...hey now." I struggled. "What are you, a wrestler? I don't go for this whole flipping thing."

"What?" Hellion sat up and smirked at me. "Is someone whining? Thought you were made of stronger stuff." She ran her hands over my face and chest. "You are one handsome butch. Thirsty? Here." She inserted a finger into her own cunt and then plunged it into my mouth, pulling it out before I could bite her. She spread herself open. "See how much I want you?"

I nodded.

"Now you just lie quiet," she said, pleasuring herself with much groaning and writhing.

With a burst of strength, I wrenched my arms free and knocked her to her back, holding her down with a gentle grip on her throat. I flung her legs apart with my other hand and cupped her cunt. "I can do so much better than you," I growled.

Carol sat at the table, startling me. "Whatcha thinking about?"

I looked at her, the remnants of the fantasy still smoking in my eyes. "Nothing. Nothing at all. Where have you two been?" I started to roll a cigarette.

Carol giggled. "Payne wanted to smoke a joint so we went outside. She'll be right back. You and Payne best friends?"

"No."

"Known each other long?"

"No."

"So it would be okay if I…" Carol held my hand, opened it, and kissed the palm. The half-rolled smoke lay forgotten on the table.

I pulled my hand away. "What the fuck? I thought you were interested in Payne. That ain't cool."

Carol giggled again. "No, I never was. I thought I could get to you through her."

"I'll be damned. Does Payne know this?"

Payne sat down. "Does Payne know what?"

"Why should she? She'll find out soon enough, right?" Carol said.

I laughed and laughed, scattering tobacco all over the table and floor.

"Find out what? Goddammit, tell me." Payne's voice was sharp. When no one answered, Payne grabbed Carol. "Let's go. *Now.*"

Carol pulled away. "Sure, I'll go, but only if Nora is ready."

I held up my hands and shook my head, still overcome with mirth.

"What do you mean?" Payne was angry.

"I mean I'm not leaving with you, I'm leaving with Nora."

"What?" Payne shouted, oblivious to observers.

"Keep cool, keep cool," I murmured.

"Fuck you, asshole," Payne snapped. "I turn my back to go socialize with my friends for five minutes and you do this just because you struck out? I don't believe this."

"It wasn't my idea. Calm down."

Payne slugged me on the shoulder. "Fuck off."

I stood up fast, knocking my own chair backward. The entire bar was watching.

"Payne, we just met. You don't own me," Carol said.

"Shut up, bitch." Payne never stopped staring at me.

"You surprise me, Payne," I said. "You're rude, you have no class, and you can't even keep the ladies interested in you long enough to give you a try." I took Carol's arm. She smiled up at me and I continued, "Share how that makes you feel inside." I walked away with my arm around Carol just as the bartender came over to break it up. Carol squeezed me and laughed happily as if she had just won a prize.

"I don't care about that bitch anyway or that no-account Negro, let them go," Payne said loudly. I was unconcerned and waved as Carol and I left. I was used to winning women, no matter who was competing. I also had a thick skin about the shame and sour grapes that made the loser attack. Nothing else mattered, I *won*.

CHAPTER FOURTEEN

I looked down at this slip of a woman, my victory fading. *What had I won?* I unlocked the car. "You need a ride home?"

Carol was confused. "But, baby, I thought...I thought we would..."

"Well, you're wrong. I'll give you a ride home, but that's it."

Carol pouted. "Why? What's wrong?"

I approached and put my arms around her. "I'm sure you're a nice person and that was really fun back there, but you're not really...I mean, there's just no chemistry. I'm sorry."

Carol's eyes flashed. "Is that so?"

I was suddenly very tired. "You want a ride or not?"

"Yes." Carol tightened her arms and pulled me close. "And a lot more," she said as she kissed me deeply.

"All right, let's go," I barked after the kiss. It had been too good to resist. If this woman wanted me that much, who was I to reject that? I would be doing a good deed, helping fulfill Carol's desires. Who was I to be so stingy and selfish? I had a gift and it was mean of me not to share when a woman so clearly needed it. Carol grinned and scampered to the passenger door and got inside. I began driving.

"Mmm, nice car." Carol looked around. "So plush. Leather seats? And so clean." Carol squinted at me with a rakish smile. "I would'nt've guessed it of you."

"It's not mine," I said. "Where do you live?"

"Really, whose is it, then? A woman's?" Carol touched my arm.

"Yes, it is a woman's. She let me borrow it. Which way do I go?"

"Your girlfriend?" Carol's flirtatiousness was bordering on sullenness now.

I braked hard and pulled over to the curb. "Hey! Snap out of it. If you want a ride home and anything else, I need to know how to get to your motherfucking house."

Carol blanched. "Fine. Turn right up here."

I drove in silence.

"Left." Carol was pouting, her arms crossed. "Second right, third left."

I said nothing, the big, smooth car easing the way. I ignored Carol's loud sulking.

"There on the right, fourth from the corner, with the gnomes."

"All right." I sighed, sliding the car to the curb, my mouth curling at the garish display of colorful gnomes cavorting in the yard. "Here we are." I turned off the motor expectantly.

"Wait." Carol's lower lip stuck out and her eyes were wounded. She looked like a basset hound.

"Yeah?"

"You were really rough back there." Carol picked up my hand and played with it.

"Yeah?"

"Uh-huh. I didn't like it." Carol was breathless. "But I did."

"Yeah."

"It's not right to treat me like that." A sly smile plucked at her lips.

"Yeah, well, you want someone gallant and whipped, you should've chosen Payne." I started the car. "See you around." I put the car in gear and waited for Carol to leave.

"But I don't want Payne," Carol said with emphatic drama.

"What do you want?"

"Don't you know?" Carol batted her eyes. "What does a girl have to do?"

I put my hand on the back of Carol's neck and squeezed. "A girl has to make up my mind. You want someone who looks like me and acts like Payne, well, that's not what you have, so now what? Am I in or out?"

Carol leaned forward and pressed herself against me. "In," she breathed into my mouth.

I gave her a stern look and turned off the car. "Let's go."

"But wait." Carol pulled back and huddled by the door.

"What now?"

"You were mean to me. You're being mean now. I don't like it."

I rolled my eyes. "We could've been done by now if it weren't for your everlasting gum flapping." I took a breath and lowered my voice. "Listen, we can do this or not. I don't care. But I'll tell you one thing, this Reluctant Lesbian act doesn't turn me on. Either you want to and will or you don't and won't. So answer carefully, because the next word you say will determine your future."

"Yes." Carol smiled bashfully. "But—"

"Forget it, you already decided. Come on!" I leaped out of the car and went to open Carol's door, dragging her from the vehicle. I jogged to the front door, Carol leaping to keep up and emitting a series of soft, insincere protestations. Carol opened the front door and waited.

"What, you want me to carry you over the threshold?" I asked, shoving her.

Inside, I went directly to the bedroom. I had a bloodhound's unerring instinct for knowing where the bedrooms were in any building.

"I've got to make a quick call," Carol said.

"Fine." I pulled off my boots, turned the ceiling fan on high, pulled the bedspread off, and went to the bathroom for mouthwash. After rinsing my mouth, I returned to the bedroom and lit what candle stubs I could find. I didn't care about this detail, but I knew that Carol would. I heard talking on the phone as Carol came down the hall.

"Payne, just to let you know, I can lend you the money. I can give you half now and half on Friday. Call me back when you get this to let me know when you want to pick it up. Bye." Then I heard Carol opening a door and a scrabbling of ecstatic claws on tile. "Come on, Foofers, come on, baby! Yes, that's mama's itty-bitty baby, did you miss me? Num num nummy, I missed you. Yes, I did, my widdle Foofer woofer. Come on, come on, come on!"

Carol came in to the room holding a small, white, fluffy, panting dog.

I watched the two of them. "I don't do it with dogs."

Carol laughed. "Of course not!" She sat on the bed and played with the dog. "Foofers is my baby! My fluffy-wuffy softie-woftie iddy-biddy baby!"

"No, no." I smiled hard. "I don't do it with dogs in the *house*."

Carol stared at me, hurt and incredulous. "Why not?"

I stretched out on my back, covering the entire bed, feeling like an indolent tiger, my hands propped behind my neck. "Because it compromises your focus."

"What do you mean?" Carol stroked the animal, nuzzling and kissing his head. "You are my beautiful Foofy, aren't you, baby puppy love?"

"I mean," I sat up and adopted a babyish falsetto, "Oh, wook at the dog? Isn't it adorable? Look, look, look, oh what's the dog doing? Where's the dog? Is the dog okay? Does the dog need a snack? Does the dog need a treat? Does the dog need to make? Does the dog need a toy? Does the dog need a bed? Does the dog need to be held? Does the dog need some love? Does the dog need encouragement? Does the dog need self-esteem? Does the dog need therapy? Does the dog—"

"Enough. I'm not like that with widdle Foofers, I promise. And Foofie promises too, see?" Carol held up a paw and said in a gruff voice, "I, Sir Foofers McRufflekins, also known as Wonderdog McRuff, do solemnly promise—hey! Where are you going?"

I was carrying my boots but stopped at the bedroom door. "I'm outta here. The whole dog love thing makes me want to puke. You're all the same."

I turned to go when Carol cried out, "Wait! I can't be alone tonight. I *can't*." She left the dog on the bed and was clinging to my shoulder.

I stared at the ceiling. "This is the dullest foreplay *ever.*"

"We don't have to do anything, just stay."

"Oh, I'm not staying just for the hell of it. If I'm here, we're doing something. Dog outside?"

"He's a bichon; he can't go out without me. I'll lock him out of the bedroom."

"What does that mean? He's unequipped to go outside? He's wearing suede boots? He just had his hair done? What? Isn't he an animal?"

"He'll stay in his bed in the kitchen, I swear."

"What is it with you, anyway? We don't get along, we don't even like each other, and you're willing to shut your dog out to keep me here. What's up?"

Carol dropped her eyes and shrugged. "I just can't be alone tonight."

"And Payne was more than willing to be the one here with you."

"I like you better. You seem…more exciting. Harder."

"In what way?"

"In every way." Carol smiled and touched my cheek.

"One word about that dog and I'm gone."

"Got it."

With lots of soft cooing, nonsensical coaxing, sweet entreaties, and treat-filled promises, Carol got the dog settled in his bed in the kitchen while I had formed my plan. Since Carol was so eager for hardness, that's exactly what I would give her. As soon as Carol entered the bedroom, I grabbed her.

"I think he's—" I smothered her words with insistent kisses. Carol groaned into my throat and arched into my rough embrace.

"You want hard, huh?" I whispered into Carol's ear. "I'll fuck you so hard you'll forget your own name." My voice bathed her neck with heat. Her eyes closed, Carol pressed her hips into my thigh, rubbing and grinding. I tore off her blouse, the buttons scattering like bright coins. Carol gasped and laughed. I took a beat to adjust myself to the tiny breasts and protruding ribs. She could be a boy, I thought incoherently. I hastily refocused and shoved her to the bed where she fell, sprawling. I dropped on her, biting one dark nipple while squeezing the other. She moaned, twisting and pushing, but pinned beneath my muscle-bound body, she had to submit. I bit and sucked with jungle ferocity. I kept grunting, "You want it hard, you'll get it hard."

Carol squeezed me between her thighs, pushing her jean-clad cunt against my hip. I sucked her nipples until they were swollen and dark red. Her neck and chest were flushed, her eyes black with desire.

"Is this how you want it?" I growled and she nodded. "That's why you picked me, isn't it? Say it."

"Yes."

"Good choice." I grinned and sank my teeth into her throat, causing her to emit a strangled scream.

"Give me that cunt." I rose to my knees and jerked off her jeans. With a smooth quickness like black lightning, I dropped a dental dam over her juicy cunt and I buried my face there. "Mmm, so wet. You do want me like this." I forced her legs wider. "You're gonna come for me and you're gonna come hard." I snapped on rubber gloves, sucked the latexed index finger and then slid into Carol's asshole. She groaned and pushed her cunt forward. "I fuck you when I say, not when you say, got it?" I took her clit in my mouth and sucked and licked, discovering how she liked it. Dams never slowed my finesse. Carol moaned and writhed, her limbs trembled, and her breath came faster and faster. Just as she was beginning to moan, I quit. Carol sat up fast.

"What the hell?"

I grinned. "Lie down." I used my free gloved hand to push her back. "Now I fuck you; are you ready?"

"Uh-huh." She groaned, thrusting her cunt to me.

As I always did, I regarded this sight for a moment, happy and smug. I had this woman impaled and spread wide and soaking wet all for me. I brushed her turgid clit. She trembled. I touched her cunt. "Oh!" Carol moaned. I slid one, two, three fingers in easily. Her thin, jagged hips rose to engulf more. I stroked her cunt slowly to start, leaving the finger in her ass still for the moment and with my free thumb, caressing her clit.

"Yes, yes, yes, yes, yes, yes, yes," Carol babbled, tossing her head. I would have her come a few times and gradually ease my fist in, using plenty of lube as needed. I was sure she had some. She began to tense, gasping and thrashing when there was a shrill bark.

Everything stopped. The dog had snuck in and was at the foot of the bed, staring up with shining eyes. I slowly pulled out and stared at Carol, who said, "Wait! I think Foofie just wants—" And then clapped her hands to her mouth.

I shook my head, stripping off the gloves and dropping them to the floor. Foofie sniffed them. I put on my boots, which was all I had removed. I left Carol's house without a word and this time, she let me go.

Chapter Fifteen

I approached Ellis's house warily. I was exhausted and therefore clumsy and didn't want to wake anyone. All was quiet. A light was on in the kitchen. I tiptoed down the hall.

"Wait!" Sayan called.

I shrank against the wall.

"Who is that dragging her sorry ass into my house at this hour?"

"Good night, Sayan!" I called merrily.

"Good night, hell, come on in here," Sayan said.

I slunk into the kitchen too spent to fight or resist. Especially a big, loud, passionate woman like Sayan, who only seemed to gain strength and stature carrying Ellis's child.

"I'm really beat, Sayan. Why don't we talk in the morning?" I attempted one of my sparkling smiles that Sayan ignored.

"God, you are a mess," Sayan exclaimed. She was standing, hands on her hips, in resplendent furious glory, her hair mussed, her satin robe only a little tight on her belly. I saw the open Bible on the table and the remains of a late light snack: cracker crumbs, tiny corners of cheese, apple parings, and a glass glazed with the frosty shadow of cold milk. Sayan brandished a flashing fingernail. "We are going to check out my *car*."

"Relax; I left the keys on the table by the door. Thanks a lot!"

"Relax nothing. I've got to see what all you did to it. Come on." Sayan tightened the robe and strode out to the garage. She flipped on the light and made an inspection tour of the car's body, scrutinizing every inch, muttering indignantly to herself. Then, she opened the driver's side door, leaned in and smelled. She glared at me and I just watched helplessly.

"Where's Ellis?" I asked weakly.

"Sleep," snapped Sayan, sitting in the car and squinting at everything. "Well, at least you had the sense to fill it up," she said, looking me up and down. Ellis must be one helluva strong man, I marveled, closing my eyes and leaning against the garage wall. At last, Sayan got out of the car and switched back to the kitchen. "Sit down."

"Really, I am dead tired—" I began and at Sayan's look, I continued, "So I'd love to sit."

"Now, Nora," Sayan said, struggling to sound calm and reasonable. She smoothed her robe over her belly pot. "I know you're Ellis's cousin and that you helped him out back in the day in some kinda way. And I love you for that."

I glanced up sharply. Seeing my expression, Sayan softened. "I do. You musta done something big for Ellis to upset me by having you stay here." Sayan smiled, so I did. "But that doesn't matter. I love Ellis and if he wants you here, I respect that. And I love you because you love him."

"But?"

"But folks joyriding all night with freaks in my car will never happen again." Sayan waved a forefinger. "And this homo drunken orgy shit don't play in my house. It's not right, okay?"

I sighed. "Anything else?"

"Yes. Something must be done. I want to take you somewhere tomorrow. Will you come? It will change your life."

"I don't want my life changed, but yeah, I'll go. Anything else?"

Sayan put her hand on top of mine. "Let me fix you a plate," she said softly.

I was surprised. I jerked my hand away. "No, no, that's okay," I babbled.

Without a word, Sayan got up and filled a dish with delectable leftovers: spicy greens, homemade macaroni and cheese, cornbread, biscuits and honey, and a couple of pieces of chicken fried with Sayan's special secret family recipe. "Here you go, Half."

"Looks like just the thing." I studied Sayan for a moment. "Ellis sure is one lucky man. I hope he knows that."

Sayan blushed and smiled. "He does."

"And that baby is lucky to have you for a mama."

Sayan's eyes filled suddenly. She blinked and looked away. "Thanks, Nora," she whispered to the wall.

When I had eaten everything, Sayan escorted me to bed in the guest room and tucked me in. I felt like a cherished child as Sayan pressed the blankets around me.

CHAPTER SIXTEEN

"Aren't you ready yet, lazybones?" Sayan bustled in, adjusting the belt on her dress.

"You're talking shit, woman. I ain't going nowhere," I said, scanning the channels on the television.

"Don't talk that trash to me, you Half and Half. I will put you back on the street." Sayan snatched the remote and turned off the TV. "You are coming with me now." She put her hands on her hips. "You promised."

I knew better than to resist further. "Where's Ellis?" I rose and stretched, feeling conscious of Sayan's hawk eyes watching.

"He's out. Business."

"Where you dragging me, Corn Pone?"

Sayan laughed in spite of her tough demeanor. "I'm not your Corn Pone. Come on, get changed."

"Changed?"

"Just come on." Sayan pushed me into her bedroom. "Try this." She held up a floral print dress.

I fell back on the bed, laughing.

"What? It's pretty."

"You don't get me at all, do you?"

"Just try it, for me? Please? Just try."

"Sure." I was willing to have a game. I stripped off my Oxford and raised my undershirt when Sayan cleared her throat.

"Uh, I'll be right outside."

I pulled on the dress and shook my head. I felt like Flip Wilson's Geraldine. "You can look now."

Sayan returned, clucking. She met my eyes. "You look like a board in that dress."

"Yes, ma'am. See, I'm not a proper fish."

"Mmm-hmm, well, there must be something here." Sayan rummaged in the closet. I dreaded an endless parade of dresses. I would have to stop this and quick.

"How about this?" Sayan held out one of Ellis's Armani suits.

"Now you're talking!" I stroked the lapel. "You don't think Hambone would mind?"

"He minds what I tell him to mind," Sayan said. "I'll be out here."

I slipped into the suit and relaxed. I didn't care where Sayan took me. I strutted in front of the mirror. I opened dresser drawers trying not to be heard and I found Ellis's socks. I stuffed a pair into my Jockeys and posed. The suit was loose, so I needed two pair. I wanted to make an impression.

Sayan came in and stopped short, her eyes wide. "You look just like Ellis." Then, this fact seemed to please her because she smiled, her eyes twinkling. "That's much better." Sayan tugged on my collar and straightened the jacket. Her eyes dropped to my crotch. "Nigga, you crazy? Get that out of there!"

I obeyed, throwing the socks to the floor. Sayan wrinkled her nose. "Now let's get going or we'll be late." Sayan clamped her hand on to my upper arm and propelled me to the car.

We drove in silence. We were leaving the city.

"Straight, where you taking me?" I asked as fields outnumbered buildings.

"Some place that is going to do you some real good."

"You gonna buy me a nasty ho?"

Sayan withered me with a look.

At last, an enormous tent came into view. While waiting her turn in traffic she said, "A revival."

"A revival of what?"

"There are only two men in my life, Jesus and Ellis, in that order. If you get saved then maybe you can get your sorry freak ass in order and find a man." Sayan began driving again, heading for the parking lot. The dust was high and thick. I clucked my tongue. We passed hand-painted signs that proclaimed BROTHER OTIS BOUDREAUX REVIVAL. The car bucked as we drove over the field. Men in bad suits pointed the way. It was as crowded as a county fair. I put my hand on the dash so my teeth wouldn't be knocked out by the car's jolting over bumps.

"Listen, Sayan, if you want me to come with you to this thing, that's fine. But there is nothing wrong with me and I don't need to be fixed. By you or by Jesus."

Sayan sucked her breath. I continued, "So just look at me like Popeye. I yam what I yam and that's all what I yam. Let's go in and have a nice time and that's it."

Sayan parked the car and we approached the tent. I could hear Brother Otis in full throat.

"And the doctors said she couldn't be healed. And the surgeons said there was nothing they could do."

A chorus of amens floated out and coated my face.

"And I said, Lord!" Brother Otis shouted.

"Oh yes, Lord," several women replied.

"I said, Lord, I know you're not finished with this woman on earth. I know she has more work to do for you right here, Jesus, *right here!*"

"Praise God!"

"Bless Jesus!"

"So I prayed and I prayed and I fasted and I prayed some more. And it gave me strength."

"Yes, Father."

"It gave me the strength I needed to use the Powah and Glory a God to *HEAL THAT WOMAN!*"

Half the audience jumped to their feet and clapped.

"Yes, that woman was healed and she is right here. Come forward, sister."

A stout woman stood, wearing a tight blue dress and wobbled up to the stage on her black pumps.

"There is such a thing as miracles, isn't there, sister?" Brother Otis held the microphone to her perspiring face.

"Praise Jesus, yes, there is, Brother Otis, and I thank you and my family thanks you because without you and Jesus, I wouldn't be here today."

"Yes, miracles do happen. And sometimes God lets us see the miracles."

Sayan and I had stopped at the edge of the tent.

"Come on," Sayan whispered fiercely.

"No, you go ahead and save me a seat. I want to take it all in…
slowly."

Sayan scowled at me.

"Go ahead," I said. "I'll be along. The devil won't swipe me to
hell out here."

"Because he's already got you," Sayan hissed and walked up an
aisle in search of two empty chairs.

I turned away and walked to the edge of the field where Brother
Otis's passionate exhortations were more comfortable. I extracted a
sweet cigarette. Cigarettes didn't have to preach and scream. Their
gospel was right inside their skins. If you were quiet when you smoked
one, it would tell you everything. I flicked my thumbnail over a match
head and sucked on the cigarette. A man in a tight, mismatched suit
disengaged himself from the knot of men and began walking toward
me.

Ah, a fellow smoker. I grinned, smoke making my eyes squint. I
felt for my tobacco pouch. Did I have enough smokes to spare? For this
guy would surely bum one. All the years I begged cigs, I figured I owed
everyone who asked.

The man looked me up and down. I said nothing, just enjoying my
voluptuous smoke, thinking how nice it would be if the smoke were
shaped like a big juicy woman.

"Uh, sir? Ma'am? *Whatever*…uh, there's no smoking here."

"Fuck off, pal."

"And no cursing either. I am going to have to ask you to leave."

I thought of Sayan and how this would break the fragile bonds we
had carefully created. "Oh, come on," I pleaded with a winning smile.
"How about if I step over this rope and into the street? Then I'm off the
property."

"Well." The man glanced at his buddies who were watching.
"Fine. But if you smoke again, you're out."

"It's a deal." I swung my long legs over the rope and stepped off
the curb. It wasn't the first time I had debased myself for tobacco and
it wouldn't be the last. I stood in the street, leaning away from cars as
they passed. It was mostly revival traffic, so I got a good many glares.

I watched the sun set. It was particularly lurid because it framed
the circus tent of Brother Otis. I heard his shouts muted by distance
and I smoked as the sun slipped lower and turned the sky from blue to

golden to orange to crimson, staining the sky pink and purple like egg dye poured into water as dire warnings against sin rose in the air.

The delicious smell of wood smoke and sweet, fresh hay overcame even my cigarette smoke. Underneath that were the more diluted smells of trampled grass and hot dust. My throat was parched. I could use a gin and tonic to strip my mouth clean.

I thought it was ridiculous that the revival wouldn't allow smoking, cursing, or drinking. If they added those enticements, the attendance and money would multiply. Weren't those people most in need of saving? Not these saintly holy people who had the Bible memorized and hit the church every time the doors opened. What a funny world, I mused as I ground out my third cigarette. Sayan must be mad as a wet hen by now, but I needed to approach this thing at my own pace. I hoped Jesus was keeping Sayan entertained. I made sure to pick up my butts. I didn't want to soil Ellis's suit, so I just held them as I ambled toward the tent.

The sun was sinking into the horizon, soon to leave me here in the darkness with Brother Otis. To the south, I saw thunderheads. The cicadas were screaming about something, probably trying to drown out the revival. The tent itself was the biggest I had ever seen. And on the supporting poles, fluorescent lights were mounted lengthwise. There were hundreds of hard wooden folding chairs set up and hay thrown down over the swampy areas. In the center there were large sections of carpet in different colors for Brother Otis to tread on. Behind the carpet was a stage elevated six feet, so all could see, and it had a metal stairway pushed up to the edge. On the stage were a podium for Brother Otis and a band consisting of an organ with a massive woman at the helm, a guitar and a tired-looking brother fussing with the strings, and a feisty female drummer with bright eyes, ready to punctuate anything Brother Otis said.

Brother Otis was marching on the carpet, ranting about Revelations and the bloody war soon to come.

I ignored him as I circled the perimeter of the tent warily. The sound of cicadas buzzing in my ears was a comforting counterpoint to Brother Otis's hammering Christianity. The air grew denser as it darkened, becoming wet and thick in my nose.

"Rain's coming," I heard one woman murmur as I walked past their backs.

I stopped to watch a group of children, all in their Sunday best, running past, yelling. Girls and boys all in a messy tumble together. I appraised the crowd. They were all dressed so fine. I checked out the men to see how I compared and then dismissed them. I concentrated on the women.

How lovely they all were. Old and young having strutted in to get God in their brightest colors and nicest shoes. The gathering as a whole reminded me of a fan of peacock feathers or a flock of tropical birds. Rich yellow, creamy orange, bright red, deep blue, dazzling teal, emerald green, royal purple, dark cherry maroon, and crisp white. And shoes and pocketbooks and gloves to match. Then there were the hats! Crowns for Jesus's royalty. There was every shape and size of hat and all trimmed to go to Glory. Fur and feathers and lace and netting and sequins and flowers and fruit and beads. I shook my head, full of love for women. Love for black women and their fierce pride. And an ineffable dignity that nothing can kill.

All this holiness made my groin stir. Just the presence of The Spirit and all this female flesh devoutly off-limits made me go breathless. "I need something to drink," I muttered, continuing to stroll.

Women held cardboard fans that Brother Otis had passed out and the audience was a symphony of rhythmic fanning. It was a beautiful silent song as the women struggled to cool their faces while remaining attentive to the Word.

Pungent wet sawdust and hay let me know I was close to concessions. A rusty meat smoker sat in the grass, wisps of fragrance trickling from its lopsided chimney. I reached the table where volunteers sat, flattened and greasy with heat.

"Yes, sir?" one asked.

I looked at what was there. Hard, crumbly loaves of bread, warm grape juice, tepid water in paper cones, and sweaty cups of cloudy lemonade.

"Got any Q?" I eyed the smoker.

"Naw, that was this afternoon. For lunch," the volunteer said.

"Huh, now ain't that some—" I stopped and amended, "Something. I'll take water."

"Here you go. Just put your love offering into that box." The volunteer pointed to a cardboard box with a slot cut into it. I could see it was stuffed with bills. I added a dollar and moved away to lean against a pole and watch the show.

I was sipping my water, trying to shut out Brother Otis when a woman stood and walked toward the concessions table.

"Oh my, oh my," I said, gulping my water and crushing the cup.

"Lemonade please," the woman said in a syrupy sweet accent. Her dress was frilly and lacy and blinding white. It was tight in all the right places. I checked out the rear view. The woman's dress hung just right, skimming her generous bottom with enough suggestion to make my fingers twitch. The woman's hat was wide and white and it curved down over one eye.

"I'll get that," I said, sidling up behind the woman and reaching to slide a fiver into the box.

The woman's one visible eye was round with surprise. "Much obliged." She held her cup with both hands.

"My pleasure." I turned on The Smile that I would never forget how to do.

The woman started to return to her seat but I barely touched her on the elbow and she stopped.

"Why don't you rest back here for a minute? Take the air. I heard a rumor of a breeze."

The woman smiled, her cheeks dimpling deep. "Well, all right."

We stood in silence for a moment, the woman listening intently to Brother Otis, but I felt the air between us vibrate.

CHAPTER SEVENTEEN

Oh, to fuck a holy woman! I imagined the unplucked splendor, the virginal sweetness. First, I would have to chase her, because I loved the chase. Instead of fantasizing about endless gallant courting, I saw the woman running and I, strong and swift and sure, gaining until I finally clasped her in my arms. She would struggle with all her soft strength.

But I was inexorable. I held fast. I could feel her heart beating rapidly, like a bird's.

"Easy, easy," I soothed. "Just relax into me."

"No, I can't! I won't!" She renewed her futile struggling.

My hot breath on her neck stilled her for a moment. I gathered her closer and laid my lips on that innocent cinnamon skin, just below her ear. We were joined forever now. She whimpered, going limp.

"That's it," I said. "Nothing to get upset about. Just going to teach you some Latin." I lowered my mouth to her collarbone.

"I don't want to learn Latin. Hebrew teaches me all I need to know!" She shoved at me, trying to dislodge my grip. I held on, meeting every thrust of hers with my own. Our thighs rubbed together. I bent her backward, achieving victory for a moment. I held her, off balance, dangling above the ground.

"I want you, and you're going to give it all up to me, understand?"

She swallowed, her eyes wide and untried. She said nothing. I pulled her upright and tight again, savoring her big curves and mountains and valleys and roads that led to eternity.

"God is my Father, Jesus is my master—" she chanted.

"I am your master tonight." I placed my open mouth slowly over hers. Our breath mingled. "I will be your Jesus tonight," I whispered to her lips. She was still and then cautious as she responded to my kiss. She closed her eyes and sighed.

"This is wrong," she moaned.

"Then why does it feel so right?" I panted, eager to devour and plunder.

"Because you're the devil and you're tempting me."

I ran my hands up her waist to her breasts. I could see the sweet nipples straining against the Sunday best dress.

"God made our bodies, right? And they're made to feel pleasure. So I'm tempting you with heaven because that's exactly where I'll take you."

She frowned, stiffening. I tightened my hold and kissed the pulse in the hollow of her throat. A small coo escaped her lips.

"You won't have to do a thing," I said. "Just let me give to you."

"No." She twisted and pushed. But her eyes were hungry. And curious.

I laughed, pinning her hands behind her back. Her breasts were thrust out. I savored the sight. "You want me, don't you?" I growled into her curls.

"That doesn't matter," she answered.

"Oh, but it does." I grinned, still gripping her wrists with one hand. With the other, I stroked one of her nipples through her dress. "You want me to whisper to you all the wonderful things I'll do?" I continued. She was silent, hypnotized. "All the sweet, dirty shit we'll do all night?" I kissed her cheek. Her breath was quick. I let go of her wrists but she didn't move. I petted both plump breasts, enjoying my power. I pinched her nipples, rolling them between my thumbs and forefingers. "This is just the start. I can make you feel good everywhere," I said, then bent and bit her nipples. She squeaked, but it was the right kind. The submissive kind.

"I will turn your body inside out," I added.

"No," she whispered.

"By that, you mean yes, don't you?" I asked, pinching harder.

She nodded.

"Then you'll tell me no all night, right?"

"No."

"That's a good start." I knocked her hat off and kissed her violently. She kissed back, sometimes moaning "no" into my mouth. I popped the buttons on her demure dress. "Yell it. Shout no!" I said.

"No! No! No! No! No!" she squealed, writhing in her deliciously modest white cotton bra and briefs. This took my breath away. It made me ache. Most times, regular women's underthings were far more erotic than that sexy underwear crap. If only women understood the sensual appeal of cotton and simplicity.

"Oh, yes. Look at you, so beautiful. Isn't it all mine?" I asked.

"No!"

I grasped her roughly. "That's right." I slid my hand down her curved waist to her generous belly to her cunt. I closed my eyes and moaned as her wet heat met my palm. She jerked and her eyes flew open wide. She shoved me away. I grinned.

"Feels good, doesn't it?"

"No."

"I know, baby. Come here." I jerked her close. "Let's have a look at your back porch." I spun her like a mannequin. She trembled, but stood still. I slowly drew down the panties that were full of innocence. Gooseflesh rose all over her lovely plump ass. I knelt and moaned. I laid my cheek against her buttocks. "Oh, yes, this needs much care and feeding." I stroked and stroked her skin. My hands made a glissando all over her buttocks. She began undulating almost imperceptibly. I smiled at her back. I lulled her into a trance of relaxed pleasure and then gently spread her cheeks. "Mmm," I breathed. I kissed her. She pulled away and turned around, fumbling for her panties, which had fallen to her ankles.

"No, don't kiss me there; it's nasty." She rolled her eyes. I drew her back, easing her underwear down again and hugging her stomach.

"Trust me. You'll love it." I kissed her plump tummy. "Just let me. You'll see." She shook her head, her legs closed and trembling. "Just try it for," I looked at my watch, "five minutes." I could see her consider it and knew I had won.

"No," she replied, pushing softly on my shoulders.

I grinned. "Come on, turn around." I spun her and was again facing the dusky round jewel that was her fat bottom.

"No," she whispered.

I began gradually. Kissing and licking and nibbling the skin was always an easy start. I kept my ears open for her response, giving unconscious permission to go further. I had to restrain myself from closing my jaws in a terrible bloody bite of her lush flesh. Oh, a woman's ass was manna from heaven! Her legs were still closed, but I heard sweet little squeaks, so I slid my hand between her generous thighs and they parted. "Beautiful," I whispered.

"Just five minutes, you promised."

"I know, baby, just don't think." I parted her slightly and bit the edges and just grazed the interior. To relax her further, I alternated this with reaching up and stroking the outside of her pussy very slowly. I enjoyed doing that until I heard a whimper. Then I used both hands and spread her wide. I lowered myself into it but started slowly. She was a beginner, after all, and I must proceed accordingly. I just kissed; the sucking, biting, probing and fucking of her ass would all come soon enough. I checked the time. Twenty minutes had passed.

"I can't stand up anymore!" she gasped.

"Good." I kept going.

"No!"

"Then by all means, lie down," I said. "Just for five minutes."

She sank where she stood, her body glistening as if it had been buttered.

"Now, on your belly." I smiled.

"No." She pouted, but turned over, her ass rising like a majestic mountain.

"My, my, my," I said, reflecting on how quickly a true "no" had become a delicious "no" and how fast she was sprawled here, nude and juicy, just for me. *Because of* me. *I am so bad*, I thought. *I am so bad, I don't even feel guilty.*

Back in the tent, I wiped sweat from my brow. "What's your name?" I husked.

"Not gonna tell you that," the woman murmured, her voice blushing. She bowed her head and sipped, two-handed, from her lemonade. She glanced at me, her lips wet. She licked away the clear dots of lemony mustache resting above her mouth. Mosquitoes whined around my ears.

"Oh, honey child, you can tell me," I purred, inching closer. I caught Sayan's horrified glance just out of the corner of my eye.

"Uh-uh." The woman grinned into her drink.

"I'm going to call you Easter Bonnet then," I said.

"No. My name's Janet." She blinked and giggled, her head bowed. I stretched my arm up the pole that Janet was leaning against so that I was close indeed. She edged away, but it was a yield, not a stop. I cupped my hand around Janet's hands holding the lemonade. She extracted her hands, her creamy skin sliding away from my experienced calluses. I drank from the cup, my eyes never leaving the dark, round ones of Janet, who stared at me in open amazement and a shiver of uncertain innocent possibility.

As I returned the lemonade to Janet, I made a smacking noise. "Tart and sweet. The perfect..." I closed my eyes and licked my lips. "Combination." I noticed that a bead of perspiration had gathered at the hollow of Janet's throat. Where her collarbones joined her neck pooled a tiny clear puddle. I wanted to slurp it. I wanted to dabble my fingers in it and taste the saltiness. I wanted to find all the other sweat trails and follow them home. I would drown myself in Janet's delicious armpit musk. I would kiss and drink every hairline. I would lick away all the salt from her thigh creases. I would nuzzle dry her navel. I would split the rosy tan melon of ass and smear myself in Janet's tribal perfume. I would replace sweat with my own saliva. I would ingest Janet and Janet would surrender to me.

Janet looked away and sipped her drink. A subtle grin rested in her dimples.

"Hot, isn't it?" I choked out with difficulty, for my mouth had gone dry.

"Not too bad," Janet answered.

"Why don't you give me your number and I'll take you somewhere nice and cool this weekend?" I said.

Janet looked at me, uncertain. Her eyes glowed with inbred goodness and obedience. Beneath that was a darker desire for some danger.

"Don't you want to experience life outside of Scripture?" I asked hoarsely.

Uh-oh, too far, too fast. Purity took over. Janet clutched the lemonade so hard her knuckles went latte. "Oh, no, Jesus is the only way. But I thank you kindly."

I leaned closer, cutting off Janet's polite response. "Don't you want to go somewhere *cold* and comfortable?" I had no idea where this would be. I could only see the two of us in a hotel room with the air conditioner turned down to zero and me raising goose bumps on Janet's skin as she lay nude, stretched out on her stomach while I traced ice all over her body. I would even put ice in my mouth, loving the chilled balloons of air that I could exhale and I would kiss Janet everywhere she was hot. "Go for an ice cream sundae, maybe?"

Janet made a tiny chirp and took such a deep breath that her chest rose and sent me directly into another fantasy.

"Mmm hmm, girl, you sure are *fine!*" I smacked her big booty and her white cotton underwear jiggled. "I'll take care of this." I hooked my thumbs in the elastic waistband and pulled. When the panties fell around Janet's feet, I stroked her huge black moon of an ass. "You've been a bad girl, haven't you?" I was gentle.

"Yes," came the reply.

"Going to have to punish you." I pinched her. "Teach you a lesson." I swatted her. Janet jerked and moaned but didn't move. "Isn't that right?"

"Yes," Janet cried.

I tickled her pubic hair, longing to plunge in deep, but restraining myself. "Spread your legs," I said. Janet complied, dragging the panties on one ankle. I ran one wet finger from clit to asshole, loving the aroused puffiness and the hot juice. Janet groaned, her legs shivering.

"Not yet." I grinned.

Janet bent forward and stared at me, upside down. "Please," she said. "I need you."

I parted her pussy to feel this and Janet closed her eyes. "Yes," she breathed.

"You want me to fuck you?"

"Oh, yes, yes," Janet said.

"Let's have some perspiration before the relaxation destination!" Brother Otis yelled, interrupting my thoughts. "Before the exaltation exclamation! We must have the castigation of the aberration! We need the inclination for inspiration! We need amplification and clarification for the deliberation of our situation!" The crowd swayed with Brother Otis's rhythmic speech. The guitar player added a thumping bass to the perky drummer's snare taps. I just watched Janet with smoldering eyes and Janet, oblivious, remained standing calmly near the bonfire of my desire without a worry.

The women sang, "Well, well, well!" and the men cried, "Hallelujah!"

I was tiring of this. I swept Janet up into my arms, Janet's white dress fluttering, and her cup of lemonade spilling forgotten into the hay already swarming with flies. I walked with Janet cradled to my chest up to the stage where I laid her down gently. The crowd disappeared. Only mine and Janet's matching breathlessness existed.

"It's finally time," I said, kneeling between Janet's knees. I raised Janet's skirt and eased her panties off. "Now my sugar angel will feel very good." I bent down. Janet was trembling. I put my whole mouth on Janet's cunt and licked her open. Inside, was her throbbing, aching clit and plenty of slick cream to tell me exactly what to do. I licked and sucked, following Janet's moans and movements. She was transported, never having had even a glimpse that such a thing was possible. I inserted a finger into Janet's eager pussy. She groaned loud. I licked and fucked, but Janet's pussy was hungrier than a finger or two, so I grabbed Brother Otis's silver cross from the podium, its ancient age having worn the sharp corners smooth and rounded. I moved to straddle Janet's breasts so I could still suck her clit and I eased the cross into her grasping cunt. Janet yelped in pleasure, her hips bucking to gather more. She squirmed, pulling more of the cross into her swollen pussy. Her ass jerked and she landed on the corner of an open Bible.

I sucked and licked, faster and faster, as Janet got filled with the cross. At last, she shrieked, grabbing me, slamming her fists on the stage, convulsing wildly, her cunt climbing the cross, bam, bam, bam, bam. The thin, delicate Bible pages tore and ripped with Janet's hard rhythm. The verses of Leviticus stuck, plastered to her sweaty hips. I marveled at the sight of the cross sunk deep into my timid virgin. The beautiful silver instrument with the burnished patina slid into the midnight flesh iris, the flower gripping and dripping. Janet was gasping and shivering. I soothed and stroked her.

"More." Janet smiled.

"Holy God!" I grinned.

"Listen to my extemporization and have the realization of the ramification of procrastination and renunciation! Have a rejuvenation of purification!" Brother Otis stomped one foot in time with his beat. Sweat poured off his head. "My recommendation is spiritualization! Hear my vociferation! Be a representation of *Jesus*!"

The lights went out briefly to indicate the powerful close of Brother Otis's monologue. The crowd screamed and cheered. I saw Sayan marching up the aisle toward us.

"I know I ask you this every single day, but, nigga, you crazy?" Sayan hissed in my ear. "You leave this alone *right now* and I mean it." Then Sayan moved to get into Janet's face. "Little girl, don't you know what you were about to do? You get your sorry slutty heifer self back to your mama this minute before I slap you silly."

Janet, accustomed to being ordered around by strong women older than herself, dropped her lemonade and scurried back into the crowd, her hat quaking.

"Half and Half, I swear, you are a piece of work. I ought to knock a knot on your head. I bring you here to clean you of sin and you turn it into Sodom."

I shrugged and smiled. "Now you will know better."

Sayan's eyes flashed. "Oh, you'll be saved tonight if I have to choke the devil myself. I will just keep my eye on you every second." Sayan grabbed my ear and began dragging me to a seat.

"Hey, sister, lay off," I said, brushing Sayan's pinch away and standing tall. "I'll sit with you a little, but don't try to change me. Let's just accept each other and have peace."

Sayan pursed her lips and squinted at me. Finally, she said, "Okay."

The sun had set and the thunderheads were growling above as I found a chair next to Sayan's.

Brother Otis was mopping himself with a towel as he walked back and forth on the carpet, his head down and his eyes closed.

"Oh, I thank You, Lord. Oh, I thank You, Jesus, for bringing all these wonderful people here to see You tonight."

The organ's vibrato voice changed chords. The organ player's dress had a dark wet patch on the front. Nobody seemed to mind how hot and humid it was. Mosquitoes were feasting. The swift, silent snap of the fans that the women held went on and on, counting off the seconds, the minutes, the Bible verses.

"And if you've got a need, oh, yes, if you've got trouble, if your heart is hurting over some problem, then I beg you to give it to sweet Jesus and He will heal you."

At this, most of the crowd raised their hands to the sky. The organ trilled out more mournful notes.

"Our good Father and His only Beloved Son will see to it that miracles happen for you if you *BELIEVE!* If you don't abandon faith in the dark times, 'cause we all surely have those, don't we?"

A chorus of impassioned amens answered Brother Otis.

"If you stay by your faith and let the sorrow deepen that faith, you will be *REWARDED!*"

I leaned to Sayan and asked, "Why are they all holding their hands in the air?"

Sayan glared at me and shook her head. "Shh!" Sayan raised her own hand. Shrugging, I leaned back in my chair, extended my long legs, admiring how they looked in Ellis's suit, and reached one of my arms up too. But it turned into a mighty stretch and a big yawn, which earned another Evil Eye from Sayan.

"What did you expect, bringing me here?" I said, unruffled. I concentrated on looking for Janet, while Sayan focused on the preacher.

Lightning flashed. Brother Otis worked this into his sermon. Thunder boomed.

"Because the devil will try to scare you. He will try to tempt you. There's nothing as sweet as what the devil offers!"

Sayan glanced pointedly at me.

"What does the devil have? He's got *everything*." Brother Otis began gesticulating. "He's got sex; he's got money; he's got fame; he's got drink; he's got drugs; he's got gambling; he's got glorious material goods; he has a life that sinners call *easy*, but those of you who are saved call *lazy;* he's got everything. He will tempt you with all that, yes, sir. That life looks easy. That life looks nice. But you don't want that life, do you?"

Ominous organ chords. A chorus of soft, "No, Jesus," rose from the crowd. I spotted Janet, her eyes closed in devotion, her cheeks wet, her arm raised, an open Bible on her lap.

I plucked my crotch and sat up. How long could this guy talk? Sin bad, God good. Done, let's leave.

"You do not want that life because why?" Brother Otis boomed.

A cacophony of voices shouted answers.

"You do not want that pretty life because the devil has *LIES!*"

At this, a few women jumped up and danced a little among the sounds of agreement from the audience.

"The devil lies and he cheats and he'll fry you up fine when your life of wealth is over. No one will hear your torment. Jesus will weep but he'll turn his sweet back because you listened to *THE DEVIL!*"

I glanced around, feeling like an observer in a zoo. Was this how sports looked to people who didn't care? I could see myself as a version of Brother Otis and my players as backup and the fans as this audience. I shook my head. Sports made more sense than Jesus.

Brother Otis toweled himself again. His forehead sprang wet right after he wiped it. His grizzled hair glistened with sweat. He stood front and center with his eyes open wide and his face earnest. His voice was soft. "You've got to choose right, people. You've got to be right now so you'll be all right later."

Chords of redemption throbbed from the organ.

"You got to choose right."

Nods and murmurs emanated from the Saved.

"Now the problem with choosing Jesus is *THAT IS HARD.*" Brother Otis commenced pacing again, daubing himself with the towel and swinging it for emphasis. "It is hard, Lord, it is hard. Do you get rich being good?"

The audience mumbled no.

"No, you do not. Do you get glory for giving your life to Jesus in this evil world?"

The audience responded with quiet passion. The organ built tension.

"No, you do *NOT.* You are heckled and reviled and ridiculed. Are your problems solved with your wayward children tempted beyond resistance? Your girls led into sex and motherhood, your boys into drugs and gangs, and every one of them headed for a dead end?"

The mothers in the crowd shouted amen. Sayan caressed her belly thoughtfully. A woman put her arm around Janet and squeezed her.

"Are all your problems solved the minute you get saved? No, they are not, people, no, they are not. You know that Jesus just helps. He is there for you and he loves us all. Oh, God, how he loves us." Brother Otis fell to his knees and stared up. "I've had my trials. Sometimes praying on my knees all night long was the only thing that saved me."

Women shook their heads and clucked. I wondered what he had been saved from. The air was so thick I felt it press the clothes onto my body. Thunder clapped.

"The devil offered me *everything*, and I know when you're low, when you're weak, when you're hurt, the devil has come to you too, selling you his slick false life."

The organ trembled at the edge of orgasm. Women clapped and stomped their feet.

"But there's one thing…" Brother Otis said, standing up. "There is one thing and one thing only that the devil don't have and never will have." He paused. The crowd drew in its breath. Lightning flashed and it was so bright that I snapped my eyes closed and saw X-ray after-images.

"The devil *DON'T HAVE GAWD!*" Brother Otis screamed.

The women, as if freed by this, launched themselves into the aisles like dervishes. The organ crashed into a crescendo, sweat pouring off the organist. My ears popped at this explosion.

I excused myself and fled the tent. Between the assault of joy on my ears and the plump air that lay in my throat like a hot snake, I needed to move. Once outside the carnival, I relaxed and breathed. My body was restless, so I strode in the tall grass, enjoying the feel of my muscles. The clouds were so low, I was sure I could touch them if I jumped. The air alternated between tense stillness and purposeful gusts. Thunder growled, louder and closer. It was full dark now. I stared back into the bright tent at the mass of devout backs. All was still. Nobody moved but the children. The atmosphere beckoned to me like something sweet and nostalgic from the turn of the century. I yearned for cotton candy and a Ferris wheel and a quilt show and piglets and pure jams made by honest farm women.

"Good people," I muttered, imagining big, tight families and huge Southern dinners and God right there in the center of it all. As long as I was a little removed, I could admire it. I smiled. I felt something on my boot. I looked down, squinting, and saw a snake slither across the leather and disappear into the grass.

"Goddamn," I said. I walked very carefully back to the tent. Just before I ducked underneath to return to my chair, a commercial jet flew over, lights blinking, and further emphasized the duality of eras. Out there was technology and modern life. I was stuck here in the marshy field with snakes and sawdust and the ancient battle of good versus evil.

I sat and Sayan smiled, relieved, and squeezed my leg. Brother Otis was still talking. Suddenly, the rain came, unleashed in full fury all at once. The tents' edges leaned and were blown, the pounding water was deafening. Rain leaked onto two dozen heads. Still, no one moved. Brother Otis knew enough to wind it up. A pair of women sitting at the back of the stage stood and supported a woman so frail and feeble that I thought she was already dead. Her mostly bald head was covered in a transparent film of scarf and what hair she had was an ephemeral white cloud. She was less than five feet tall and she weighed about sixty pounds. But there she was in her resplendent floral dress, hobbling inch by inch toward the donation box.

Brother Otis was shouting good night and to please bring family and friends for his final day tomorrow.

"And here is blessed Mother Robinson. Here she comes. Mother Robinson, holy Mother Robinson to give the Lord her tithe."

People were transfixed as the women nudged Mother Robinson closer and closer. She held a fistful of money clenched in her tiny ropy gnarled hand.

"Oh, thank you, Mother Robinson, you are my guiding light. You are an angel on this earth. May God bless you seven times seven times seven, pressed down and overflowing. I can always count on dear Mother Robinson to show up and contribute to my work for Jesus."

At last, Mother Robinson was close enough to fling her money into the box. It caught the light and fluttered briefly like green butterflies. Mother Robinson and her two support women had already turned and were shambling cautiously back to their seats of honor.

The believers burst into applause. Brother Otis grinned and declared, "We will sing this one out tonight. This is Mother Robinson's favorite song." And with that, everyone stood and began singing and dispersing to their cars. Thunder and rain did not deter them whatsoever.

Sayan sighed and smiled at me. "That was so good. Ready to go?"

"Am I ever."

Sayan frowned and shook her head. "I swear, Nora, I never knew a person to be so unchurched."

I stretched. "I went to college instead."

Sayan paused. "And just what does that mean?"

I waved my hand. "Nothing, nothing, forget it, okay? I'm Popeye, remember?"

Sayan softened. "All right, Popeye, let's run through this downpour."

"There are snakes. Want me to carry you?"

"Hmph. I will stand on my own two feet and Jesus will look after me."

"Suit yourself." I glanced around for Janet but she was gone.

We joined a long line of cars returning to civilization. Through the rain as we waited in traffic, I watched the crew clean up, turn off lights, and retire to their waiting mobile homes.

CHAPTER EIGHTEEN

My skin felt electric. I knew I needed to go out for some fresh air. My legs were jangly; my heart raced. I knew this feeling—my body was on the hunt. I dug through my suitcase looking for my strap-on. I threw clothes all over the room in my frantic search.

At the same second that I held the stiff black penis victoriously in the air, Sayan opened the door.

Sayan emitted a series of clicks and finally muttered, "Oh, Lord." Then to me, "Sorry." She closed the door quietly.

I shrugged and stripped as I dashed for the bathroom. In the shower, I shaved my scalp and scrubbed my skin, getting more and more pumped. I was too restless to let even my fear of the swamps slow me down tonight.

When I finally emerged from the bedroom, I was ready to conquer.

I had shopped at an extravagant men's boutique earlier and had acquired a new style. My previous style had been conservative and mainstream. Abercrombie, Ralph Lauren, the occasional FUBU. But a store down by the river and run by Latinas caught my eye this afternoon. When I went inside, they swarmed, seducing me with the lie that these clothes were from Cuba. That musicians and rebels and pimps wore them. So I bought six new shirts: a purple iridescent, a bright red, a shiny green, a rich blue, a liquid gold, and a luminous stripe. All so delicious and loud. I also bought several twill trousers, some pleated, some not. I couldn't quite take the plunge to wear bright matching pants…yet. Stay away from Los Angeles long enough, I could see myself a luxurious tropical parrot, strutting proudly with my new plumage.

"See y'all later," I called to Ellis and Sayan, who were cuddled together on the couch watching television. "Don't wait up."

He grinned. "I get you."

Sayan unlooped herself from Ellis's embrace to follow me. "I know you're not borrowing my car, Half," Sayan said, dragging me into the kitchen.

"Nope." I threw my keys in the air and caught them behind my back. "I got my ride. No worries, puddin'." I chucked Sayan on the cheek.

"Uh, the reason I...what I wanted before, um, was, I opened your door because...to see if you wanted any of these leftovers?" Sayan opened the refrigerator door and peered in, studying with great interest.

"Forget all that. I'll check it tomorrow." I closed the refrigerator door, my high spirits dancing like flames in my face. "How do I look?"

Sayan's eyes traveled over me, avoiding my crotch and fixing on my forehead. "Fine."

"Naw, naw, baby, look at me," I said, sidling close. "Ain't I finger-licking good?"

Sayan brushed me aside and sat at the kitchen table with a slam and a huff. "Your resemblance to Ellis is amazing. It really is."

"Does that mean you like me?" I was all eager friskiness.

Sayan made a mouth. After rolling her eyes, she finally spoke. "What do you...I mean...do you *use*...I mean...what...that's just sick...I can't...okay...don't you see, you wish you were a *man*!" Sayan said the last word in a harsh whisper.

I laughed, easy and comfortable. "No, I don't, Sayan. It has nothing to do with that. Penetration feels good to *everyone* and some women love to penetrate and others love to be penetrated and some others do both. The point is *women* doing to *women* what feels good. Not trying to be a man, or imitating straightness, just using every tool for pure pleasure."

Sayan's eyes goggled. "Do they...? Never mind. Seems like y'all are just sinning when you could get all you need from a natural man."

I grinned, feeling free and playful. "Now what did I just say? What did I just tell you? Chicks with dicks are a whole different vibe."

"Mmm-hmm. No more." Sayan sniffed. We regarded each other, Sayan wary, me hot and fine in my best butch posture.

"Hey, baby!" Ellis called. "Can you bring me some of that cold chicken when you come back, please?"

"Sure thing, darlin'," Sayan answered.

"Sayan, you leave Nora alone, you hear me now?" Ellis called. Sayan and I both laughed. Sayan stood and fingered my shirt.

"I will say this, your clothes are fine."

I smiled at her. "Good enough, puddin'." I strode to the front door saying, "Later, Hambone," to Ellis, who gave me an approving nod.

"Don't get too wild, T-Bone, you gotta work tomorrow."

"Yeah, boss," I said.

I decided to bypass Marcie's even if I could find my way, which was doubtful. I would drive to New Orleans and try my luck at a straight bar.

After driving for half an hour, I approached downtown New Orleans. I had a nose for clubs and knew the right one would turn up. Downtown was dead. I headed for the river and the French Quarter. Plenty of hunting there. I cruised by the old Jax brewery, St. Peter's, and Café du Monde. Luck like no other favored me when a car pulled out of a space and I swerved the vehicle in.

At last I was walking. My legs sang with movement. I must start running again and play more one-on-one in the driveway with Ellis; my high-octane body was getting sluggish and twitchy. I operated best when I exhausted myself with vigorous exercise and slept long and hard. Otherwise, I was disoriented, wobbly, and weak. I was strong enough for tonight; that was all that mattered now. I saw ferries, lighted to blazing like floating birthday cakes, gliding up and down the black river.

The myths and legends attached to the mighty Mississippi were too much for me to get my mind around when I saw it. I just walked to the edge and smiled at the water.

Tourists passed behind me, people in the throes of drunken merriment. If attending a convention they were free of the spouse, the family, and for a time, the job. Drinking in the Quarter of the Crescent City gave people visions that they were cowboys and rock stars and supermodels and all dangerous.

Down an alley, I glimpsed a faint light. Ellis had specifically warned me against alleys, but that just made it more exciting. I boxed the air a couple of times, doing the quick step. "I can take care of myself," I declared in a whisper.

"Hey, handsome, need a date?" A long maple drink of water emerged smiling from the shadows wearing only stiletto heels and a g-string. I grinned my widest.

"Mmm mmm mmm, I do need a date, baby, look at you. But I never pay for my dates."

The woman stopped, her smile dropping. "Then you can fuck *yourself.*" Faint tittering sounded from the blackness.

"That's right," a woman called as the hooker switched back toward the shadows.

"Listen, honey." I spread my arms wide. "You don't want me to pay you anyway."

The woman turned and scowled at me over her bare shoulder. "Come again?"

"I'm a jasper and I would turn you inside out." I tilted my head and rocked on my feet. Hooting from the shadows.

The hooker approached me and pointed with a bright, dagger-nailed finger. "Do you *have* money? 'Cause that's all my job is. I don't care what you are or what you *think* you would do. It's all the same to me, know what I'm saying?" The woman sniffed.

I bowed my head, conceding the point. The woman put her hands on her naked hips. "Now, do you want a date?"

"No, baby, I'm just on my way somewhere. I never pay."

"Then why are you talking to me?"

"Why are all of you hiding here in the dark?" I squinted in the direction of the laughter.

"We're on a work slow-down. Labor negotiations." The woman smiled. Titters from the dark.

I strode to her, grabbed her hand, and kissed it. "Good luck, baby."

"That will be ten bucks." The woman snatched her hand back and shook her breasts.

I laughed and handed her a bill. Surprised, she took it, held it over her head, and danced back to her colleagues. I headed alone down a wide, dark alley toward the light.

Halfway down, a bar revealed itself. There were large storefront windows and inside, leather banquettes and dim lighting and a large gleaming bar. A plump, choice blonde perched on a stool sipping something dark while chatting with the bartender. The small, wooden sign outside said THE SNOOTY FOX.

"Just the kind of woman I'm looking for," I said and went inside.

I sat on the stool next to the blonde. "Gin and tonic."

"Sorry, mate, this is a brew pub. Fancy an ale? How about a Guinness?" the bartender replied.

"What's she having?"

"Mead," the woman answered, her familiar voice curling like hot smoke.

"One of those. Large," I said, then digging in my pockets, turned to face Julia. I flipped the business card on to the bar and smiled. Julia's slightly crossed eyes gleamed. I thought again—Siamese cat. I affected a soft falsetto. "You've got to stop following me or I'll tell Ellis!"

"How did you know I would be here?"

"Get over it. I didn't. I'm out looking for action."

"And you think you've found it with me?" Julia asked incredulously with a withering sneer. She was wearing a god-awful power of jewelry.

"You're still sitting here, aren't you?" I said, laughing at Julia's haughtiness. The glass of mead came and I raised it to my mouth, very aware of Julia watching with her crossed Siamese eyes. I took a large mouthful and almost choked. The drink was room temperature, thick, dark, bitter, and sour, but also yeasty and sharp. I swallowed, my eyes watering, and shook my head. Julia giggled.

"That shit is nasty," I said and then grinned. "But good." I drank again. "Just like you, baby." I licked away my mustache.

"Check!" Julia called, then to me, "I don't know how you dare to face me."

I put money on the bar for both of us and I gulped half the drink, breathing heavily. I tapped the business card with my forefinger. "That's how, dumplin'."

Julia reached to retrieve the business card but my finger pressed it on the bar.

"That was just…that was only…that wasn't…" Julia shrugged.

"I know," I said, taking Julia's arm and helping her off the stool. "Where do you want to go?" I walked her toward the door.

"St. Louis."

"What?"

"Thanks, guvnor. See you next time, Julie-pie!" the bartender called and Julia waved at him.

On the sidewalk, I noticed again how the streets were identified by their names in tile set into the concrete. Magazine, Napoleon, Tchoupitoulas, Bourbon, Chartres, Dauphine, Canal, Annunciation.

Julia removed her keys from her poufy little bag. "It's not far, I'll drive."

I checked myself, adjusting slightly and following Julia around the corner.

Once in her Jaguar, I asked, "Why do you go to that bar?"

Julia started driving. "Because it's in the Quarter, the tourists don't know about it, and I get to meet the most interesting people."

"So you're a regular."

"No, I'm highly irregular."

I was a little woozy from the drink and laughed myself breathless. When I calmed, I sank into the leather seat, resting my head and closing my eyes.

"Don't fall asleep on me," Julia said.

"I'm not," I said dreamily. "Nice ride."

"I hope so." Julia grabbed my crotch.

I was too relaxed and experienced to be shocked, so I patted Julia's hand and held it there. "See? I'm all ready for you, bitch." Julia pursed her lips and pulled her hand away to shift.

"Come on, get out," Julia said as she turned off the car.

I opened my eyes. We were parked at a cemetery. "What the hell?"

"St. Louis. We're here." Julia grabbed her purse and marched to the entrance.

"You crazy, baby? What the hell am I supposed to do in there?"

"Same thing you do everywhere else. But extra good tonight."

My crotch throbbed. It always overrode my decisions in my head. Graveyard? Mighty fine. I leaped out and followed Julia, slowing my long stride because high heels caused the Siamese cat to mince steps. The darkness was palpable. I squinted to read the names off the ornate crypts. Le Doq, Chevalier, Mendez, Gonzalez, Taliaferro. The cemetery was an enormous suburbia of tiny stone homes for the dead. Each had a little yard, a front door, windows, and a cross or an angel on top.

"How far are we going?" I asked, my cock drooping a little bit as we walked farther from the gates.

"Not much farther." Julia smiled at me, the brilliant moonlight making her teeth look like fangs. Our footsteps echoed down the little sidewalks, through the silent marble neighborhoods. My skin began to crawl. We saw another couple disappear around a corner. I suddenly knew what being a lab rat in a maze was like. Julia led me deeper and deeper, turning, walking. The quiet was spooky.

I grabbed Julia and shoved her against the nearest tomb. "I need you now, baby." I nuzzled behind Julia's ear, getting poked by her gaudy earrings and scraped by her necklace. I had to get this going or leave this creepy place at a run. Julia gasped and gurgled laughter. She shoved me away.

"Not yet, sweetie." Julia took my hand and we stumbled back onto the walk, continuing. "New Orleans is below sea level, did you know that?" she asked as she pulled me along.

"That right?" I watched for bats and vampires.

"Yeah, that's why the graveyard is set up like this. We can't bury anybody in the ground, they just float to the surface. Funny, huh?"

"Yeah." I listened for footsteps.

"So you buy six inches of space in a mass tomb. They lay your body inside, carve your name on it, give you a few months, and when you're decayed, they press your bones into the back and lay another body in and so on until it's full. 'Course, if you have money, you don't have to share."

"Uh-huh." I was jumpy, my skin prickly.

At last, Julia stopped and lay on her back on a large, flat concrete plot with dozens of names engraved. I tried not to think of the collections of skeletons beneath.

"Here we are, stud." Julia raised her skirt and spread her legs. I grinned at what I saw. Even in the shadows I could make out a naked muff and plump, stocking-clad thighs.

"Oh, yes, you nasty whore." I ran my hands down Julia's thighs, pinching and slapping.

"Call me Blondie," Julia breathed.

I shrugged. "Okay, Blondie." I enjoyed seeing Julia writhe on the tomb, her legs spread wide, aching for me to plunder. I snapped on rubber gloves and caressed Julia's cunt to see if I needed to add lube, a sample size of which I always carried along with my latex goods. Julia was swollen and wet so I shoved my fingers inside her pussy. I groaned as her cunt sucked me in. Julia undulated, straining to gulp more of me deeper.

"Get in my purse," she grunted, thrashing on my fist.

"Why? What do you want with that right now?" I laid on top of her, staring into her face, but not kissing her and continually stroking her cunt by clenching and unclenching my fist. With my free hand, I covered her turgid clit with a dam, bent down, and sucked it.

"Oh, oh, oh, oh!" Julia's eyes clamped shut and she tried to shove me off. "No. Not yet. Not yet!"

I stopped and Julia opened her eyes. "Get the knife out of my purse and put it against my throat."

I was too aroused to care what this crazy bitch wanted so I did as she asked. I removed my hand slowly and carefully fumbled in her purse until I found a large folded knife. I unfolded it and placed it close to her neck. Being aggressive and promiscuous, I had seen and done it all. It was against my principles to deny a hot pussy anything she desired.

"All right, Blondie, you bitch. You're gonna get fucked now." I fell on her, pinning her to the tomb and rubbing my large black cock on her clit.

"No, please, don't!"

I pulled away. No means no.

"You silly idiot, come here and fuck me right. If I want you to stop, I'll say, 'acquit.' Come on, come on." Julia stretched her legs high in the air. She fondled her cunt, spreading her lips. Furtive footsteps crunched by, everyone ignoring each other.

I got a condom out of my pocket. "Here, bitch, put this on me and hurry."

Julia sat up, smiling and obedient. "God, you are so sexy," she said, staring up at me and I just glared at her. She rolled the condom down slowly and then lay back, raising her knees to entice me. "You have that Greek god look like he does."

"Forget that, Blondie, roll over and get on all fours."

Julia's eyes widened. "But…"

I grasped a fistful of her hair and held the knife to her face. "Do it."

Julia smiled and complied.

"Now raise that skirt."

Julia did as she was told, her delectable, giant beach ball behind glowing. I approached, my cock standing stiffly. I rubbed the head on the wet entrance of her cunt.

"No, no, no!" Julia pressed against my cock. I deftly avoided her.

"Now grab your ankles," I ordered.

This wasn't part of the game. "What? Do you know how old I am, you jerk? I can't do that. I'm already on my knees, now just do it."

I swatted Julia's ass. The smack echoed off the headstones. Julia jumped and sucked air. I held the knife where Julia could see it. "What did you say, Blondie? I know I didn't hear you say that." Julia's eyes widened. I smiled.

"You want your jungle cowboy to service you? Well, he needs you to grab your ankles before you get his prick."

Julia nodded, mute. She struggled to slide her arms along her legs toward her feet. She gasped and grunted.

I stepped close, grabbed the delicious meringue-mountain hips, and slammed my dildo in to the hilt. Julia raised her head and bellowed. I slid in and out, varying the speed and depth, drawing out our pleasure. Several times, Julia was on the brink and I stopped completely. The first time, she was pleased and played along. Then I spooned her and stroked her throbbing clit as I thrust into her dripping pussy. The second time, she got snarly and tried to force me to continue. When I wouldn't, she rubbed her own clit, trying to come. I stopped that by spanking her hard until she lay still. Then I was gentle and slow, building, building, building until I felt her ass riding my cock hard and her breath quickening. I stopped.

"Oh!" Julia whimpered. "Please? Please let me come. Please, please, please. I need it so bad. I need to come on you. Please."

"Shut up."

Julia was quiet, her head down, her breathing muffled by pillows of hair, her ass naked, red and wet, high in the breeze. Her hands lay helplessly next to her calves. She was a delicious triangle.

"Turn over."

Julia scrambled to obey. My mouth twisted. I wondered if she had ever moved that fast for anybody in her life.

"Spread your legs for me. Open up your pussy."

She did as she was told, panting in eagerness. I retrieved the abandoned dental dam and dropped it on my shoe so I wouldn't forget to throw it away. I put the penis tip to Julia's hungry slit.

"What's my name?" I asked.

"Killer!" she cried.

"No, wrong. What's my name?"

Julia looked at me standing there, ready. "Nora. Nora Delaney," she answered rapidly.

"Good girl!" I said, sliding all the way in.

She trembled and shrieked. I held her ankles and stroked her long and sweet. My hips swiveled and dipped. Julia twitched and groaned. I was close too. I let go of one leg and picked up the knife and sliced open her blouse. The cloth cut cleanly.

"Show me," I barked. Julia jerked her bra up to her neck, her heavy breasts plopping out. I fell on them, licking and biting greedily. Overwhelmed, Julia just lay there, being fucked and sucked, her arms akimbo. "Oh, yes," I moaned, quickening my pace.

"Oh, yes, oh, God," she cried.

"Yes, yes, yes!" I said as I came, plunging fiercely into Julia, who finally exploded into screams so loud I had to smother her voice with my rubber-gloved hand. "Shut up, shut up!" I growled as I held Julia's mouth but continued to fuck her. Oblivious, she shook and bucked, her eyes screwed shut. Her hands clawed the air, scraped the concrete, and finally scratched my arms, bringing threads of blood.

At last, when Julia was calm, I looked into her face to make sure she was all there and okay. Her crossed eyes were soft and bright. Satisfied, I withdrew very slowly, removed the condom and glove, and stuffed them with the dam into my pocket. Then I helped Julia sit up and straighten her clothes.

"Goddamn," she whispered.

"Get me a cigarette, baby," I said, sitting close. Julia fumbled in her bag, lit one, and with shaking hands, passed it. I pulled the smoke into every crevice of my brain as if it would knock me out.

"That was phenomenal." Julia's voice was small and meek. "I've never—"

"Shut up," I said. "Just all in a day's work. Don't talk about it." I looked at this voluptuous virago so forceful and intimidating in life, willing to lick my boots for a good fuck. Same old story. I blew the smoke out with a sigh. "And don't start following me around and thinking this means something, you got it? Your money's on the dresser, cunt."

Julia smiled, her face naked and radiant. She nodded happily as if my stern words were a flirty marriage proposal instead of a rejection.

"No, I mean it. I don't hook up. Ever." Flashes of The Redhead. I shook my head to dispel the vision. "So you need to know this."

"Yes, sir." Julia grinned, clutching my arm. I pulled away, dragging deep on my cigarette.

Another deaf femme. I gave them the true word and they didn't hear it even as I said it. I gave thanks again that I couldn't knock boots and become a baby daddy. I stared at the stars and then at my feet, wondering at the situation I had gotten myself into again. I needed Julia only long enough to walk me back to the graveyard gate. I fell back on the tomb. Maybe I was too old for this dogging around, breaking hearts. Here was Julia, married and in her forties and ready to tattoo me as hers, for good. I was determined to break that dream right now. I touched Julia's back. "Listen."

Julia fell back with me. "Shh, don't talk."

I rolled my eyes but gave up. Why can't sex be clean and simple? Why can't they all be like me and see lust and fucking as just that and have a great time? I flicked my cigarette butt away in an arc where it landed in a tiny explosion of sparks on the sidewalk.

"Why do you come here?" I asked.

"I go where I won't see anyone I know," she answered, her voice husky. Then she was seized by a fit of laughter. I watched her, suddenly chilled. Her voice rang out like a voodoo priestess, a ghoul, chapping my ears and skin. When she settled, I pulled her up.

"Let's book," I said.

Julia hugged me, clinging too long. I pushed her away and held her chin in my fingers and stared into her cat's eyes.

"Can you remember what I just told you?"

"Yes, but you don't seem to take me into account at all, and that won't do."

I gestured to the tomb. "I just *took* you into account. There's nothing more."

Julia snaked herself around me again, grinning. "There's so much more. I am dangerous to mess with. Best you come along and do as I say."

It was my turn to burst into laughter. I doubled over, resting my elbows on my knees. As Julia stared at me, her mouth shrank to thin and hard. As soon as I stood up to my full majestic height, Julia pasted on a smile.

"Yeah, baby, I saw how dangerous you are. Mmm-hmm." I sniffed.

Julia blinked like a lizard in the sun. "Slow eyes, fast mind," she said as she took my arm and guided me to the cemetery entrance.

CHAPTER NINETEEN

I stood at the pawn window, bored. I was used to having an all-consuming sports career and living an urban pace, not having slow days of leisure handing money for objects to hard luckers and being hidden away in a small backwater town.

"Take it easy," Cleo rasped from the card table. It was an admonishment he commanded of me several times a day.

"I don't want to," I answered. "I want something to be difficult." I watched the traffic at Tassie Pie's. A car pulled in among the crowded lot. It had a bumper sticker that read SUPERVISE THIS! I smiled. Then I saw a woman come out of the restaurant wearing painfully short denim cutoffs. Her ample thighs jiggled. My mouth watered. I looked at the woman's crotch where her vulva was clearly split wide by the tight seam of her shorts.

"Mmm, nice camel toe, baby," I muttered to the glass and grinned.

"My man needs some new panties!" Drew exclaimed.

I sighed and turned from the window. I glanced, irritated, at the pawn's browsers, men who were always on the hunt for an amazing bargain but never bought much. They spent hours curled over guns or stereos or tools, murmuring approval but really just using the pawn to congregate and escape wives.

"You got that right, Drew." I punched him on the shoulder, hoping to jostle some action out of him.

"Say, say, man, siddown." Drew brushed me away. He had a bag at his feet that he kept checking. Cleo was doing a crossword and smoking. He looked just right with his silver hair and dark freckles on his walnut skin.

"Anybody ever tell you how much you look like Ellis?" I asked, trying to provoke Cleo.

He looked up and squinted at me. "Anybody ever say the same thing to you?" He returned to his crossword. I glanced at the words he had filled in: tappan, re, gnu, pettifog.

"Drew, what do you say we go cruising?" I asked.

"My man, you're on the job."

"Well, what do you do when you're bored stiff?"

"Knit."

"What?" I waited for the joke.

Cleo smiled at his puzzle, unconcerned.

"Yeah, man, I knit. You got a problem?" Drew bent down and finally removed the contents of his bag and it was indeed a ball of yarn, needles, and a square of knitting. I was too shocked to ridicule and just watched as Drew arranged his supplies and began. "I'm from Haiti," Drew said softly as if that explained it. "I was raised by my grandmother. I was the only child and she knitted and I had to help her. So I picked it up. You should try it."

"I don't believe it," I said.

"Knitted a whole blanket for me last Christmas," Cleo said. "Wasn't that felted merino you used?"

Tickled, Drew said, "Sho 'nuff. See, this here is chunky wool. I like it. It's got heft but it's so warm, you'll feel like you're sitting on the sun." Drew rummaged in his bag. "My favorite is, oh, I can't pick. I love to work with slub and vrille, but angora is so soft. Silk is très élégant, no?"

"I wouldn't have any idea." I was charmed and baffled.

"What stitch you doing there? Quaker ridge?" Cleo asked.

"Ha, good guess, my man. It's knit two, purl two ribbing. On my next thing, maybe a sweater for little brother here, I'll use garter or stockinette."

"A sweater for me?" I was strangely touched.

"Made a sweater for Ellis and a baby blanket for Sayan," Drew added.

The crowd of browsing men finally approached the counter. One of them held a Craftsman screwdriver. "What's your best price on this?"

I rolled my eyes. "Listen here, boys."

"Ten percent off, that's the lowest we'll go," Cleo said, concentrating on his crossword.

"Oh, come on. You can do twenty-five," the man said. The rest agreed.

"Not on a small item like that," Cleo countered.

"Buy more and we'll see what we can do," I said.

The man shrugged and put his money down. I gave change and started to sit at the table.

"I'd like a receipt," the man said.

I complied, glaring at the crowd of utterly useless and pleasant men. I headed for the table again.

"I'd like a sack," the man said.

I began muttering to myself and slammed a paper sack on the counter and then sat at the table, willing the man to ask for something else. He didn't. One of the others was observing Drew knit.

"Sure appreciate that scarf and hat you gave me, Drew. Came in handy when we went to Chicago last year," the man said.

Drew smiled and nodded. "Mighty fine, mighty fine."

After the men left, wandering across to Tassie's to re-hash the purchase, I stood at the window again.

I wished I were hungry, thirsty, or in need of a smoke. Anything to lift this numbing inertia. I saw an old beater truck park at Tassie's. NOT FOR HIRE it said on the back window. The truck was rusty and dented with piles of miscellaneous metal equipment in the truck bed. I couldn't tell if it was a winch, a tow truck, lawn maintenance, or what. Definitely some kind of difficult labor vehicle. The man that got out was tall, even taller than me, and heavy like a former football player. He wore no shirt, stained threadbare overalls, and a battered baseball cap, dark with sweat. He was a rough, hulking brute. He had a long silver beard and gnarled horny hands. He limped like he was used to arthritis every day of his life. He went to the order window and got two soft-serve vanilla ice cream cones. My eyes sharpened. The man lumbered back to his truck and leaned against the bed. A dog leaped up, propping his front legs on the truck side, wagging his tail and behind in a fury of happiness and laughing into the man's face. The man held one cone out to the dog while he ate the other one, the dainty cones almost disappearing in his huge hands. The dog lapped, the man ate, companions in silence. When the dog was through with the ice cream part, the man gave the cone to the dog. The dog disappeared into the truck bed with it in his mouth. The man continued eating, his eyes smooth. They finished their cones at the same time. When the dog jumped up again, the man held the dog's head close to his own for a moment, then ruffled his neck and lurched back into the driver's seat. The dog sat obediently as the truck jerked and shuddered and popped. The dog's eyes were closed, his face turned to the sun and his pink tongue rolling from side to side. The truck disappeared with a cloud of smoke. My throat was tight so I said nothing to Cleo or Drew. I closed my eyes and when I opened them, there was a horse parked at Tassie's.

"Hey!" I said, clearing my throat, "Look!"

The men looked and nodded. "That's ole Sol," Cleo said. "He comes in to Tassie's every once in a while. Refuses to drive. His land is not too far."

I turned to watch as a slim, wiry man in jeans and cowboy boots and hat carrying several white paper sacks mounted the large chestnut and gently eased him out into traffic, oblivious to the cars. As they walked, the horse's rump undulated, the tail swished, the man sat erect and stiff, and the vehicles kept a respectful distance.

"Now I've seen everything," I said.

"I doubt that," Cleo replied, his eyes sparkling. "You ain't lived here long enough."

"I know what my man needs," Drew stated, setting his knitting on his chair and dashing to Tassie's.

"I don't need anything they have over there," I snapped to Cleo, who ignored me.

Drew returned, carrying three large cups. He handed one to me and I took a huge gulp. Drew sat and he and Cleo watched as I began coughing and sputtering and choking and beating the table.

"Fool, why didn't you just sip it?" Drew asked and he and Cleo laughed.

I sucked air, my eyes watering. Cleo shook his head and Drew still laughed.

"What the fuck?" I wheezed.

"Lime Drag," Drew said. "It will cure what ails you." He and Cleo both sipped theirs.

"Jesus!" I gasped. "What's in it?"

"Crushed ice saturated with salt, then pure lime juice poured over it. Good, ain't it?" Drew drank more, licking his lips.

I wiped my nose. I took a small mouthful. My eyes screwed closed and I shuddered. "Yeah, it is. Thanks."

"No problem, my man." Drew smiled.

The phone rang. Cleo didn't move. I didn't move, still studying my drink. "Could use some tequila."

"Naw, naw, have it pure."

"There's something difficult to shift your boredom. The phone," Cleo said.

I swaggered over to answer it. "Pawn."

"Yeah, yeah, say, this is Lullabye Baxter, and I'm gonna need Ellis to give me an extension on my stuff."

"You made a payment lately?"

"Naw, naw, 'cause I can't. But tell him I'll be there soon as I can. Cool?"

"No, we can't give you an extension without payment," I replied sourly. Didn't people know business was business?

"Ah, listen, man. Ellis does this for me from time to time. It ain't no big. You get me?" The man's voice had an edge.

I was sick of being the ignorant newcomer and I wasn't going to be pushed around. "Well, that's the policy and that's the agreement you signed."

"Is Cleo there?" The man was exasperated.

"Yeah, but—"

"Put Cleo on the goddamn phone!"

I held out the telephone.

"Who is it?" Cleo asked without looking up.

"Lullabye Baxter."

"Oh yeah, tell him it's cool. We'll hold it all. Just with the regular fee."

I was angry and embarrassed but passed on the message. Lullabye was cordial again. "Thanks a lot, man. Y'all real good. I 'preciate ya."

I hung up. "What the hell?"

Cleo lit up another cigarette. Blue smoke flew from his mouth like an arrow. "He's good for it. He's a pimp and he's in prison."

I nodded, incredulous, and walked back to stare out the window.

CHAPTER TWENTY

I handled the booklet carefully, whistling. The book had red printing on stiff ivory paper covers. "Ham, you do this right up, don't you?"

Ellis smiled, flushing with pleasure. I read the front again, this time out loud: "Sixth Annual Dinner Dance and Auction, Saturday, September twenty-third, nine o'clock p.m., Delaney-Winthrop Liquidators, Incorporated, New Orleans." Then I pinched my nose and read, "The Important Collection of English Silver belonging to The Notable Mrs. Huey Harwood, French Furniture, Bronze Dore and other Objets D'art, Gold and Silver Watches and Bibelots, Miniatures, Savonnerie and Other Rugs, Tapestries, Old Porcelains, and Queen Anne Furniture from the Estate of the Late William Harrison." I released my nose and thumbed through the catalogue of photographs and descriptions. "Man, how do you do all this?"

Ellis shrugged, grinning. "Well, I started with just the other pawn, you know, here in the Bayou."

I nodded. We were at the kitchen table, Sunday morning, after breakfast and before church. Sayan was dressing. When they left, I would go to the pawn.

"Then the rich white folks started coming in because I gave a better rate and they thought of me as being more confidential. You know, outside the city, small operation, sweet-talking black man who didn't know no better; all it takes is just one good word-of-mouth recommendation. Once you're in with one of those people, they all use you, so I started accumulating lots of high-dollar items and I needed a safer place to put it all. T-Bone, you would not believe how those damn fools burn through money. They have all these antiques and jewelry and cars and shit, but not two dimes to rub together because they're careless and stupid with all of it."

"White privilege," I said.

"Yeah, so I rented a place on Canal in the city and made it secure, 'cause you know, I can't keep diamonds and sapphires out here." Ellis laughed. "Soon, I couldn't house it all. It was too crowded with the riches of the glorious antebellum past. Which I was pretty happy about, you know. I thought of all those black hands that had cared for this shit over the years and here it was, all mine!" Ellis crowed. I nodded. "I didn't want to have to rent a warehouse, insure it, and hire people to guard it. That's nonsense. All that merchandise just sitting there, not earning its keep and costing me money to store it where nobody even uses it. So after I let Sayan have her pick…"

I looked around the house as if for the first time and smiled. "She's the Winthrop," I said.

"You know it. She picked that name out of a hat. A very white hat." We laughed. "So after she was through, I had an auction." Ellis whistled and shook his head. "I made so much money, it scared me. Really, no lie. Turned my skin pale and gave me goose bumps." We laughed again and bumped fists. "And I got to noticing how everybody liked to stay afterward and talk. So I added some food. You cannot do anything in the South, especially down this deep, without food. And that worked well. And then liquor and that was slammin'. Then Sayan noticed how everybody dressed up and we changed it to a party. Then added the dance as a lagniappe."

"Sayan loves to dance?"

"Oh, does that girl love to dance." Ellis slapped his thigh. "So she gets to invite her family, dress up, dance, and play Queen Bee all night."

"I play Queen Bee every night," Sayan said, entering the kitchen and embracing Ellis from the back.

Ellis turned his head and looked at her, his eyes liquid and tender. "That you do, baby."

I turned away as Sayan kissed him.

"Well, T, we got to go," Ellis said, rising. "You sure you won't come?"

"Yes, Nora, I'm going to get you to come sooner or later, you might as well give up," Sayan said.

"Church? Nah, I've got to work. Repay your hospitality," I said but thought, Thank God I have an excuse.

They walked out, arm in arm, Sayan giving me the stink eye as they left. I breathed a sigh of relief and opened the refrigerator. I carved off a large hunk of Sayan's meat loaf, wrapped it in white bread and a napkin, and ate it as I drove to the pawn.

Chapter Twenty-one

I shoved open the door to the tune of tinkling bells. Cleo was at the counter, examining a tuba that a woman with her back to me was trying to sell.

"You're late!" he called.

"Traffic was terrible," I joked. I had been the only one on the road. The knot of pleasant men was looking at drum sets. Drew wasn't there.

"Check the books, see who's overdue this month," Cleo said.

I took the large heavy ledger to the table and rolled a cigarette. The woman at the counter took her cash and left. Cleo put the tuba in the back room to be cleaned and checked and priced.

When he returned to the table, he was shaking his head. "Tuba." He chuckled. "What kind of a horn is that?"

I just watched him, listening.

"It's something for a circus or the military, but nobody with any grace or finesse plays a *tuba*." Cleo inflated his cheeks into balloons like a struggling blowfish. His skin stretched, thinned, and lightened with his effort. "We'll never sell that thing unless Bozo comes in here."

"I'll keep a lookout. Red shoes, right?" I smiled.

"Roll me a cigarette, little brother," Cleo said after he patted his pockets and found nothing. Even though I had perfected my technique with so much practice over the past few weeks, I still trembled at the request. I sealed it and he lit up with a smile. He poured his dominoes out of their scuffed box and stirred them thoughtfully.

Drew entered, carrying a sack lunch and his grocery bag of knitting.

"Do you work here?" I asked, wanting to have some jovial sparring.

"Do you?" he retorted. Cleo laughed. He and Drew bumped fists.

"I need a hat." I swiped Cleo's ever-present stained but elegant fedora and put it on. Drew gasped. Cleo just stared at me until I placed it back on his head.

"You never take a man's *hat*," Cleo said.

"That's right. Don't you know that?" Drew asked.

"Well, while you ladies crochet and play mah-jongg, I've got to run this business." I stood and ambled over to the pleasant men who had moved to chain saws. They glanced at my approach, sidling uneasily away like a fleet of gazelles in the path of a lion.

"What can I help you with today, boys?" I boomed.

They shrugged and smiled and mumbled, shuffling toward air compressors.

"Deep discount? Just today, just for you, boys, I can do something very special!"

Their eyes downcast, they nodded, not tempted. "We'll let you know," one said.

I returned to the card table and opened the ledger. I made notes on the new items that needed to be reported to the police. I also made notes on the delinquent accounts and wrote a list of names on a tablet. Ellis would decide whether to contact them, give an extension, or sell their belongings.

"Never take a man's hat," Drew whispered.

I threw down the pen to chew his ass and saw both he and Cleo were laughing. "All right, all right." I waved at them.

"Say, little brother." Cleo held a domino close to his face and squinted at it. "Ain't you got a birthday coming up?"

"Or just passed?" Drew added.

I stared from one to the other, frowning as I rolled another smoke. "No, I—"

"'Cause I been thinking about the perfect gift for you," Cleo went on. "Your very own set a bones." His arm formed an arc and he slid the whole set slowly to rest in front of me in a pool.

I looked down in amazement. My throat was dry, my tongue confused. My cigarette remained unlit. The domino dots swam in my eyes until I blinked and coughed. "You can't be serious?"

"Happy birthday!" Drew said.

Cleo's steady eyes met mine. "You go on and take 'em. I need me a new set and I've been wondering what to do with these old things." Cleo caressed one with the tip of his finger. It was silky with wear and stories.

"But I can't." I tried to push them back.

"No," Cleo said, his voice iron. "It's right."

"It is right," Drew echoed.

Cleo cleared his throat and stood, making his voice cheerful. "I never saw anybody try so hard."

Drew laughed, re-rolling a yarn ball. "You right about that. Nora wanted to beat your black ass at bones."

Cleo laughed while I protested.

"Listen, I'm a go get a Crush. Anybody want one?" Cleo jingled coins in his pocket. He studied the sky above Tassie's. "Hurricane's comin'."

"Cleo, let me." I tried to stand but Cleo pushed down on my smooth skull.

"Lemme go."

I nodded, wondering if he meant more with that sentence, feeling my heart pause with fear.

"Yeah, I'll take a cream soda," Drew said, his needles clicking in the complicated weave of bright red yarn.

"I'll uh, I'll have a grape," I said. After Cleo left, his fedora jaunty on his head, I asked Drew, "Is he sick?"

Drew didn't even look at me as he sped up his knitting. "Naw, uh-uh. The man just knows the life of things."

"Huh?"

"You know, the proper way. The expiration. Those dominoes are dead for him but alive for you. Can't you see that?"

I picked up a polished domino. "No. So what...how does—"

Drew set down his knitting, his brows clenched. "Can't you be peaceful for a second? Why don't you get a hobby and quit talking so much? Lord!"

I lit my cigarette at last and sat back with a sigh. Me, a hobby. So I could retire here and be a kook like this crowd, collecting stamps or whittling. Bullshit. But the idea sounded good, too. Rest at last. Somewhere to belong and relax.

"We want to talk to you about this turntable," one of the pleasant men said.

I slammed out my cigarette, grinding it into the ashtray. "Coming, boys."

"You don't take a man's hat," Drew muttered.

CHAPTER TWENTY-TWO

The front door burst open and a man stood there, pointing a rifle at Ellis. "You sold my granddaddy's watch, you son of a bitch!" Ellis was with me behind the counter, collecting a bank deposit. I dropped to the floor and tore at Ellis's pants, grappling with his legs to try to bring him down with me. The pleasant men scattered, spying on the scene, their eyes insectile with curiosity. Cleo and Drew just watched, never moving. Drew never dropped a stitch.

"You never came to redeem it, you goddamn fool," Ellis replied.

"But why didn't you—"

"I did!" Ellis bellowed. I was astonished that Ellis had mastery of the situation, so I peeked cautiously over the countertop. "I phoned you every month. I visited you at work. I talked to your wife. I took you out for a beer before I sold it," Ellis said.

Tears coursed down the man's face. He cocked the hammer. Tension rose in the silent room. I held my breath. Cleo's lighter flared, startling everybody as he lit a cigarette. Ellis, as if reading my mind, pressed down on my shoulder, stopping me from rushing the man as I had been planning.

"That's the only thing my daddy left me," the man blubbered, the rifle barrel quivering.

"Put that thing down, you dumbass cracker," Ellis said and held out the box of tissues.

The man set the rifle on the floor and mopped his face with the tissues. "I'm sorry, Ellis, I just…"

Ellis went around the counter and held the man's shoulder. "No problem."

"You know who got my watch?"

Ellis shook his head. "Man, you shouldn't pawn things you want back and then stay drunk until they're gone. Ain't cool. You know I'm in business here, right?"

The man nodded, hanging his head.

"I don't have time to babysit your shit and give you money. That's for your mama. A deal is a deal and you gave me the shaft. I've gotta protect myself and my family, you know?"

The man nodded. I slowly stood. The pleasant men were burbling over a set of tires. Cleo watched Ellis with a bright, proud smile. Their fedoras were cocked identically.

"So don't come in here and pull that shit. I've got money for *loan* and you don't pay me, what am I supposed to do?"

The man shrugged.

"So, you see? I did what I had to do. I'm sorry about it, man, but I can give you a great deal on another watch. Look just like it, okay? Now go on home and dry up." Ellis squeezed the man, turned him in an about face, and pushed him toward the door. Cleo picked up the rifle and removed the bullets, pocketing them before handing the gun back to the man. The man waved weakly as he stumbled out, dragging his gun on the ground.

"Ellis," I said. "I'll be damned."

"My man!" Drew cried.

"Naw, naw," Ellis shook his head. "Don't be too impressed. He comes in like that about every two months. Damn rifle has probably never even been shot."

"You mean he's still not over his gran's watch and he threatens you regularly?" I asked.

"Naw, what happens is, he pawns stuff all the time and never pays it out. He puts that rifle in my face about all of it."

"I'll bet he pawns the gun next." Drew laughed.

"Yeah," Cleo said. "And, little brother, everything he owns is some precious heirloom from his daddy. It can say Wal-Mart right on it and he still has a sob story about how it was passed down."

Ellis laughed, his teeth gleaming. He slapped Cleo's back. To me, Ellis had never looked stronger, handsomer, or more powerful. In my mind, he grew tall in respect and deep in legend.

"And, Nora, if he ever comes back looking for a watch," Ellis rummaged in the storage cabinets below the display cases, "show him this one. Mark it up another hundred and fifty percent and then come down fifty percent *slowly*, all right?"

"But it's already marked up…" I trailed off, everyone waiting. "Oh, okay. How do you know it looks like his daddy's?"

"'Cause it *is* his daddy's." Ellis smiled, his eyes hard.

"Don't say nothin'," Cleo said to me.

"My man, my man, my man, mmm, mmm, mmm," Drew said. I nodded.

"Okay." Ellis clapped, brisk to the bone. "I'll take this." Ellis zipped the bank bag fat with the deposit. "And see you all later."

After Ellis left, I straddled a chair and lit a cigarette, still shaking over the morning's drama. I massaged my scalp, trying to integrate everything. "How did he do that?"

"It's his business. Anyone would do the same," Drew said.

"No, I wouldn't," I declared.

"You're blood, ain't you? You could do it," Cleo said.

I regarded him sourly through my fingers as I held my head. "You're wrong, old man. I do well when my opponents only have a ball."

"Or a pussy." Drew cackled.

"You enjoy it, though, don't you? Having opponents?" Cleo said.

"Yeah, but that's my job."

"Same thing."

"My man is right," Drew said. "Ellis is successful because he's a dirt gatherer and he doesn't look or act like he's a dirt gatherer."

"And he knows how to keep his mouth *shut*," Cleo added.

"And all that's in you too," Drew said.

I removed my hands from my face. "What do you mean, he's a dirt gatherer?"

Cleo shrugged. "Look around. Pawn is a dirty business. Useful, necessary, but dirty. There are problems, tragedies, failures, losses all through here."

"And that's not all," Drew said. Cleo glared at him for a second.

"Well," Cleo said, scratching his head underneath his hat.

"Tell me, Cleo, I'm blood," I said. I hated to use the relativity card, but I would to find out what the hell this was about.

"There's more." Cleo rose and led me to one of the back rooms where Ellis kept his office and there was a wall of battered metal filing cabinets. Cleo removed a key ring from his pocket and unlocked one, pulling out a drawer and removing a manila folder.

"What is this?" I said, seeing the label marked "Threats."

"Ellis ain't stupid. He keeps a record of all of them just in case. I told you, pawning is dirty."

I leafed through the notes. Some were just Ellis's handwriting recording an unpleasant phone call. Others were notes scrawled hard in anger and threatening property damage. There was a police report of a stabbing.

I held it up to Cleo's face. "He got stabbed?"

Cleo took the report, squinted at it, and nodded. "Not serious, though."

"But stabbed?"

"Only in the leg. Ellis knocked him down. The nigga pulled a knife and went for anything close."

"My boy was stabbed," I said.

"Pull yourself together. It was years ago."

"Who was it?" I snatched the report, belligerent and ready to kill. Cleo pinched it back and returned the report to the folder.

"Calm yourself. It's all settled. You're not in it."

"But...was he? Sayan..." I stammered.

"It's the South. You got to expect things like that. You're not from here. You wouldn't understand. So don't try."

"The South? What the hell does that mean?" I yelled. Cleo gave me such a look that I subdued myself. I looked at the filing cabinets. "What is up with all this?"

"Oh, you know how it is...small town, a black man with money. You sell your shit for a little relief, then the money's gone, your shit's gone, and you start to blame Ellis for your troubles."

"But he needs protection."

"That's why he saves all this. For evidence, just in case. Don't you worry none. Ellis can handle himself." Cleo replaced the file, slammed the drawer, and locked it.

"There's more," Drew said.

"Tell me," I said, surprised to hear that old familiar tone in my voice that I had used on my players. Cleo and Drew stared. It pleased me. I felt big. I straightened my spine, threw back my shoulders, planted my feet, squared my jaw, fixed my eyes, and repeated, "Tell me."

Wordlessly, Cleo motioned for Drew to watch the store as Cleo led me deeper into the back to a closet. He opened the door and exposed an enormous safe. Cleo knelt and twisted the dial, jerking the handle down; the thick, heavy door swinging wide. I held my breath. Cleo leaned on the safe's door waiting to see if I would understand it.

"Envelopes?" I reached in to remove a fat 81/2 x 11 envelope. *Chappelle* was written across the top in Ellis's hand. The envelope was sealed. "Are they stocks? Bond? Confederate notes?"

Cleo shook his head. "Secrets."

"What kind of secrets?"

Cleo shrugged. "Anything. Everything. Whatever someone knows and shouldn't know and needs a loan. Now this is serious money." He gestured to the stacks and stacks of innocent-looking envelopes.

"I don't believe it." I said. "This is filthy, nasty."

"You think he can turn a profit on unwanted vacuums and used, broken-down TVs?" Cleo snorted.

"Other people do, don't they?"

"Maybe. Don't really care." Cleo started to push the safe door closed.

I stopped him with a grip on his arm. "For real, what is all this?" I regarded the envelopes again.

"Like I told you, it's people's sins. Where the bodies are buried." Cleo laughed at his own joke. I was mute. "Embezzling, thievery, assault, sexual peculiarities and peccadilloes, who is whose daddy, stuff like that. Regular humanity as it has been since before Jesus."

"How does it work?" I still couldn't absorb it. Ellis, a blackmailer! I hoped that if I could get Cleo to explain it then I could prove it false and point out where he had gone wrong. A misunderstanding.

"Well, they come to him. He never solicits this sorry trade. I don't remember how it started, but let's say a husband needs to confidentially cover a whiskey debt. He has nothing to pawn but information. So he gives Ellis all the evidence of some foul doing, signs the contract, and takes the money. If the secret isn't eventually bought back, Ellis goes to the victim to sell it and reclaim his money. If the secret is redeemed, all the evidence goes back to the seller, no questions asked, no further action. No copies are ever made and Ellis forgets he saw anything. Slick, huh?"

I felt queasy. "Are you sure that's what this is? Cleo, are you certain?"

"Shit, all that is enough of a scandal powder keg to blow us to Kingdom Come." The tinkle of bells rang faintly.

"Customer!" Drew called.

"I gotta take a walk," I said.

"Sure, you go on." Cleo returned to the front with a smile. I let myself out of the back door, my head spinning.

CHAPTER TWENTY-THREE

That night at supper, Ellis and I sat at the dining room table alone as Sayan, in the den, caressed her belly and stared at the television, which issued continual weather warnings about the approaching hurricane.

"Baby, come away from that," Ellis said. "Everything is getting cold."

"You two go on and eat," Sayan called back. "I'm just fine."

"You've go to eat. Come on now," Ellis said.

I just watched, trying to assimilate my new unsettling version of Ellis. How much did Sayan know? Would she care? I was undecided about mentioning anything to Ellis. What could I say? He was a grown man, successful and supporting my own sponging black ass while I regained my bearings.

"Why are you so quiet?" Ellis asked as he spooned peas on to Sayan's empty plate first, mine second, and his own last.

Startled, I shook my head. "Nothing. Hard day at the office." I tried to look into his eyes for some guidance but he was dishing up food and yelling for Sayan.

"Baby, please come eat with us. I'm not playing. The hurricane will be there after supper!"

"Just a minute," she replied.

"Don't make my food sit wrong," Ellis said.

I smiled, marveling at the stubborn little battles of marriage.

"Don't make me snatch you bald-headed for worrying me to death," Sayan retorted.

Ellis slapped a heap of sweet potatoes on each of our plates. Then he scooped some tomato salad next to that. Last, he dished up the chicken and rice Sayan had baked that afternoon. I started eating until Ellis's gentle unblinking stare stopped me. After all these meals in all these weeks, I still wasn't used to the seemingly constant prayer. I dropped my fork.

"Right. Sorry." I mumbled and bowed my head, taking Ellis's hand. Ellis shook me loose.

"Not without Sayan," he said. "Kendake Sayana Kibibi, turn off that TV set!"

"I'll eat out here. It says the storm is gathering strength in the Gulf and it's headed straight for us."

Ellis sighed, rolling his eyes. Then he winked at me. "Jesus!" I pressed my lips together in muted amusement. Sayan was in the doorway in a flash, her brows knitted together. Ellis grabbed my hand and we bowed our heads.

"Ellis, what have I told you—" Sayan bellowed and seeing us praying, she finished meekly, "Oh," and joined us, clasping our hands and closing her eyes.

Sayan stayed for the entire meal and we ate in comfortable silence. All of us went to bed early.

The next morning, I woke to the smell of bacon. I slipped into a T-shirt and shorts and padded to the kitchen where Sayan sat at the table and Ellis, in a pressed shirt, suit pants, and an apron, tended several pots at the stove.

"Nora, you need to go shower," Sayan snapped. I looked down at myself, puzzled. "You got to get the funk out of your face."

"Don't mind her. I cooked breakfast as a surprise and I didn't know bacon would make her sick," Ellis said.

"Yeah, I got my man making me throw up on one side and a freak making me ill on the other. Y'all two peas in a pod and both nauseating."

"Your oatmeal is almost ready, baby," Ellis said.

"You want coffee, Sayan?" I asked, aching for a breakfast of cigarettes and caffeine.

"Fool, you know I cannot have coffee," Sayan replied as she turned the pages of the *Times-Picayune* spread all over the table.

"Maybe get her some juice," Ellis whispered as I poured myself a huge steaming mug of chicory java. I filled a dinky glass with orange juice and set it in front of Sayan, who picked it up, sniffed it, scowled, and set it with a bang away from her.

I stirred sugar into my coffee and slipped onto the patio with my cigarettes. I thumbed a match into fire and sucked a smoke down to a roach before I even took a seat or had a sip from my cup. I sat astride a picnic bench and gazed at the azure sky, warm and cloudless. Hurricane. Not likely. I rolled a fresh cigarette, admiring its plump perfection. I admired my fingers: long, thin, and strong. I thought of all the women I had been with and all my hands had done, and as I enjoyed the panorama of images, I put the unlit cigarette on the table and kissed each fingertip. Then I darted a glance around, cleared my throat, and drank coffee. I stretched, my back popping. Reluctantly, I admitted I could get used to this. I lazily lit the cigarette. Usually by this time of the morning, I had gone through two rounds of training with my players before they dashed off to class; I had had a pot of coffee; made dozens of calls; dictated a memo to my assistant, and was deep into reviewing game films. But this! I closed my eyes and let the blue smoke drift up my nose as the sun baked my head. I would have a slow breakfast, wander into the shop, and lie low all day. Just like a vacation. I finished the mug of coffee and cigarette before anyone called me inside to eat.

"Just you and me, cuz," Ellis said, removing the apron from his waist. "Sayan took some dry toast and will be going shopping with her sisters."

"Sure thing." I sat down with a grin to eggs, grits, bacon, toast, and more chicory coffee. "You got to let me clean up," I said, my mouth full.

"Yeah, you do that." Ellis threw his tie over his shoulder, tucked a napkin into his collar like a bib, and leaned carefully over his plate.

I leisurely turned the pages of the paper Sayan left on the table. I was feeling fine, fat, and lazy. I begged something in the articles to catch my eye and keep my interest.

"Today, you and Cleo have to clean up over there," Ellis said between bites of bacon. "You know, wash the windows, sweep the sidewalk, sweep and mop the floor, clean the glass on the display cases, stuff like that, you get me?"

"Mmm-hmm." I turned page after page. Sports, International, Careers, Classified.

"I mean it. The place has got to be kept up."

I looked at Ellis. "What's wrong with you, Hambone? Don't you notice a damn thing? Cleo and I do that stuff every day. The place looks sharp. We even cleaned the guns and polished the instruments yesterday. Do you think I'm not pulling my weight? What's up your ass?"

Ellis dropped his eyes. "Sorry, Nora. I'm just..." He shrugged. "Everything is moving so *fast*, you know? I been in control for so long and now I'm about to have a baby and it's all..."

I waved my hand, smiling. "You're just PMS-ing. I get it."

"Yeah, you and Cleo are the best."

"And the cheapest," I added. We laughed. I reached the local section in the paper and began flipping through it. Sayan clattered out of the bedroom looking fresh and rosy in a soft sleeveless top, pedal pushers, and sandals. She was fastening a necklace as she read over my shoulder. As I turned the page to the society section, I froze, glad I didn't have food in my mouth or I would've choked. There was a glorious color photo of Julia in a spectacular evening dress that was nearly obscured by the sparkling cape she wore. She had one arm looped through her husband's and the other hand at her throat as she laughed, surrounded by a small crowd of over-groomed glitterati. I just sat, immobile, trying to remember to breathe, the remains of my breakfast congealing on its plate. Sounds from the St. Louis cemetery filled my ears. Julia splayed out and me sunk deep inside her muff, Julia shrieking and screaming and shaking, biting down as I smothered Julia's cries with my gloved hand, Julia's pelvis pumping hard, me fucking hard, Julia's tits bouncing, her neck and chest flushed, the knife shining...

"Hey," Sayan said, pointing. "Ellis, isn't that one of your snotty white clients?"

I made a grunting sound, trying to find my voice. Ellis looked over and snorted.

"Yeah. She's in the paper all the time. What's she doing now?"

"Ballet Benefit," I said.

"Say, what the hell?" Ellis stood suddenly and came to squint at the photo.

"Ellis, I thought we talked about cursing," Sayan said.

"The baby's not born yet," Ellis muttered, distracted.

"What is it?" I asked.

Ellis whipped a loupe out of his pocket and bent close to study the photo. "This doesn't do me any good. All I can see is damn dots." He straightened. "But I'll be good and goddamned!"

"Ellis!" Sayan said.

"That motherfucking, shit-eating, white bitch!" Ellis put the loupe in his pocket, kissed Sayan, and left. The two of us heard the car start and roar out, tires squealing. Sayan and I looked at the picture again.

"I don't see anything, do you?" Sayan asked, her forehead furrowed in worry.

"No, ma'am, not a thing." I stared hard at the photo.

"Well, I'm late." Sayan grabbed her purse and kissed me on the cheek as she left. I was confused beyond utterance and could only look at the picture in the paper and hold my cheek where Sayan's lips had been. Finally, I stood, put on an apron, and cleaned up.

Later, I was still shaken by the photo and what it might mean to Ellis. I let myself in the pawn through the back door. I heard drilling and found Cleo attaching sheets of plywood to the window frames.

"What the hell are you doing?" I set my mug of coffee on the wooden bench and cupped my hand around a match as I lit a cigarette. Cleo wiped beads of sweat from his forehead with a handkerchief and set down the drill.

"Preparing for the worst and hoping for the best," Cleo said, lifting the cigarette from my lips and taking a deep drag.

"What, you mean the hurricane?" I sat on the bench and rolled another cigarette. I noticed that none of the other businesses along the street were boarded. The cordless phone next to me rang. Cleo hefted a second sheet of plywood into place over the second plate-glass window. The iron bars preventing robbery had been mounted on the inside, allowing for just such a weather eventuality.

"Get that, will you? Sayan has called twice already. Tell her I'm doing it and not to worry."

"Pawn," I said, my voice more tender in anticipation of Sayan's concern and feminine flutterings.

"God damn you to hell. I'll get you," a voice said and hung up.

I rested the phone on the bench and smoked.

"Well, what did she want?" Cleo used the drill to put bolts into pre-drilled holes in the brick building.

"Wrong number," I answered, sipping cold coffee, wishing I had my sunglasses and a hat like Cleo's.

"Done," Cleo said, stepping back to look. Painted on the plywood, which had evidently been used for this purpose before, was DELANEY PAWN with the hours of operation on one sheet and CASH FOR ANYTHING, BEST TERMS ANYWHERE on the other.

"Sayan make you do this?" I asked.

Cleo removed his hat and scratched his head. "Yep. Every year. She and all her people are from here. I don't know where she gets her jumpy, it's like she's from Los Angeles." He settled his hat more firmly on his head.

I laughed. "You have to do anything else?"

Cleo grunted. "Not right now. Let's have a break. Play bones?"

I shrugged. "Sure. Where's Drew today?"

"Oh, he'll be in, don't you fret none."

Inside the pawn, which was now even dimmer and had the creepy atmosphere of being the inside of a smothering box, Cleo and I sat at the table and I washed the dominoes. Cleo set his hat down and wiped his skull and hair with his handkerchief and then replaced the hat on his head, after inspecting it minutely and brushing off invisible dust.

"Where could I get a hat like that?" I chose my dominoes.

"Can't. My wife had it made for me on our anniversary when Ellis was just a baby." Cleo held his dominoes lined up all across his palm in a peculiar, seasoned grip.

"You've known Ellis all his life?"

"Sure I have." Our eyes met and held. "I don't know why you and I never met, bad timin', I guess, but I heard a lot of you over the years. Saw your prize fight on TV that brought you here." Cleo put down a domino. "That's a time."

My jaw tightened and I hung my head, sliding a piece out to join Cleo's.

"Naw, naw, it's not like that." Cleo smiled and his face glowed. "That was something." Cleo laughed and shook his head. "Smack! TKO! That girl went down like a sorry sack of shit."

I grinned, feeling wide in my chest. I pushed out the double five.

"Uh-oh, get back! Twenty-five points for little brother!" Cleo wrote the hieroglyphics.

"Now I got you," I said.

"We'll see. Don't celebrate yet." Cleo studied his hand, his gnarled fingers curled around his dominoes. "Easy does it." With his other hand, he tapped the table absently as he studied the layout. "Paint my wagon, Nettie," he whispered to the zigzagging black trail. "And fifteen for me."

"How's that?" I said.

"Hey, now, you won't punch me, will you? I'd hate to tangle with your tough."

I smiled. "All right, all right, you sweet-talking cheat." I set down the two/three.

"Who are you calling a cheat? Oh, now I'll have to kick your black ass. You whupped a girl, but I'm still a man."

"What are my points?"

"Five."

"Well, mark it down in your secret code."

"You telling me what to do?"

"Yeah, and in a minute, I'll take your hat."

"Take it, then." Cleo plopped it on me. Even on my bald head, the hat fit as I already knew. It felt warm and comforting, like a good daddy hug. "Why, you look fine. Just like Ellis does in his."

I tipped the hat at an angle. "Tell me something I don't know."

Cleo laughed. "Zip for me. Lotta money on that other end already. Harem scarem hickum slickum, slide all that to me."

I put down the one/four. "Not fair using voodoo."

Cleo slapped his forehead. "Dang! You cleaned up!" Cleo wrote on his pad.

"I did?"

"Yeah, don't you see? Right here. All this." Cleo traced the print line.

"Well, I'll be damned." I grinned.

"I bump," Cleo said gloomily.

"Oh, and I have the perfect place for this right here." I placed my last domino. "I won!" I stood up. "I won! I won, right? Did I win?"

"Yeah, you won." Cleo totaled the points.

I slammed the table with the flats of my palms. "I won! I won! I really won! Did I really win or did you rig it?"

Cleo smiled into my face without answering. "Musta been the hat."

I removed the hat. "Hat hell, it was *me*. I did it. I can beat you now, old man. Let's play again with bets this time."

"Naw, let's not. Lemme just sit here and smoke a minute."

"Hey, roll me one, will you?" I asked.

"For the victor?"

"Yeah." I took my seat, beaming. "Wait till I tell Ellis and Drew!"

"Watch yourself, buck."

"Why? I won, didn't I?"

"Ellis has never beaten me. Might take it hard."

I watched Cleo roll the cigarettes. "Okay then, this is just between you and me. But I'm gonna do a victory walk." I strutted all over the store, waving to admirers as Cleo cackled.

"You sure are a good sport about it." I sat and lit my cigarette.

"Well, I'll tell ya." Cleo snapped open his silver lighter of such distinguished age and markings that I wished to give up my thumbnail match habit. "You're almost like family."

"That's right. Almost like a woman and almost like a man too, eh?"

"That's none of my business." Cleo leaned back in his creaky chair and stared into space. "The way I see it," Cleo picked tobacco off his tongue, "I trust God completely."

"What?" More religion. I leaned back, put my feet up, and stared into space, copying Cleo to maybe be in a tandem mindset with him.

"God makes everything and everybody on this Earth, and He don't make mistakes."

"Well, now, there's something about God I can agree with."

"God lovers burned you pretty bad, huh?" Cleo asked, still dreamy.

Startled, I glanced at him. "How—?"

"From time to time, Ellis would tell me of some of your problems while you were coming up. Don't be upset, Ellis came to me for advice about everything. We just stuck together, him and me, from when he was a boy."

"You know his mama?"

Cleo nodded slowly, both the couple's eyes still distant. "Yeah, I knew her."

I liked this new feeling that we were easing down a gray smoky path going deeper and deeper into each other.

"I knew her too. She was always my sweetest auntie. She had loads of children, but just knowing her for five seconds, you knew Ellis was her king."

Cleo closed his eyes and sighed.

"'Cause he was her firstborn, I guess."

"That's not why," Cleo said, his voice sounded slow and wet.

I waited, smoking the last of my triumph cigarette.

"I'm his daddy, but he don't know it."

My feet dropped to the ground as I gaped at Cleo. He finally faced me with watery eyes. I had to remind myself to breathe.

"This is a story you've got to tell," I whispered, scared to break the spell. I prayed the phone wouldn't ring or a customer wouldn't barge in on us. The pleasant men were absent and they better stay that way for a while, I vowed.

"Yessir, I got to tell it," Cleo said, dabbing his eyes with his handkerchief.

I rolled two more cigarettes to have something to do. They remained untouched in the center of the table. I straightened the dominoes and replaced them in their scuffed box.

"Sidcoe...Sugar, I called her...y'all call her Sugar too?" Cleo asked.

"Yeah, Auntie Sugar."

"Sugar and I were an item. I was going to marry her when I had to go away."

"The war?" I said, just guessing.

Cleo didn't reply to my question but said, "When I came back, Sugar was married to your Uncle Smoky and on her fifth child. So I courted her cousin Jet and found I could love her and was married happily to her till she died, God bless her. And Smoky looked something like me, dark and tall and lean with fine features. I guess Sugar liked that type, so it was never too suspicious, and we all got on fine. But she was my woman."

"Did Smoky know?"

"No."

"And Ellis has no idea?"

"No. And don't help him figure it out, hear?"

"Sure. No, I mean, I won't."

"That's why I stay close. To keep an eye on my boy and that grandbaby coming. It's my only home."

I held a hand over my heart; my eyes felt like they were bulging like hard-boiled eggs. "But doesn't that break your heart? Aren't you busting to tell him?"

Cleo shook his head. "Leave off talking that junk. I don't speak that language. My life has been lived the best way I can and I get to see my boy every day. I been a part of the family. He took me in when nobody had a reason to and I'm not gonna shake things up now. Smoky was a good man."

"But Sugar and Smoky and Jet are all dead. What would it matter?"

"Listen, I'm closer to that end than to the beginning and I guess I come from a different time. It would just hurt their memories and maybe cause pain. Why do it?"

I shook my head, uncomprehending. My heart felt big and fluttery. Cleo put his horned hand on mine. "When you're as old as I am, think on this again. I'll bet different things will seem important to you too."

"Oh, Cleo!" was all I could manage. We both reached for the cigarettes and Cleo lighted them with his silver lighter. His hand didn't shake at all.

The phone rang and Cleo smiled in such a way that I knew the dreamy secret time was over and we were in the world again.

The door pumped open and the pleasant men arrived, chatting about the approaching storm.

I answered the phone, spoke for a few minutes, and hung up.

"Hey, y'all." Cleo greeted the men. They nodded and smiled, looking over the DVDs.

"That was Sayan. She wants us to tape the smaller windows. And she says they're sandbagging all over town. She wants me to go home and help her move her furniture upstairs."

"Then you do that, little brother. You helping Sayan is helping Ellis, which is helping me. So you go on. I'll tape the windows."

"Right on." I stood, feeling rushed but not wanting to leave Cleo. I wanted to hug him and smell his shirt or punch him on the arm or pat his back or something. All I could do was stare at my hands. "Cleo," I began.

Cleo stared at me, level and calm. "You go on."

"But I just..."

"It's time to go. You're out of sync with the proper order of things, aren't you? To be safe in the storm, you gotta be flexible. And if you're not with Sayan in ten minutes, she's the biggest storm you've ever seen."

"Yeah, okay." I gathered my tobacco pouch and hesitated at the front door where I saw now that much had occurred during our talk. Tassie's was boarded. The streets were empty. "Cleo, I—"

Cleo cut me off by waving and walking into the back room for the rolls of tape.

CHAPTER TWENTY-FOUR

As I drove home, I glanced with increasing concern at the horizon. Navy and purple clouds warned of what was coming. I had seen hurricanes on TV and never dreamed I would be a part of one. The sun was now blocked by fat cloud banks and the wind was picking up. It stirred my blood with excitement and I wanted to stand in the storm face-first to see all it had. I suspected hurricanes were like sassy femmes. They just needed sweet-talking and good loving to be gentled down.

As I neared the house, I saw the streets were being sandbagged by many volunteers. Far in the distance, I saw a line of cars heading north for higher, drier ground. I wondered what Drew, Ellis, Johnny, and Payne were doing.

When I approached the driveway, I saw Sayan standing in the middle of it with her arms crossed, tapping her foot. I debated honking at her as a joke and changed my mind when I saw Sayan's face.

Sayan's expression was thunderous irritation and queenly displeasure mixed with terrible worry, and as soon as I approached, it all melted into a pleasurable, relieved smile.

She needs me, I thought, astonished. I'm the Ellis substitute; not quite a man, but close enough. Good enough to take care of her and make her feel safe in the storm. Man enough to move furniture. My mouth twitched.

Sayan walked alongside the car as if escorting me to a parking place. "Thank goodness you're here. We need to get started right now. I've tagged what all needs to be moved and you should start with the bigger stuff. It's labeled where it goes, so everything is ready. When you're finished—"

I turned off the car. "Slow down, puddin'. Let me come inside."

Sayan pulled open the car door, grabbed my arm, and tried to lift me out. I laughed, easing myself to standing tall. "Just calm down, little mommy."

Sayan's eyes blazed and she pinched two fingers hard on to my ear. "What are you laughing about? Don't you know what time it is? Get your sorry ass in the house. There is work to do."

"Whoa, hold up." I pried Sayan's pincers off my throbbing ear. "Don't treat me this way, baby."

Sayan stepped back, putting her fists on her ample and outraged hips. "What? I do not believe what I am hearing. Don't treat you like what, a lazy good-for-nothing, too stupid to know when a disaster is coming, or don't treat you like the ignint child you *are*? Which is it? Or both? Oh, Jesus, help me through this. I've got my hands full a work and my house full of disrespect." Sayan entreated the darkening skies. She put a finger in my face, her neck going Cobra on me again. "Nora, I swear, you better do me right today or I'll put you out. I will! I'll set all your shit right out in the 'cane and not look back, you hear?"

I tried to back away but was trapped by the car. "Cleo warned me," I muttered, wondering how to solve this.

Sayan heard. "Cleo…Cleo *warned* you? Warned you about me when I am just doing my level best to get through this in one piece and keep our home safe and our things protected and me and my baby secure and the shop dry and Ellis and Cleo and you alive!" Sayan's voice cracked. "And all Ellis had worked for." Sayan took a gasping sob. "And our future—" Sayan collapsed on the ground, crying. I knelt beside her, realizing I shouldn't have poked a pregnant tigress.

"Easy, easy, baby, I'm sorry," I murmured over and over until Sayan leaned on me and cried herself out. The wind blew leaves and trash in torrents over us. I lifted Sayan and we walked into the house with our arms around each other. I was docile and obedient for the rest of the day. And amid all the TVs blaring the dire forecasts, Sayan worked me like a pack mule.

Late in the afternoon, I was sweating and panting, and stood before the television as the weatherman announced that the hurricane had been downgraded to a tropical storm. Extreme caution was still advised and preparations for flooding and wind damage were still recommended. Evacuation was voluntary.

Sayan called out from the kitchen where she was preparing supper. "You finished?"

"I need a break, Sayan," I said.

"All right, but no smoking."

I trudged into the kitchen ripe with cooking aromas that made me sick with envy to smell. How I would love to have a wife taking care of the vitals: cooking in our kitchen, spoiling, pampering, and petting me. I sat across from Sayan. Me, having nothing to do, drummed my fingers on the table under Sayan's stern glare. "Where's Ellis?"

"Taking care of business, I'm sure." Sayan looked at the clock. "That should be him now."

As if synchronized, Ellis voice called out, "That smells so good. Where's my baby?" The door closed and Ellis stood in his fedora, big as life, smiling at Sayan, who ran into his arms. He rocked her for a few moments. They murmured to each other. I studied my fingernails.

When there was no sign of change, I stood up. "Well, I'll just…"

Ellis rested his chin on Sayan's head and grinned at me. "She been slave driving?"

"No, not too bad." I wanted to wink at Sayan, but Sayan's face remained on Ellis's chest.

"Well, I've got a situation to discuss with you," Ellis said to me. "Come outside?"

Sayan jerked away from Ellis. "I know what that means. Trouble. Don't go hiding your tribulations from your *wife*, Ellis Abraham Delaney."

Ellis kissed Sayan's forehead and stroked her back. "No such thing, baby. It's only a small something I want Nora to handle just so she knows how in case she decides to expand our business someday."

Sayan pressed her hands against Ellis's chest to look up and study his face. "And why can't that happen in here with me?"

Ellis sighed as if he were drawing on vast supplies of patience for a beloved child. "You know Nora needs to smoke. You probably haven't let her eat or use the bathroom all day."

"Mmm-hmm," Sayan grunted, unsure but deciding to concede. "I expect you both on time at the table for supper."

Ellis looked at his watch and nodded. "What are we having?"

"Your favorite, baby." Sayan snuggled against him again.

"Pot roast, mudfish étouffée, and pie!" Ellis licked his lips. "You can do no wrong, Sayan."

"You either, baby." Sayan seemed to melt and I saw, just for a moment, the tender soft side Sayan concealed behind her fireball exterior. Without warning, I got images of Sayan's lovemaking, hot, intense, and oh, so feminine. I rattled my head, disgusted with my involuntary fantasy. I didn't desire Sayan at all; Sayan was my sister and I felt about her that way. But I was jealous of Ellis and his cozy home life and beautiful, passionate wife. I needed to go to the Sayan store, I thought, wondering where and when that might be. Or I just needed to get laid.

"C'mon." Ellis left his hat on a peg by the door and went to the backyard. I started to follow, fumbling for my tobacco and matches.

"Be careful out there. Storm is still coming," Sayan snapped.

"Yes, ma'am," I answered, meek with desire for a woman of my own to boss me, worry about me, tend me, and mend me.

Sayan brushed my shoulder as she passed by, hot pads in hand. "You're not so bad, are you?" she said to the pot roast as she checked on it.

Belatedly, I realized Sayan was addressing me and I said, "No, ma'am," and followed Ellis outside.

Ellis stood, hands in pockets, his clothes whipping like flags in the wind. Once I was next to him, we both squinted into the gale as we watched trash cans and lawn furniture of Ellis's wealthy neighbors get tossed.

"Aren't you nervous?" I asked, putting a cigarette in my mouth but realizing it would be futile to light up. I desperately pulled air through the cigarette, trying not to swallow too much loose tobacco but getting a faint satisfying taste. Sayan, with her comfortable domesticity and love like a sun, made me go limp with longing and ravenous for cigarettes.

"Gimme one, will ya?" Ellis asked.

I glanced back at the house and held my pouch out to Ellis. "Hambone, you don't smoke."

"So don't worry about it." Ellis tipped his head at me, his caramel eyes meeting mine. He shook his head and looked off in the distance. "Love lies."

I knew instantly what Ellis was telling me. Love lies, the rationalized justifiable fabrications told to women to protect them from harm and hurt. I had never been much of a liar myself because I had too many women to keep track of to risk complications of that magnitude. But I knew many who did lie out of love and I understood it. I held my cigarette pinched between forefinger and thumb. "What fibs you been telling, Ham?"

A patio umbrella sailed through the air, the weather a counterpoint to our quiet, intimate conversation.

Ellis sighed, twiddling the unlit cigarette in his fingers. "To Sayan back there. It is trouble, and lots of it. Mrs. Clyde."

I felt my armpits go hot and my spine cold. "What's the story?"

"She's crazy, and I don't mean in a cute wacky sense. I mean dangerous. Loco."

I wondered if all this was about our night at the graveyard. I had brought my doggish disgusting habits into Ellis's clean, organized life and as thanks, brought strife and difficulty onto the man who loved, sheltered, fed, and employed me. My toes curled and I shut my eyes against the wind. What had Julia told him? How would I repair this? How could I possibly apologize enough? My cheeks grew warm with shame as I imagined Ellis trying to protect me against the disappointed look in Sayan's clear, shining eyes. "Look, Ellis."

"Turns out the bitch has been taking me for years."

I opened my eyes. I felt a drop of rain on my skull. "What?"

"I just can't tell Sayan all this because she told me not to do business with that raggedy heifer. But everything has been cool all the years I've known her, I *thought*. And now I'll look a fool if I tell her. I can't do that, can I?" Ellis spread his hands, asking for my approval.

"No, no, of course not. What's all this about?"

Ellis took a deep breath. I could sense his embarrassment to confess even to me.

"Listen, Ellis, don't worry about talking to me. You saw what a damn fool thing I did to fuck up my life and land me here with you."

"Yeah, but that's different. That was vigilante justice. And it was cool. You're infamous for that now. You got the glory with it. And I like having you here. Feels nice. Right somehow." Ellis pinched his nose and cleared his throat. "All I got was cheated by a skeeze white thief."

"But look at everything else you have that I don't," I said. I gestured to the upscale neighborhood and the charming home behind us, my cold cigarette like an accusing pointer. "And Sayan," I choked out. "And your baby. And Cleo." I stopped before I said too much. I sucked on my unlit cigarette and gathered myself. "So fuck your pride, man. Anybody would take all you got for that easy price."

"Sho 'nuff, huh?" Ellis grinned.

"Tell me, man," I said. "And let's go where I can light this goddamned thing."

"We'll go to the other shop. Let me tell Sayan."

"Don't want Cleo to know either?"

Ellis raised his chin, defiant. "No, I do not. That okay with you?"

I held up my hands, cigarette dangling from my lips.

I didn't know how Ellis convinced Sayan that it would be all right for us to leave in this weather and this close to suppertime. Love lies getting bigger, I surmised. He had grabbed his hat too.

In the tony shop, we sat in the dim light in luxurious chairs, all quiet around us. I was amazed by the contrast between Ellis's two shops. The pawn where Cleo and I worked was a chaotic rat hole compared to this. Ellis's regular pawn did all it could to speak poor. Concrete floor, rattly, battered filing cabinets, a touchy, temperamental cash register, scuffed cigar boxes of paper, squeaky ceiling fans, homemade cinder block shelves, and a hand-painted sign. I settled into my overstuffed wingback chair. This is more like it, I thought.

Ellis had deadbolted the door behind us and had only turned on one beautiful, fragile lamp that cast a warm yet eerie glow in the rich silence while the wind howled outside.

I had the feeling that we were hiding from a hunter. The door to this place was nondescript and all customers were viewed by camera and then buzzed in if they had an appointment. Outside, the door was solid metal with a plain brown façade. Next to the door was a brass plate with a buzzer. That was it. No identification or windows or awnings or signs.

Inside, the walls were striped gold damask; the thick carpet was black wool, and heavy gold velvet draperies covered the back wall and the entrance to Ellis's office. There was no direct lighting except at the antique table where Ellis examined proffered items with a brilliant halogen lamp, several magnifiers, a loupe, and several other tools. On a side table was a small bar with crystal decanters of whiskey, brandy, gin, and vodka. There was a tray of lovely glasses that were so clean they seemed to sing. Also on the table, there was a humidor, matches, ashtrays, and a cutter. Everything was immaculate.

Ellis poured each of us a glass of brandy and offered me a cigar, which I took and watched Ellis clip the end and puff on a match until the room was fragrant with tobacco smoke.

"Don't inhale, T-Bone, you'll get sick. Can you do it?"

"What's the point?"

"The point is, you'll feel like a fat, white CEO banker man."

I smelled my cigar with a smile. Ellis instructed me how to clip and light it. As I applied the wooden match to the plump cigar end, my smoker's instincts took over and I sucked deep and began coughing immediately.

"Now, Nora, what did I tell you?" Ellis chided as spit flew from my mouth and my eyes rolled. Gasping, I took a large swallow of brandy and my coughing spasm continued as the alcohol burned all the way in. I crouched on the floor on all fours, my cough like a feral yelp. Ellis, cigar perched between his teeth, laughed and slapped his thighs. He tossed me his handkerchief. I returned to my chair, knees wobbling, hands shaking, wiping my mouth and eyes. I was not at all amused. I plugged the cigar in my mouth and pulled gently, letting the ripe smoke nestle on my tongue and curl out between my lips. I took a cautious sip of brandy and fixed Ellis with a stern eye.

"What did you want to tell me, cuz?"

Ellis swirled his brandy, staring into its topaz depths. "I've lost a lot of money with that cross-eyed bitch. A lot."

"How much?"

Out of discreet pawning habits, Ellis wrote the number on a slip of paper. I looked at it and smacked my head.

"Do you realize how many zeroes are here?"

"Just one." Ellis pointed to his chest. "Me."

"Ellis, how did this happen?"

The wind screamed and yowled around the building. It sounded like rain was driven to ground at all angles like bullets.

"She was one of my first big clients, Nora. She's honky trash all the way. Been ridden hard and put away wet, but she used her skank toot-toot to snare some dumbass rich bastard who smothered her in furs and choked her with jewels and kept her in the life that royalty is so accustomed. I guess his gamble paid off because she cleans up nice and took on that role of bored, spoiled rich wife. She started all that useless shit that important people do: interior decorating, party planning, charity work with the movers and the shakers of New Orleans, you name it." Ellis took a breath.

I remembered that night at the graveyard. No matter how much Ellis thought he knew, he didn't know the half of it.

"But old habits die hard for a greedy bitch like that. So, she started stepping out. But she had to be careful 'cause her husband kept her on a short leash and he expected a lot. She could live like a queen, but she had a strict schedule and absolutely not a penny for herself. Everything was in his name and anything she needed or wanted, he had to approve and she charged on his accounts. So she was going crazy in this plush prison, so she started fucking all the male servants. Young, old, black, white, no matter."

"How you know all this?" I asked, only slightly annoyed that Julia wasn't a lily-white virgin until our night together.

"Well, since I've been wised up, I've been nosing around. Help talks. It's not hard to find. She's a kept whore, so her nasty doings are really of no consequence to anyone but herself and her husband, who knows a lot more than he lets on. So people give up info and it's easily researched."

"Mmm-hmm." I puffed my cigar and tasted my brandy. Mighty fine once I got the hang of it.

"So her husband changed all the service people to female," Ellis said.

I looked up.

"That worked for a while. But then more trouble started. With the women, there were broken hearts and lots of hostility. The house was in a constant uproar over this lousy piece." Ellis shook his head.

"Then what?"

"He got rid of the women, hired new men, but made them sign a celibacy clause to work for him." Ellis laughed. "Ain't that some shit? White folks."

I snorted. "Why didn't he just dump Julia and start over?"

"Good question, T. What I found out is that the silly jackass loves her. Is mad for her sweet stuff. I don't get it. You know what I'm saying?"

I pursed my lips, reflecting on that poon. I had had better. I had missed out on better.

"It's all mixed up. She was a hard-luck case, she sexed him up, he gets addicted to her but wants to save her from herself, they marry and he controls everything about her and she has several secret lives she must keep confidential to keep this gourmet meal ticket."

"You mean there's a point where he'd give her up?" I asked.

Ellis nodded. "He's a vain, touchy rich man and he likes his pride. Julia has done well by him so far with her volunteering and community service and being the adoring wife at all events, but I have it on good authority that one breath of actual scandal would bring down this house of cards and she would be on the street turning tricks for grits."

"But if he's so touchy, what about her sexcapades?" I was certain that was the only time in my life I would use that word.

"No, I'm talking real scandal like public shame from the news and exclusion from society and embarrassment from his peers. The fact that he has a wild nympho wife whose legs he struggles to close just adds to his machismo. I think he likes the gossip." Ellis shrugged, turning his finger around and around at his temple. "Sleeping with the mechanic and the butler ain't the same as fucking his golf buddies, you get me?"

"So where do you come in?"

Ellis sighed. He relit his cigar. His phone rang. His face got soft as he answered the call and convinced Sayan to hold supper. He hung up and finished his brandy, pouring another for himself and freshening mine. "When I started my pawn, I knew I could make a good living. And that was fine. But I saw a rich market go begging just because there was no resource with the capital and with the confidentiality. So that's where you came in the second time." Ellis smiled at me and I returned it warmly. "To stake me for this place. So I had the experience, the funds, and now I needed the business. Julia was referred to me by Payne Phillips. You know her?"

Not breathing, I nodded.

"Turns out, when Julia can't get enough freak, she's a voracious gambler. Her husband puts the cuffs on her in one way and she busts out in another. She has a curfew all the time and a guardian most of the time. But she slips out and loses at the tables as often as she can."

I steepled my fingers. "Uh-huh...and?"

"Well, she and Payne go way back even though Julia's a lot older.

Payne's from the hood and had done a few transactions with me, a drum set, a toolbox of Craftsman, shit like that, so I trusted her referral and I thought this was my big chance. So I laid down the deal for this nouveau riche bitch and she bit hard. She has a lot of important Jewelry with a capital J. You ever hear of the Claren-Stein rubies?"

"No."

"Well, they're magnificent. She's got them mounted in a ring and matching earrings. Ever hear of the Turkish Fires?"

"No." I pulled on my cigar, enjoying the large coal crackling and climbing up the shaft.

"Opals." Ellis shook his head. "Opals the size of walnuts. And brilliant. Oh, you should see the way they glow. And opal is so very fragile. She has them casually set in a gaudy necklace. I swear." Ellis punched his fist into his other hand. "That shit is wasted on that no-account trash. *Wasted.*"

"Where do you come in?"

"You ever hear of the Parker brooch?"

"Yes, I have, as a matter of fact. Emerald, right?"

"Not just any emerald. This one is amazing not only because of its size, but also because of its color. It would take your breath away."

"I get it, she has a lot of flashy jewelry." I sipped my brandy feeling warm and fine.

"All right, all right, I won't get into her diamonds. So Julia starts pawning these magnificent irreplaceable pieces."

"Only they're not, right?"

In response, Ellis rose and drew aside the heavy velvet curtain that covered the rear wall. I smiled with surprise. It was a wall of safes. Two dozen small, six medium, and three large. Ellis chose one, turned the dial for the combination, opened the door and turned the dial for the safe inside the safe then opened one more door and pressed a combination on the touch keypad, opened that last door and removed a long black velvet tray. Even from across the room, I was dazzled by what I saw. The jewelry seemed like royalty sparkling there. Just as Ellis had said, there were stunning rubies, incandescent opals, glittering emeralds, and flashing diamonds. I held my breath, my hand involuntarily reaching out to touch. I suddenly understood why there were thieves: this all seemed like pirates' booty to be found on the ocean floor or in a museum.

"Can I?" I asked before my hand closed around the opals.

"Go ahead." Ellis tipped the tray and everything dropped to the carpet sounding like golf balls falling. I gasped, hoping the jewels weren't offended.

"Ellis! You'll hurt them." I was on my knees, rescuing the pieces. Ellis laughed, his voice harsh. "No, I won't. This is what I'm saying. This is paste. These are fakes."

I sat cross-legged, hugging the jewelry. "Fakes?" I held one to my eye. All I saw was twinkling color.

"They're excellent fakes, but fakes just the same." Ellis looked as if he'd like to smash all of it. "That dirty whore."

"What? How?" I was hypnotized speechless by the jewelry.

Ellis sat on the floor with me. "Julia had them made. Three complete sets. She had one made in Dallas, one in LA, and one in Chicago. I know this because I found out that two other brothers, one in New Jersey and one in Florida, have the other two sets and all of us are convinced we have the real things."

Ellis let that sink in. I weighed the pieces in my hands. The wind screamed around the corner, rain drummed on the roof. We could hear things flying down the street bumping and hitting as they went. "What can I say? She had become such a good customer with such frequency that after a while, I quit checking the jewelry so closely. She always redeemed it on time, so I started trusting her more and more. Turns out, those jewels haven't been out of her husband's safe in years."

"But she pawned the real stuff to you the first few times?"

"Yeah, because I was real cautious at first. It was a lot of money. I don't know how she snuck it out, but what I saw was authentic. After about a year, I quit examining so hard."

"How do you know about the husband's safe?"

"Because help knows and help talks."

"And you believe them?"

"Mmm, let's see, believe them and all the evidence I got here, including those pieces of crap," Ellis indicated the baubles, "or believe a cross-eyed, lying sack of shit."

"So what happened?"

"This last time, she ain't been back for them. I got lots of money tied up in these and I called to tell her she's got to give me the cash or I'd sell her stuff. I never heard from her. So I went by her house and told her I needed the money or that I would get it from her husband, but I wasn't going to be left holding the bag on this deal. She can't do me that way."

"What did she do?"

"Flew into a rage, threatening me and blaming me if she ends up on the streets. Screamed so loud the butler asked me to leave. Sayan saw her photo in the paper and then I got to looking at these gems because if they were real and I sold 'em, I'd be sitting pretty on the plus side. But they're just very good fakes. Expensive glass and semi-precious stones. Beautiful but not worth a fraction of the real and nowhere near what she borrowed on them."

"What now?"

"She's been trying to buy time with stalling and promises and she still threatens me. She's even sent some clowns around to rough me up."

I stood, the jewelry dropping forgotten. "Who?" I said. "I'll go fuck them up right now."

Ellis laughed and punched me in the arm as he stood. "Good old T-Bone. S'awright, I can handle myself." His cell phone rang.

"It's Sayan. We need to go," I said.

But Ellis's voice was sharp and angry. "You crazy bitch! You think you can cheat me and get away with it? Where are you now? That right? Well, you leave me no choice! Bring me the money now and your husband never finds out. Otherwise, I keep my appointment with him tonight, storm or no storm." Ellis closed his phone and snapped off the lamp. "Let's go. Suppertime."

"What's she gonna do?"

"Who knows? I can't worry about it." Ellis tidied up the room and replaced the fakes in the safe.

"Why don't we swing by and pick up Cleo and invite him for dinner too?" I said.

"Now that's a good idea." Ellis smiled. "Let's do it."

CHAPTER TWENTY-FIVE

On the road, Ellis swerved, struggling to maintain control of the car. I gripped the door, my legs stiff and tense, pressing against the floor. We were both soaked from the run to the car and we were panting softly in tandem.

The wipers beat the water back at a furious pace but didn't help visibility at all. The only other traffic on the road was the occasional emergency vehicle screaming by. Many roads were already flooded and blocked off.

"Shit!" Ellis jerked the car to avoid a picnic table rushing at us.

"Listen, maybe we should just—" I began before Ellis plowed into a group of trundling metal garbage cans. It was an explosion of sound and papers that were not yet wet puffing into the air.

"Just shut up for a while, all right?" Ellis barked.

I scowled at him. "Not cool, cuz. I'll drive if you're too nervous." I unbuckled my seat belt.

Ellis closed his eyes and sighed. "Sorry, Nora." Ellis opened his eyes and stared at me. "Sayan will be frantic. I'll sleep on the couch for days."

"No, you won't. My man's not getting knocked off the honey pot. C'mon, slide out. I'll handle this." I shoved Ellis out the door and into the storm as I moved to the driver's seat. He ran around to the passenger side and got in, fresh water rolling off him as if he'd emerged from a pool. "I need a hat like yours," I said, again admiring his fedora, from which water streamed.

"Why? To keep your hair dry?" Ellis quipped.

I backed up, dragging a trash can for a ways, and then I stepped on the gas, tires screeching.

"Whoa, Nora, slow up." Ellis's hands were balled into fists.

But now that I was in control, I finally relaxed, dodging obstacles and swinging the car around water ditches and parked vehicles with ease and holding the car steady when it hydroplaned. Tree branches and moss flew through the air like missiles. I smiled, totally focused. I fumbled in my pockets for a cigarette to smoke while driving. Then I could really relax and enjoy the ride. I let go of the wheel and looked down, searching.

"Shit!" Ellis cried, grabbing the steering wheel. "What the hell you doing?"

"Smoke," I replied tranquilly.

"I'll get it for you. Fuck. Just drive!" Ellis rummaged in my pockets and placed a wilted cigarette in my mouth. Rain beat on the vehicle as if it were a kettle drum.

"Match?" I asked placidly.

"Match," Ellis muttered. "She wants a match. The whole state is being blown off the map and she wants a match." He extracted a broken wooden one from my breast pocket. I thumbed it to flame and sucked fire into the tobacco.

"Ahhhhhh," I sighed, settling into driving. I increased our speed. Rain sluiced across the windshield, the wipers unable to keep up.

"Exciting," I said. "Just like a video game."

"But it *isn't*," Ellis said. I grinned and patted his leg.

"Which way?" I asked. I had not even tried to learn my way around the serpentine weaving of roads that was Bayou La Belle D'eau. Too spooky and swampy. I had memorized the streets from Ellis and Sayan's house to the pawn and that was all. We squinted in all directions. Trees bent and whirled. Everything looked under shallow water already.

"Maybe we should just go home," Ellis said. "Cleo can take care of himself. I'm worried about Sayan."

"No, we're close, right? You know he would like a hot home-cooked meal tonight. Fifteen minutes, we're home. Which way?"

Ellis pointed.

I sped off. When the pawn was half a block away, the car lost control and spun in doughnuts. "Wheeeeeeee!" I shouted, letting go of the wheel.

"Goddamn it!" Ellis yelled, clutching the dash. "We're hydroplaning!"

We came to rest crossways in the street, our headlights pointing at the pawn. A news van raced around us toward the Gulf.

"You crazy!" Ellis cried, glaring at me. Then he frowned at the pawn. "It's dark."

"Maybe he locked up and went on home," I said.

"Naw, naw, he always leaves the lights on over the register."

"Power's out?"

"Could be." Ellis tightened the belt on his leather jacket. "Something is wrong."

We ran up to the door, getting soaked to the knees and down our backs. The door was unlocked.

"Uh-oh." Ellis pushed me behind him as if to shield me. "Stay back," he said.

"Like hell I will," I answered, shoving past him and yanking open the door, then charging into the darkness.

It was too quiet. The smell was wrong too, but I couldn't pinpoint it. Ellis stood silently next to me. "Nothing is missing," he said, looking around.

"Cleo?" I called. "Drew?"

"Cleo!" Ellis shouted. "C'mon, man, time for supper. Sayan is waiting." Ellis had drawn a gun and began creeping through the store.

"Cleo?" I flicked the light switches. Nothing. "Power's out." I headed for the back rooms. Near the filing cabinets, I stumbled over something. My stomach knotted. I knelt. It was a cold hand. "Ellis!" I yelled. "He's in here! Call nine-one-one! Get a flashlight! Heart attack!" I sat at Cleo's shoulder and felt my way up the arm to his head. I rested my hand on his cheek. I could feel him barely breathing. "Cleo, hang on. Everything will be all right." I heard Ellis speaking to 911. He rushed in, brandishing a flashlight whose beam bounced crazily over the walls, making a lurid picture and creating a nauseating vertigo in me.

"Cleo." Ellis sat beside him. "How you doing?" When he shone the light on Cleo, his eyes were open and he was drenched in blood. "Oh my God!" Ellis jumped away. The flashlight fell to the ground. "What the fuck happened to you?"

I picked up the light and shone it on the ceiling so it wouldn't be in Cleo's face. "Ellis, go outside and wait. Flag down the ambulance when they come." I knew the emergency techs might never arrive, considering the storm. Familiar with taking the lead and directing others, I convinced Ellis to go. On his way out, I heard him call Sayan and start sniffling, his voice wavery.

"Cleo," I said softly.

He looked at me and smiled. "I took the bullet for him. Tell him, okay? I took Ellis's bullet. She thought I was him."

"Don't worry. You'll be all right."

Cleo shook his head. "Lemme go."

I felt punched in the throat and I labored to breathe. "But...no, you can't..."

Cleo nodded. "Lemme go. It's okay," he repeated, exhausted with effort. He closed his eyes and concentrated.

I couldn't do anything more, so I just sat with him. "Cleo, tell me who did this," I finally said. "Who shot you? Was it Julia?"

His eyes remained closed. "No, not her," he said. His breathing stopped. I kissed his cheek, turned off the flashlight, and just sat with my hand on his chest until the ambulance arrived. When I heard Ellis bringing them in, I stood, turned on the flashlight, and filled my eyes with the sight of my beloved Cleo. As my smashed heart struggled to beat, a canyon of dark agony opened up in my chest and boiling blood surged through me. I spied Cleo's crumpled fedora flung against the far wall. I scooped it up, put it on, and fled out the back door and into the fierce stormy night.

CHAPTER TWENTY-SIX

I had no idea where to go or what to do. I only knew that with Cleo dead, nothing mattered. I also knew I couldn't return to Ellis's home and be marinated in their grief on top of my own. I would not be able to tolerate Sayan's soft crying, Ellis wiping his eyes, his hands hanging limp and useless. My entire being was now composed of a thin bubble shell of fragile glass, and any family around would shatter me. I couldn't stand the long, wet, soulful looks, the inane talk trying to make sense of it, the shrugged shoulders and repetition of how it must be God's will, the extra-long hugs, the dark suits and arm slapping, the praise of how brave everyone was being and how strong we must all continue to be. And most of all, I couldn't take the smiles and the stories. How everyone would gather and tell loving funny tales about Cleo. How women would eat the salads and desserts, the men would eat the meat from the lavish death buffet, and all would sit close over their plates and reminisce, laughing, nodding, slapping thighs, brandy and cigars toasting Cleo, crying a little but in a sweet way because Cleo was in a better place now and didn't we all just love him to pieces and wasn't he a helluva good black man and didn't he bless us all our lives and we were so damn lucky to even know him and he'll be our angel in heaven watching over us and hot damn we had some good times, remember this? Remember? Remember?

I ran, not caring where, the fedora jammed tight on my head. Cleo shouldn't be a "remember." It violated my soul that he was. I ran. I ran, not heeding the driving wind, not caring about the scary swamps, not noticing the churning levees, indifferent to being swept up into a hurricane or blown out to sea. I didn't mind the wet. The rain attacked me from above like hooves on my back, and from below, like hard spray as I ran, laboring, splashing through the water sometimes as deep as a bathtub.

I ran, not knowing where, not caring. As I ran out of town, I saw the chaos of the storm: people's belongings flying everywhere, things floating and things crashed and flattened, cars abandoned in the rising floodwaters, the empty homes with boards and tape over the windows, the water lapping at the miles of sandbags, a dog swimming with the current, police cars and roadblocks.

Gradually, the homes thinned and all was wilderness. I ran on the road, keeping my eyes down. After a long time and many near misses with vehicles that honked me into the flooded ditch, I realized I must rest awhile. Just for a bit. The storm was weakening the farther I traveled. I began looking for homes where I might sleep in the car.

I finally found a house that looked empty but had a carport. I sank to the wet concrete floor, huddling into the corner. My teeth chattered so hard I bit my lip and drew blood. I stood and found a greasy tarp and wrapped myself in it as I tucked back into the corner. I shivered myself warm enough to fall into a light, uneasy sleep.

"Sir?"

I opened my eyes. A policeman stood there with a bearded man. The owner of the house, I supposed.

The storm had passed. A diluted sunshine lighted the world as if through wavy water. The sky was white.

"Sir?"

Though unbearably weary, I met their eyes and struggled to stand.

"Sir, do you know your name? Do you know where you are?" the policeman asked.

"You know, I work nights. Up to the city. If the storm hadn't passed, I would'nt've come home. But like I told you, I found this guy when I got here. I don't want any bums hanging out. There are places for that," the man said to the cop, then turned to me silent, staring, and repeated loudly, "There are places for the likes of you!"

I nodded and dropped the tarp. I mumbled, "Sorry," and started to walk.

"Wait a minute, sir," the cop called. "You need a ride to New Orleans?"

I stared off into the distance, Cleo's hat still damp on my head, a ruined past, a devastated future, and a painful present. "Am I being charged with anything?"

"No, I'll just help you get where to need to go if you like. I'm headed that way."

I shrugged. "Sure." I held out my hand to the man under whose carport I had slept. "Sorry." He shook my hand and I led the way to the squad car, settling myself in the back.

As I watched the scenery pass, I willed my mind to think of nothing. I was dull as I watched the miles flow. There was debris everywhere. Suddenly recognizing Ellis's neighborhood, I shouted, "You're going the wrong way, pig!"

The cop didn't say anything but pulled into Ellis's driveway. Ellis and Sayan came out of the house and hugged me. I remained stiff.

"Thanks, Officer. We were so worried," Ellis said.

"My pleasure, Mr. Delaney. And I'm sorry about your uncle. We'll do our best to solve it."

"I know you will, thank you. And anything I can do, I will," Ellis said. Sayan dabbed her eyes with a wadded tissue. The policeman returned to his car and left.

Ellis studied me. I felt like wood. My eyes felt like specimens in jars.

"C'mon home, Half." Sayan threaded her arm through my rigid one and gently tugged me into the house. "Go on, lie down. I'll fix you a little something." Sayan pushed me onto their king-sized bed and wiped her own leaking eyes. With her sodden tissue in one hand and a blanket in the other, Sayan covered me up to my neck. She closed the door behind her, leaving me in the silent darkness. I lay, immobile, listening to the soft purr of Ellis's and Sayan's voices in the kitchen.

Soon, Sayan returned with a tray. There was a shrimp po' boy, chips, and an orange soda. She set the tray on the floor. I sat up and Sayan sat next to me.

"You know," Sayan said, shrugging, "Just in case you are hungry."

I was unresponsive. I dared to dart my eyes to Sayan, who was massaging her stomach.

"Oh!" Sayan groaned. "This got to be a boy 'cause he's kicking my butt from the inside out. Thought I'd name him Cleo." Sayan noticed my eyes on her. "Oh, baby." Sayan's hands flew to my face and I jerked away with a gasp. I stared at Sayan, furious and panting. Our eyes locked. Sayan began weeping, shaking her head. I didn't look away as two large tears rolled down my own cheeks.

"It's okay," Sayan said. "It's okay. Let it out. It's okay."

"No." My voice was steel.

"You've got to. It's not good for you. Come be with us. Be together with your family."

"No."

"Well, that's just fine," Sayan said, dashing her hands across her face. "Don't think of anyone but yourself. Do you know what we've been through while you were gone?" Sayan's voice cracked. "Ellis thought he had lost you too. How dare you be so selfish?"

I lay down, turning my back to Sayan, who struggled to stand.

"I can't," I moaned.

"Sure." Sayan closed the door behind her.

I heard the phone ringing. I heard visitors arrive. I heard wailing. I heard Drew shouting. I willed myself into unconsciousness.

When I opened my eyes, it was dark and I knew someone was in the room. "Cleo?" I asked.

"Naw, T, it's me," Ellis answered.

I sat up. I could barely see Ellis but I felt his calm sorrow. He wasn't jagged and fragile like I was. For once, pussy and cigarettes and booze wouldn't blunt my pain, but I wanted them anyway. I heard the commotion of grieving all through the house.

"Where's my hat?" I said.

Ellis stood and handed it to me from the dresser. It was still damp and slightly misshapen. He also laid the box of dominoes on the bed. I looked away.

"I know you need to leave and it's okay. Here." Ellis dropped some cash. "Don't get proud, it's what I owe you for working."

I nodded, my face burning.

"Well," Ellis sighed, "See ya." He hugged me roughly. I closed my eyes. As soon as the door closed, I folded the blanket and force-fed myself the lunch Sayan made. I wasn't hungry but I knew I needed fuel. I gathered the hat, the dominoes, and the money and slipped unseen out the back door. I walked into town straight to the bus station. I bought a one-way ticket to New Orleans.

Once there, I asked a cabbie to take me where the whores were. He took me to the Quarter. After I paid him, I found a liquor store and a terrible, run-down dive called the Royale and checked in. I placed my hat on the nightstand, the dominoes on the desk, and I lay down. I lit up a cigarette and drank gin straight from the bottle. Both the smoke and the alcohol were sweet going down. The street noise provided enough distraction so I left the television off. After a while, I opened the box of dominoes, removed one and returned to bed. There I lay, swigging booze, smoking, and sniffing the domino.

I kept myself poisoned and insensible to the point of losing track of days. I lived at the seedy hotel with my door open because nothing could hurt me. I had no fear left of anything that might come after me. My open door dared something to try. I didn't even need the warning of a knock on a closed door. Plus, it helped pizza deliveries find their way and it facilitated a great many tipsy friendships. With my door open, the lively, monkey, chattering drunks wandered in, told their life stories and ended up sobbing and being comforted by my room-temperature Tanqueray. I was popular because I never said a word, I had a free hand with money and a heavy hand when pouring drinks. Soon, every resident ended up in my room each evening. There was warm camaraderie, blissful group singing, and the center of it all, there I was like a black hole. When I rolled cigarettes, my hands shook but no one asked why. Everyone's hands shook who lived at the Royale. My eyes felt like ice picks. My head began to grow fuzzy hair and I never changed my clothes. I had Cleo's blood on my shirt, but none of the stew bums asked me about it.

One night, during a party of gleeful drinking, wise advising of what was wrong with the world and exactly how to fix it, and big-headed boasting, I opened my box of dominoes.

"C'mon, let's play bones!" I shouted, cutting the din to absolute silence. The first words I had spoken. They all stared at me, uncertain.

"You there, get a table. You, what's your name, find some chairs! Let's go, let's move!" I dumped the dominoes in the middle of the bed and was washing them vigorously. Their loud hard clicks were like teeth slamming together. It was the only sound. Still no one stirred. "Doesn't anyone know how to play?"

They shuffled their feet, stared into their cups and glasses and bottles. "Come on, you trash. Gimme a game."

There began an angry muttering.

"Get out," I said softly. They all looked at each other, shrugging and whispering. This was sudden and out of nowhere. *"Get out!"* I bellowed, standing. This group, obviously accustomed to being hassled and shaken and chased, knew how to clear a room. Almost by instinct, they picked up items as they fled; all things I bought: jars of peanuts, sticks of jerky, bags of chips, beer, vodka, wine, pretzels, even my own pet bottle of gin, which was stained greasy with fingerprints. The crowd left me nothing except trash and my dominoes and hat. Even my shoes were taken.

"Worthless motherfuckers!" I screamed to the group of backs running away down the hall. I fell on the bed, breathless and sick. "Ow, goddamn it!" I wrenched up, exposing the pool of dominoes. I sat on the bed hurling one after the other at my reflection in the pitted old mirror that hung above the dresser. I hoped it would shatter, but it didn't.

CHAPTER TWENTY-SEVEN

S omeone was knocking on the door. *Hello? Who's there?* I didn't know if I was speaking out loud. The knocking continued, so I knew I hadn't.

"Ah!" I tried to find my voice. It had died somewhere in my chest. "Heh…eh…mmm…" I ran my tongue over my teeth and sat up, holding my head. "Who's there?" I slurred, my voice creaky. If it was another drunk wanting money, I would put my foot in his ass. If it was the landlord, I would slap him upside the head.

"Drew."

"Drew who?" I asked then cackled, a sound that surprised me.

"Drew Ekalibato, you dumb motherfucker. Open this mother-fucking door."

"Drew Ekalibato of Haiti?"

"I'm a break this door down!"

"Go ahead, I don't care. There's piss in every corner, the roof leaks, and the bed squeaks. Can't hurt."

"All right. You making a tired old black man bust into your room? That's ill."

I stared at the door for a while wondering why he was here and what it would cost to see him.

"Fine. I'll leave, then. Forget you, nigga."

I leaped up and flung the door wide. "What do you want?" My voice was clear but my eyes felt wild.

Drew seemed taken aback by my appearance. He cleared his throat. "Lemme in, little brother." He brushed past me and looked for a chair. "Hm. Ain't no chair." He sat on the bed. "Come in here. Close the door. Time for you and me to talk."

I stared off into space. "I don't think so."

Drew jumped up and seized my neck with one hand and slammed the door shut with the other. "Get in here." He pushed me onto the bed. "What the hell's happened to you?"

I looked at him, my chin trembling and my eyes watering. Just seeing Drew without Cleo and seeing Drew in this hotel and not in the pawn brought the terrible reality to rest on my heart. Drew handed me a white cotton handkerchief. I lay down, holding the handkerchief over my face with both hands.

"What the hell's happened to you?" Drew repeated. "You gone pirate?" He fingered one of the wide gold hoops I had in each ear.

I remained silent, my face concealed and tears secretly slipping out of my eyes.

"What the fuck, man?" Drew just noticed the dark marks on my biceps. He pushed my sleeve up and squinted. "You got a goddamn tattoo?" He traced over the scabs. "Who is Max?"

I shook my head.

"Let's see…you've got a domino…that's cool…number ten, Michael Jordan? That's cool…who's Max?" he asked again.

I kept shaking my head. "I'm going to remove it," I said, my voice muffled.

"How did you do this?"

"Payne came by and took me out."

Drew laughed, pinching his nose. The sound was profane to me, but under my grief, I longed for it because his laugh was good: clean and warm. "Man, she fucked you up but good. She must've had some excellent shit, huh?"

I lowered the handkerchief and glared at him.

Drew held up his hands. "I ain't gonna play no more. I came here to talk to you."

I waited.

"You need to go home to your family."

I covered my face again. "Forget it. Leave me alone."

"Not yet I won't."

"Why do you care anyway? Just get out!"

"Why do I care? *Why do I care?*" Drew stood over me, pointing his finger. "Why do I care? 'Cause I love Ellis! I been knowing him since he was born. I love Sayan and I love her baby that is coming soon. And they are in pain. They are in pain over their loss and they are in pain over your sorry ass." Drew sat down. "And I loved Cleo. He was a fine man."

"Don't." My word was a barb.

"I'll say what I came to say. I loved Cleo and he's gone to glory and we're stuck here with each other. And he mad at you."

"DON'T!"

"Shut the fuck up. You'll hear this if I have to sit on you to do it and then I'll be free cause I'll know I did what I could. T-Bone, you know you're wrong. You know Cleo wants you to be there with Ellis and Sayan to help them through their trouble. And that helps you too even if you're too big a chicken to recognize. Wasn't Ellis there for you?"

I rolled into a ball, trembling.

"You're shitting on Cleo, man. This," Drew swept his arm around the room, "ain't showing your love. This is breaking Cleo's heart, and he loved you too. Hell, we all do. And Cleo would kick your raggedy ass if he could. Maybe I will."

"Go ahead. I won't hit back."

"Nora, get yourself together. This ain't right and you know it. Get your constitution laid out. Stand up and be strong. You know what Cleo would want you to do. Doesn't that matter at all?" Drew rose and picked up my various gin bottles and poured the liquor down the bathroom sink.

"Shouldn't be telling you this…" Drew shook his head. He placed the bottles in a neat row by the door. "I shouldn't but I'm gonna." Drew crossed his arms and leaned against the dresser. "You know Cleo was Ellis's daddy, right?"

I was unresponsive.

"Well, Ellis knew too. Ellis knew and didn't want to let on because he figured Cleo wanted it that way and you gotta respect your daddy."

Barely breathing, I watched him with one eye.

"What you don't know is how good care Ellis took of Cleo. I

know only because Cleo told me. If we were brothers we couldn't've been closer."

I waved the handkerchief in the air like a surrender flag and Drew grabbed it and honked into its center.

I pulled a stale pillow over my face.

"See, Ellis *set him up*. Cleo died rich 'cause Ellis didn't want him to lack nothin'. 'Course, it all goes back to Ellis now, but Cleo could've bought anything." Drew took a shuddery breath. "Ellis did all that 'cause being the dirt sniffer he was, he knew Cleo would have a hard time on his own." Drew shifted. "I guess it can all come out now… Cleo was in prison…in the pen at Angola…a long time ago and for a long time."

I grunted.

"He killed somebody and did his time. And you know what he told me? That his family made all the difference. That they stayed together and backed him all the way. He would've died in the pen if they hadn't."

"Cute story," I said.

"Every word is true."

I sat up and rubbed my eyes.

"My man!" Drew smiled. He waved his hand by his nose. "You're funky, you're ashy, you're crusty, your hair, you've grown some nasty hair. I'll wait while you shower."

"I don't know."

Drew grabbed my neck again and thrust me in the shower. "You can do this easy or you can do this hard. But make no mistake, you're cleaning up and coming with me."

"Take your hands off me, you old fool. Let me get my clothes off. And these are dirty, but they're all I got. You sit out there on the bed."

Drew looked at me a moment. Our eyes were soft as we stared at each other. "Now you're not gonna turn on the shower and then climb out the window, are you? Because if you do, just keep running. I can guarantee you, *no one will come after you this time*." He closed the bathroom door.

❖

"Look what washed up in the Quarter!" Drew guided me into the kitchen. Ellis stood, looking lost. Sayan, hugely pregnant, jumped up, ran to me, and folded me into her arms.

"Oh, baby," she said.

Finally, I cried.

CHAPTER TWENTY-EIGHT

Sayan had me by the collar and was jerking me. We were in the kitchen and Ellis was smothering his laughter and shaking his head.

"Now all my sisters are coming over here and I don't want you embarrassing yourself or us. Don't be acting a fool. Behave and act like somebody. *And you know exactly what I mean.*" Sayan's eyes were blazing.

I hid a grin, my eyes rolling with the vigorous shaking. "Yes, ma'am. No, ma'am. Yes, ma'am."

Sayan gave me a stink eye and released my shirt.

"I won't sleep with more than half of them," I added.

Sayan slammed down the wooden spoon she had picked up. "Ellis!" she barked. He sat up straight but shrugged. Sayan turned her back to us. She raised a finger and said, "I am too big with this baby to be worrying over the two Delaney children. Y'all bad."

"Oh, sweet pea, c'mon now," Ellis said. Then he and I saw her fist closing around the wooden spoon. "Git!"

We both scrambled to escape, but when Sayan whirled around, she was like Shiva with multiple arms and all of them strong and angry, wielding the spoon like a paddle.

"Ow, ouch, ow, quit baby, ow, now quit." Ellis tried to edge away.

"We were just playing. Ow, ow, Sayan, stop it." I contorted myself and dodged.

"Get out of my kitchen and stay out!" Sayan said through gritted teeth. She whacked us once more, Ellis on the behind and me on the back of the head.

"Whew!" I was panting and rubbing my skull as we hid in the family room.

"We better go to town." Ellis wiped his brow.

"And get her a big bunch of flowers?"

"My thoughts exactly, cuz. Let's roll." Ellis returned to the kitchen door. "Sayan, honey, we're going out for a while."

"Don't let the door slap your sorry fannies," she said.

"I love you too, sweet pea."

After filling his car with lavish bouquets, Ellis and I drove home. We had discussed the idea of going somewhere for a beer and a smoke, but since Cleo's murder, neither of us really had a taste for that. We both wanted to stick close to home and never go far and never leave for long. We told each other that we felt protective toward Sayan, but in truth, it was her presence that protected us. We needed to be near. She was so earthy and powerful and real, we felt calm and safe.

"You remember we're having this family reunion thing, right?"

I nodded. Sayan's talk had been of little else since Cleo's funeral. I knew it was just Ellis's way of opening the conversation.

"Well, ever since…" Ellis glanced at me and the silent sound of Cleo's death pulsed between us. We were pretty normal when Cleo wasn't the subject. But when his name or the space where his name should've been arose, it uncovered our grief.

"Uh-huh," I said, looking away.

"Well, Sayan has got this bee in her bonnet—"

I snorted. "'Bee in her bonnet'?"

"Bug up her ass? To start this reunion thing. To keep family close, she says. So it's going to be a monthly affair. What I'm saying is, the house is going to be full of brothers. And…"

"I'm gonna lay low and be cool, how's that?"

Ellis let out a shuddery sigh. "Naw, naw, I don't give a shit. You're fine. That's not what I'm saying."

"Then say what you're saying, Ham."

"Coach me some before?" Ellis's voice was high and small. "It's been a long time since I've played real hoops, and I know some of these guys can jam. They really get they ball on, you know?"

I grinned and nodded, watching the scenery pass. "Sure, Ham, we'll start tonight."

"You know Drew is moving in with us?"

I reached around roses to punch Ellis's shoulder. "That's wise, man, that's good."

Ellis smiled. "His girlfriend and son will probably come too, eventually, but for now, Sayan thinks he'll be great with the baby and helping to cook and clean and all, but I don't know."

"My man!" I boomed. We laughed together.

When we reached home, the driveway was already full of cars.

"Her sisters," Ellis said with an ominous tone.

"How many are there?" I asked, balancing bouquets of tulips and mums.

"Six. Seven daughters total. Agrafina, Wynetta, Tanitta, Taheerah, Ajaunia, Ubiqua, and Sayana."

I whistled. I looked Ellis up and down. "How you've survived all this time is a mystery to me."

"'Cause I am Hambone Delaney," Ellis replied, strutting up to the house. As we approached the kitchen, we heard the happy din of women. There was the clatter of plates, the music of spoons, the stomp of knives on cutting boards, the sizzle of onions and garlic, the rush of water and laughter. When we stepped inside everything stopped in a thunderclap of silence.

"Hey, y'all," Ellis said, his voice small but trying to be hearty.

"Ellis!" everyone yelled back and swarmed him. Sisters took the flowers Ellis was holding and set them in the sink and along the countertops and took turns embracing him, kissing his face, looking him over for signs of fatherhood, and patting his head. I cowered in a corner, hiding behind the bouquets in my arms, peering out between the blossoms.

"And this here," Sayan threaded through the crush and brought me forward, putting my flowers on the floor, "is the freak laying up in my house I been telling y'all about. She is Ellis's cousin Nora, so we love her and treat her right."

There was a collective gasp and six pairs of black, penetrating eyes picked me over, from my gleaming bald head to my face so like Ellis's, to my large graceful hands hanging limply, to my long giraffe legs and back to my goofball ingratiating smile. I felt at once exhilarated to be submerged in such a powerful tribe of beautiful females and scared witless that there would be some secret signal and they would grab me, gut me, and fry me up. I giggled involuntarily.

"See?" Sayan said. "I told you she was a fool. Nora, here are my sisters: Agrafina, Tanitta, Taheerah, Ajaunia, Wynetta, and Ubiqua."

I nodded to each, staring hard at Ubiqua, wondering where we had met before. Ubiqua flushed and looked at the floor. Sayan switched away, checking something in the oven.

Hurt by Sayan's assessment, I dropped my eyes. The women began a gentle murmuring of "Glad to meet you, Nora. How you doing? What you know good? Heard a lot of nice things about you." I shook hands with everyone. They returned to their tasks, chattering about greens and meringue, Ellis and me forgotten. A couple of them found vases and containers for the flowers and were clucking with admiration over their arrangements.

Ellis motioned for me to follow him outside where we might take a nip, but I was hypnotized and awestruck. I wanted to watch their strong, succulent bodies move in those amazing woman ways; I wanted to eavesdrop on their sacred speech; I wanted to be wrapped in their warmth; I wanted to be petted.

"Ladies," I said. "Can I help?"

Sonic boom of silence. Cheese sauce dropped from a suspended wooden spoon. Sayan bustled up. She pushed me outside with Ellis. "Women only. Go on, go on, don't be getting underfoot and making a nuisance of yourself." She looked me in the face as if speaking to a toddler. "Why don't you have a smoke?" Then she glared at Ellis as if he should know better and for him to handle this immediately. Then she blew him a kiss. "Thanks for the flowers, baby."

The back door closed and I heard the lock turn.

"Did she just put us out?" I jerked my thumb at the kitchen.

Ellis was laughing. "No, I walked out on my own. She put *you* out, T-Bone."

"No, no, she didn't," I said. "She put me out! Damn if she didn't put me out!"

"We might as well have a swallow and play some hoops." Ellis withdrew a flask from his car.

"What you got in there, Ham?" I grinned.

"Just some smooth sipping whiskey."

"Pass the Jack and get the ball," I said.

Ellis handed me the flask and went into the garage, emerging with a soft basketball that he proceeded to inflate. Even with all the sisters' vehicles, the driveway was generous enough to accommodate a ball game.

I drank two large swallows and coughed hard and long in appreciation as the liquid Kentucky heat spread through my body, relaxing everything as it went. As the coughing subsided, I withdrew my tobacco pouch and deftly rolled a cigarette. I held it out to Ellis in question. He glanced around and nodded, opening his mouth. I placed it between his lips and struck a match with my thumbnail and held it to the end. Then I rolled a second one and lit it.

"How do you do that?" Ellis smiled.

"Cleo taught me." His name sounded rough on my tongue. I looked at Ellis, checking for pain and we puffed smoke in unison.

"Ready to lose?" Ellis was an ungainly Sasquatch, flailing and eventually hitting himself in the face with the ball.

"Lord, Lord, Lord, man, you expect me to help you? I got nothing to work with. Are you sure we're related?" I couldn't help laughing. We ground out our smokes on the driveway and I threw the butts in the garage trash.

"C'mon now." Ellis rubbed his nose. "Everyone will be here tomorrow; I need to *shine*." He waved at a passing car.

"Okay, well first of all, you need to control the ball." I jogged after the ball that was bouncing through the lawn. "Let's just practice that." I was astonished that I didn't miss coaching as I dreaded I would. I heaved a sigh of relief as I chased the ball. Any area of life that could be grief-free, I welcomed. As I prepared to help Ellis, I was proud of my sports and coaching abilities and my knowledge that were second nature. My acceptance of my career loss was a bright surprise made more so by the contrast of my having expected deep misery.

"Naw, I want to do some three-pointers, lay-ups, jump shots, all of that." Ellis dodged and weaved.

"I can't work miracles. My advice, make sure I'm on your team. I'll make you look good, okay?"

"Yeah, okay. But can't you show me something flashy?"

"Sure. Do what I say." I tossed Ellis the ball. "Pass to me." The ball hit me in the mouth. "Jesus Christ! Are you retarded?" I tasted blood on my lips.

"Shit, I'm sorry, Nora." Ellis tried to stifle his chuckles. "Are you okay? Let me see."

I waved him away. "Let's you and me lie down here a minute." I stretched out on the sun-warm driveway. Ellis joined me, his knees up.

"Can you pass me the flask without blacking my eye?" I asked. We each had a swallow and lay quiet.

After a few minutes, Ellis asked, "Is this part of the training?"

I ignored him, wiggling my front tooth. "This is loose! You broke my tooth and now I'm going to have to get a gold one and you're going to pay for it."

"Yeah, sure, whatever. I've got a box of gold teeth at the pawn shop that no one came back to get after they pawned them. Take your pick. Just show me some moves so I can smoke those turkeys!"

"Ellis, believe me, you will be awful. I'll do what I can, but you gotta recognize."

"No, Nora, I gotta be smooth. Sayan will be watching and there's our entire family to impress."

"Ellis, you'll just have to settle for being rich and successful with a beautiful wife, a son on the way, and a lovely home."

Ellis sighed, petulant and fidgety. But I felt just right. Quiet and still inside and floating on a little buzz.

"Hey," I said, "let's talk."

Wind blew over us, making me close my eyes and smile. I could smell Sayan's gardenia shrub, the bougainvillea and wisteria that wrestled each other up the trellis that was mounted on the east side of the house and was so thick with bees that to stand next to it, I would always fall into a trance.

"What do you want to talk about?" Ellis's voice was sulky.

"Julia. Cleo."

"Let's not." Ellis let out a heavy sigh.

"No, man, I need to."

"When are you gonna get rid of those sorry tattoos and those raggedy pirate earrings?"

"It will be *after* we talk. Have you heard anything from the police?"

"No. They're investigating all the leads they have. They'll let us know."

"What about the pawn?"

"Drew is running it. I may have to hire," he answered carefully. "You know if you hadn't been wasted and in New Orleans, you would've found all this out at Cleo's funeral reception."

"It's not hurting you any to tell me now. What about Julia?"

"Disappeared. I think her husband hopes she's dead. He paid me in full."

"You saw him?"

"Yeah, I went over there with tapes, receipts, records, and a gun, everything I could think of. But when he saw me, he just went to the safe and got the money. Turns out he's been visited by many unsavory associates of Julia's that he just pays off."

"Good going, cuz."

"But it didn't save Cleo. You're sure she did it too, aren't you?" Ellis asked.

"Yeah, but Cleo said she didn't," I said.

"But it doesn't matter when she's gone."

"What proof do you have?"

Ellis lifted his shoulder. "Don't worry about it."

"Ellis, don't do anything stupid."

"Now who are you to tell me that, killer?"

I stopped breathing.

"She told me. She was hoping for...oh, who knows what. She was desperate. You know what else she said?"

My breath was stuck in my throat.

"She said, 'Ellis Delaney, I like to gamble and I like to fuck. Don't get in my way.'" Ellis laughed ruefully. "Poor Cleo."

"You know I loved Cleo and wish he were alive. But he had a long life. So better him than you. Neither Cleo nor I could live with ourselves if you'd been killed."

Ellis cleared his throat. We didn't look at each other.

"It was Johnny, you know," Ellis said casually.

I raised on my elbow. "The hell you say! I'll never believe that weenie would have the balls to kill anybody."

Ellis laughed. "T-Bone, it don't take no *cojones* to pull a trigger.

And the district attorney called me in as a potential witness in a case they're building against him. It doesn't look good."

I lay down. "I still think it was Julia. She's scarier."

"I know that's right." Ellis laughed. We bumped fists.

"Boo!" Sayan called.

Ellis winked. "That's short for booty," he whispered to me. "Yes, sweet pepper?" he called.

"Come on in here and taste this for us, okay?"

Ellis got up with a groan and dropped the ball to me and I flinched.

"I'll be back," he said.

"Hey, leave that flask." I held up my hand. I lay there, nursing the whiskey with a little bitterness that I hadn't been invited. Eventually, I heard a rattling truck pull close and shut off with a series of coughs. The horn honked until I raised my head.

"My man! Get your wrinkled ass outta there and stop worrying my nerves."

Drew was grinning as he approached, carrying an ancient threadbare carpetbag, his knitting bag, and a few books. He wore clean, faded overalls, a pressed white shirt, a straw boater, and freshly shined black shoes.

"C'mon down here, have a taste." I offered the flask.

"Good to see you here, Nora. Sure is good to see you." Drew set down his books, bags, and hat, then proceeded to lower himself to the ground with a complex series of groans and a three-point system, possibly involving invisible pulleys.

"I need a chair. I am too old for this shit." Drew lay next to me and took a sip from the flask. "Oh, yeah, that fixes me up fine. What are you doing out here?"

"Trying to teach Ellis a little." I spun the ball on my finger.

"Where is he?"

"In there with his Boo."

Drew didn't comment.

"So I hear you're moving into the Big House? That's something."

Drew laughed. "Yeah. No worries. Say, when are you gonna settle down and buy a camp around here?"

My eyes opened wide to the sky. "I doubt I will, old man."

"You're not thinking right. Whatever's out there cannot compare to what you got right here with the people who know you and love you anyway."

We burst into laughter.

"Think about it. For me and Sayan and Ellis and Little Cleo."

"Leave it be, old man."

"Ohhhh, Nora." Drew smacked her hip. "Just *think* about it."

Ellis returned, licking his lips. "Mmm-mmm, I do love sweet potato pie!"

Drew sat up. "They got sweet potato pie in there? I better go on in and see what I can do."

"No, man, nothing's ready yet." Ellis patted his stomach. "Y'all will just have to wait."

"You sorry sucker." Drew grinned. "I gotta put my bags away and everything. I'll see y'all." Drew climbed to standing with considerable difficulty, retrieved his things, and went into the house.

Ellis and I watched and waited, expecting him to come out at a gallop, his stuff scattering and measuring cups and spatulas raining after him. But nothing happened. We shrugged.

"So, let's practice, huh?"

Sighing, I worked harder than I ever had before, coaching Ellis very gradually and very gently. In my career as a coach, I had always just been provided gifted and talented recruits who already knew the game, loved to play, and could handle the ball. Before now, I never realized how easy I had had it, focusing instead on how far they had to go and all their weaknesses. I wished I could pay Ellis the ultimate compliment, "You play like a girl," but he was far from it. "You play like a white male lawyer," maybe I could sincerely say. But Ellis didn't have the rhythm for basketball, a fact that still astonished me. There was a heartbeat to it and you had to hear that, feel it in your blood to really understand the game.

"No, don't jump yet; don't do that one-handed, don't run with the ball, don't try to hang on the basket, and please do not try to fake me out. I can see everything you have done, can do, and will ever do," were some of the orders I shouted as we practiced. I was drenched in sweat. Playing an actual game with a peer wasn't this hard. When my head began throbbing and my knees started shaking, I stopped. "Let's quit for now." I panted.

"C'mon now, I think I've started to get the hang of it. I'm getting goooood." Ellis pounded the ball out of my hand and chased it down the driveway. I shook my head and limped back to the house, cautiously entering the kitchen.

There, on a throne, was Drew, grinning like a cat in the cream, being fed tidbits and having his mouth wiped as he praised each and every treat he was offered by his personal bevy of beautiful handmaids who cooed over him and smiled into his face.

"Jesus H. Christ," I muttered. I staggered into my room, ran a scalding bath, and afterward collapsed into a deep sleep.

CHAPTER TWENTY-NINE

The next day, the day of the big reunion, Sayan and Ellis's home began filling with the warm chatter of family very early. I tossed and turned, burying my head in pillows. I wanted to run out and hug everyone while also wanting to hide in here all day. I felt the familiar ache of loneliness that always signaled to me that it was time to move on. Either to change homes or more likely, to dump whatever girlfriend I was with when this pain infused my soul. I realized this wasn't my home and in spite of what everyone said, there was no place for me. Their lives were healing, knitting seamlessly together after Cleo's death: with Drew moving in and taking over the pawn; Sayan about to have the baby; Ellis having recovered his financial loss and now looking to strengthen his contacts and improve his expensive pawn. Who was I? Nobody. A poor prideless relation sponging room and board and gumming up the works. I had to leave and make my own way again. This had been an excellent rest cure. I truly loved Sayan and Drew and adored my puppy cousin who had grown into such a wise man. I would visit, I promised myself. But now, the shame of staying on began to grow larger than the benefit. I must get my constitution together and get to steppin'.

I got up, my bones heavy and weary with sadness. When would I stop moving? When could I settle in a home, in a woman?

In the bedroom, I removed the hoops from my ears and threw them in the trash. A drunken lark I now hoped would grow over. I put a large rectangular bandage over my tattoos, not to appear more conventional for the family reunion, just to feel more myself. The Nora

I knew who didn't live in a bum's hotel in the Quarter, drinking more than breathing.

I shaved, dressed, and squared my shoulders as I emerged into the joyful fray.

CHAPTER THIRTY

I got surprised into a hugging line and I was passed from hand to hand, arm to arm, moving down the line of relatives. People welcomed me and murmured over my resemblance to Ellis. They patted my back, held my chin, squeezed my shoulder, rubbed my head, punched my arm, and kissed my cheek. I was further surprised by meeting Drew's girlfriend and baby boy. By the end of the gauntlet, I was worn out and weepy.

I escaped outside and crouched between the lilacs and the magnolias, rolling a cigarette with shaking hands.

"POW! You're a dead police!"

I flinched. The tobacco that had been resting in the paper showered to the ground in soft, pulpy flakes. A boy with a toy rifle grinned and ran away. I slumped against the trunk of the magnolia, closed my eyes, and breathed deeply. When I opened them, four little girls clothed in bright dresses and holding hands were staring at me. Their eyes were like chocolate satin and I thought of four Bambis.

"Scram," I said, trying to roll another cigarette.

They didn't move.

"You're not supposed to smoke," one said.

I smiled at them, squinting through the gray cloud. "That's right. I'm not supposed to drink either, so why don't you…" I dug in my pocket for a dollar bill. "Go get your cousin a big, cold gin and tonic?"

"Are you a boy or a girl?" another asked.

I looked at them, suddenly laughing, my heart wide. The girls were clothed in identical brilliant floral dresses: pink, blue, green, and yellow. They were scrubbed and shining, their hair in beaded braids, their skin warm and soft, their plump little feet buckled into blinding white sandals.

"A girl," I replied.

"Okay," one answered before snatching the money and darting away. The others followed, their lacy underpants flashing like bunnies' tails. I heard rumbling bass laughter and knew the men had come outside to advise Ellis and Drew about the proper smoking and grilling of meat.

I smoked, enjoying the shade, the smell of barbeque smoke, and the sound, thinking with comfortable pain about how Cleo would have loved this.

The little girls edged back to me, one holding the drink that was frosty, full of ice and dripping and the other girls tiptoeing alongside with their hands outstretched at the ready to help if needed.

"Here." She held it out to me. I took the wet glass and sniffed. It was gin and tonic with a wedge of lime submerged in the cold, clean depths.

"Who gave this to you?"

"Uncle Drew," they sang in unison.

"Thank you." I drank.

The girls stayed, twisting and shuffling.

"You're not getting a smoke or a drink," I told them gruffly.

"We know, dummy." The little girls giggled. "You want us to do anything else? For money?" They all grinned.

I laughed. "Well now." I dug in my pocket for a twenty-dollar bill. "Here. For this, why don't you fetch me things all day, whenever I ask?"

They gasped, their eyes big and round. "Yes, ma'am," they chorused.

"First order, don't call me ma'am."

"Yes, ma'am," they answered.

"Hey," I said, sitting on the ground. I gestured with my cigarette. "Whose are you? Are you quads?"

The girls looked at each other. "Huh?"

"Who's your mommy? What are your names?"

Pink dress stepped forward with the confidence that comes from familiarity. She had done this many times for parents, teachers, and strangers on the street. "I'm Quanice Charmaine, that's Syncee, that's Lynetta and Coco Tasonda. Syncee is my sister and our mom is Tanitta. Lynetta and Tasonda are sisters and their mom is Ajaunia."

"Are you all twins?"

"No, I'm ten months older than Syncee. Netta and Coco are twins."

"Well, thank you, Quanice."

Syncee, in the blue dress, held out her hand.

I laughed, shaking my head. "I already gave you money and you don't get paid just for answering questions. Now why don't you all go see if there's something to eat?"

"What do you want?" Coco in the green dress asked.

"Whatever's ready."

Three of the girls began to walk away but yellow dress Netta stayed and asked, "Are you Uncle Ellis's sister?"

"No, cousin. I'm Cousin Nora."

The three waited on Netta, whose eyes widened, and upon hearing my name, she screamed and ran, inducing panic and screaming in the others. Shrieking, they fled like a herd of startled gazelles. There was nothing like a little-girl screech to penetrate the very center of the brain.

I drank half of my gin and tonic, trying to cool my echoing head. As I rolled another cigarette, I noticed more black eyes watching me through the lilac branches.

"Come on outta there, fellas," I called, knowing that news of my presence had spread to the boys.

Instead, with a great rustling and clattering, the eyes disappeared. I heard a lot of fierce talking that passed for boys whispering.

"You ask her."

"No, you do it. I can't."

"Let's run."

"No, let's squirt her!"

"I'm a tell it you be in trouble."

I crept up to the lilacs and yelled, "Boo!"

The boys that didn't leap into the air yelling almost fainted. I retreated, chuckling around my cigarette. The boys scampered away.

I took another large swallow of the gin and tonic. "Most excellent," I said, hearing tiny girls giggling.

Quanice bought me a plate. "This is all I could get." There was a spoonful of sweet potatoes and one hot crumbly biscuit.

"Thanks. You're not scared of me?"

Quanice threw out her chest and locked her knees. "I ain't scared of nothing."

"Good." I nodded, closing my eyes in bliss as I bit the biscuit. "Stay that way."

Quanice left and Tasonda brought me a plate. "This is all I could get," she said. On her dish was a small, but still sizzling piece of ham.

"Thank you, darlin'." I smiled.

Tasonda curtsied. "That was funny what you did to those boys," she said and walked away.

Syncee approached with a tiny tablespoon of macaroni and cheese. "Here." I set it next to the others, chewing happily.

"Aren't you going to say thank you?" Syncee asked.

"Thank you," I replied.

"It is impolite to talk with your mouth full," she said and left.

I was eating bits of everything when Netta crept up, holding two fried chicken legs.

"Are both of those for me?" I asked.

Netta shook her head, her eyes large and black and silky.

"Do you want to sit down?"

Again, Netta shook her head, munching on one of the drumsticks.

"Well, what do you want?"

Netta flung the remaining chicken leg into the dirt at my feet and ran away. I picked it up, brushed it off, and bit it with relish. As I looked at my food collection, I realized they were all children's portions. The food had been doled out small because the kitchen ladies thought the food was for the daughters.

I finished everything, stacking the plates and draining my drink, wishing for seconds, thirds, a toothpick, a tit, and a nap.

I closed my eyes, drowsily considered getting up, then rejected the idea. I just loved listening and smelling. There were the lilacs and magnolias scenting the air like candy, the smoke of the grill smelling musky dry and masculine, the clean, fresh scent of newly mown grass, and the sounds. Sounds of men boasting and insulting, children laughing as they played, and occasionally, the rap of a woman's reprimand ringing out. I could only enjoy this from a distance. If I entered the scene, I would change it. I drew immense comfort from it remaining the same and me, an aloof observer in the distance.

"What in the world are you doing hiding out here like a bum with my good dishes?" Sayan cried. "Get up this instant!" She tugged on my arm. "And you've been having my nieces run your errands? Oh, I could whip your hide."

"Let me alone. I like it out here," I said, irritated and cranky at Sayan's everlasting meddling.

"When and if you ever leave my house is the only time I'll let you alone. Come outta there and join the party."

Glowering, I stood.

"Quit your pouting and pick up my wedding china." Sayan rubbed her own back. I did as I was told. Sayan took my arm, leaning on me for support, and led me around to the back deck. "I'll bring you a plate of something myself," she murmured sweetly. She pointed to a large comfy deck chaise. "Look. Saved the best chair for you." I sat, handing the dishes to Sayan. With her free hand, Sayan reached into a bin and plopped a straw hat on my bald skull. "That's to protect your silly old head." She kissed my cheek and went inside.

I was glad for the hat because my cheeks burned with embarrassment. Sayan just undid me. Her fire, her ice, her unexpected kindness kept me off balance.

Ellis, wielding tongs, winked at me. Drew pulled up a chair next to me. "That Sayan is something, ain't she?" He grinned, taking out his knitting.

"She sure is and don't you forget it," Sayan said as she presented me with a plate piled with steaming food. "Are you not supervising any more?"

Drew shook his head. "I've done what I could. Let those amateurs ruin everything."

Sayan laughed. They watched the men crowd around the grill, poking, prodding, suggesting, and shouting. "Men, meat, and fire," she mused, shaking her head as she returned to the kitchen.

The rest of the day, I lay low, comfortable in my chair, coaxed only once to play a game of croquet at which I beat everyone soundly to their good-natured boos. I retreated, smiling, to my chair and enjoyed treats the nieces eagerly brought, their attitudes having changed, I guessed, for the dual reason of seeing Sayan kiss my cheek and not wanting to be asked for their money back. A little boy barely out of diapers sat on my lap for a while, sucking his thumb and going to sleep. His mother, Wynetta, eventually lifted him off me and my lap was then cold from his missing warmth.

Sometimes Sayan passed and rested, leaning her hip against my shoulder for a moment.

The food lived up to my dreams: exquisite juicy barbeque patiently created by Tanitta's husband to the tips and jeers of the other men, rich creamy macaroni and cheese, sunny potato salad, spicy greens, melt-in-your-mouth biscuits, jalapeno skillet cornbread, hopping john, seared ham steaks, curls of fried bologna, dirty rice, cheese grits, sweet potato pie, peach cobbler, apple pie, decadent chocolate cake, and coconut cream pie.

I stuffed myself and indulged in the only remedy for a full belly: a luscious nap.

Drew settled in beside me. "In Haiti we say, now we turn our bellies to the sun. True, no?"

I closed my eyes, and lulled by the sounds of happy family, I relaxed and slept peacefully for the first time since Cleo died.

I woke to Netta jerking my sleeve. "Uncle says wake up. Time to play."

I stretched, rubbed my eyes, and yawned, facing a semicircle of men, watching me. Ellis held the basketball.

The sun was setting in lurid orange.

"Better wipe off that drool," Drew told me.

I grinned, bumping fists with him and rising slowly.

I was tired and the game was fierce. I had forgotten how good street players were, and I was pleased. I set Ellis up for several shots, all but two of which he missed. But he made such a fuss over those two, no one forgot them.

The dark came fast. The only sounds were panting and grunting. Shirts were shed. The ball flashed through the air, through the basket, from man to man, round and round. Pass, dribble, jump. Someone sprained his ankle. Another got an elbow in the eyes. Another hit the pavement bloody. All kept playing hard. After putting away the food, wives came to watch. Sleepy children sank to the grass, nodding. A couple of older boys, yearning to join the game, mimicked the moves on the lawn. Fireflies swooped and soared.

I sank a beauty, staggered back, and said, "Time. I need a smoke." They all groaned.

Sayan stepped up, looking at her watch. "Time is right. Time for y'all to clear out and go on home. The kids are asleep and we are bone weary. Y'all can have a rematch next month. C'mon now."

Ajuania's husband, holding the ball, muttered, "Lucky break," because Ellis's team was ahead. Ellis heard, charged him, and slapped the ball out of his hands, sinking a three-point shot, catching everyone off guard.

There were shouts and protests and the game was back on. Sayan sent me in to break it up.

"Hey!" I ordered in the voice used for recalcitrant, arrogant freshmen. "Knock it off!" I grabbed the ball. "Or I'll make you do laps." I threw the ball and effortlessly swooshed through the net. "Showers!" I barked, catching the ball and smiling at Sayan, whose mouth hung open.

Like obedient pups, the men trotted to their families and the long good-byes began. Ellis was strutting around saying, "I kicked your black ass!" until Sayan pinched his ear and sent him to help load cars.

Sayan's parents approached me. They were imperial. Her father was distinguished with a short, white afro and a matching beard and mustache, the ends of which he waxed into large curls. He was tall and slim with warm intelligent eyes and graceful hands. Her mother wore a towering, intricate headdress, voluminous vivid skirts, and bracelets similar to the one my grandmother gave me. Sayan's mother had cherrywood skin, high cheekbones, and a voluptuous, powerful body. Both of them could still a child or win a war with a look.

Sayan's mother grasped my hand. "I am so glad to have met you. Sayan has shared so many sweet stories with us."

Her father nodded. "I'm sorry we didn't get to spend more time with you." His eyes swept the families busy leaving. "Such a joyful day. I understand you're moving here, so I'll count on seeing you often. Good-bye."

"Good-bye, sir. Good-bye, ma'am," I said, dazed. The royal couple strolled to their vehicle, holding each other close. "Oh, Sayan, dear," I called, annoyed.

"Later, Nora," Sayan replied, smiling as she helped herd children. Drew stayed in the house, washing dishes.

I stood in the driveway, just now noticing the crickets and the frogs calling and calling, filling the night air with song. Sayan returned to the house.

Ubiqua, who I finally placed as the militant dyke at the gay bar, emerged and headed for Ellis. She was holding hands with a stunned-looking man she'd brought and had been showing off all day. I had tried to speak with Ubiqua, but she had deftly avoided me, continually putting food, duties, or people between us.

"You are gonna be a great daddy," Ubiqua said to Ellis, who grinned and kicked the ground. "Children have to have a strong daddy. Or else they turn out bad." She cut her eyes to me. I was listening and rolling a cigarette.

"I've never known girls to turn out right unless they have a good father," Ubiqua said.

"My baby's a boy," Ellis said.

"This one, maybe, but surely, you'll allow a girl or two, right?" Ubiqua punched Ellis lightly. The man at her side was fascinated with my cigarette ritual.

"Sure, sure." Ellis was restless.

"Just look at my family," Ubiqua said. "Seven strong girls and not a freak among them."

I narrowed my eyes and lit my cigarette with a wooden match. "Now just a minute. I seem to remember—"

Ubiqua grabbed her man's hand and kissed it. "Not one freak," she repeated, interrupting me. "I'll see you in church." She and her date left.

"Whatever, Beek, whatever, baby," Ellis muttered, rolling his eyes. Ubiqua and her man were the last to leave, the car's tail lights disappearing in the distance and emphasizing the sudden silence. The yard was so empty.

"How about a game?" Ellis fetched the ball and dribbled it.

"Haven't you had enough, Junior?"

"Nope, c'mon, T, c'mon."

"I'm done. Let's you and me go in back and talk." I led and Ellis followed, whispering a litany of color commentary about the phantom game he played, jumping and feinting.

We sat in deck chairs, the only light coming from the kitchen where we could see grizzled old Drew still washing and rinsing pots and pans that wouldn't fit into the dishwasher. We could see Sayan, alternately helping, bossing, and resting.

"What is it, Nora?" Ellis leaned forward, his hands dangling between his knees itching to pick up the ball at his feet. I enjoyed sitting in the deep blackness, feeling hidden and only visible by the red coal of my cigarette glowing.

"You know I'm grateful for your hand up all this time, right, Ellis?"

Ellis waved me away. "It ain't nothin'. Is that what this is?" He started to stand.

"Wait." My voice was a quiet command. Ellis sat. "This isn't my home. I know everybody thinks I'm gonna stay here, but I'm not, and I want you to know that for sure."

"Why don't you stay? What you need that you ain't got here?"

"I don't know. I don't know where my home is. Maybe I don't have one and never will. Maybe that's what's wrong with me. But I'm leaving. I owe you big for—"

Ellis shook his head. "You know that ain't so," he interjected. We watched Drew and Sayan wipe their hands and share the last piece of coconut cream pie right out of the plate.

"Okay," I continued, "I'm mighty grateful. You saved me in so many ways. I love you. I love Sayan. I love Drew. I loved…" I paused. "I've loved everything here. And I know I don't belong. But I'll visit."

"Sure you will," Ellis said sourly. "Just do me one favor."

"Anything."

"Tell Sayan." Ellis turned and walked to the house.

"The hell I will!" I yelled after him, but he was inside, urging Sayan to come out and speak to me.

I puffed hard on my cigarette, inhaling it to ash by the time Sayan sat down, holding her belly. There was a lone bird chirping in the dark. The air was damp and smelled of magnolias.

"What is it, Nora?" Sayan's voice was serious as if she already knew.

I swallowed, attributing my shaking hands to fatigue. "It's time for me to move on." Silence. I busied myself rolling a new cigarette I didn't want. I willed myself to wait for Sayan.

The bird continued to sing, its solo voice underscoring my loneliness. Finally, Sayan sighed and said, "I know."

I relaxed.

"I've seen it on you. Your skin is itchy; your feet are hot. You need to go."

"I'm sorry," I said for lack of any other ideas.

"You have nothing to be sorry for. I've enjoyed having you here and—" Sayan's voice broke off.

I paused for a while and asked at last, "Are you all right?"

"Shut up," Sayan snapped, sounding nasal.

We sat quiet until Sayan continued, "You need to find a place that fits. This town doesn't fit you. It is perfect for me, but you're not Bayou La Belle D'eau. You go out there and find a place if you can."

My throat tightened. I played with my unlit cigarette. "I'll visit."

Sayan struggled and stood. "If you want to, that's fine. You're always welcome." Her response was nonchalant because we both recognized my lame lie. "Come here, you nasty freak." Sayan embraced me and we held each other. Sayan let me go just before I started to cry, so I was relieved.

Drew came outside. "What the hell's going on? Ellis is mad and stomping around the house, and, Sayan, you're crying and you two are out here talking secrets like thieves. Tell me!" For the first time, I noticed that Drew looked old and small. His mouth was wrinkled and sunken with worry; his back was bowed and his legs were spindly. I wanted to cradle him and give him vigor and strength.

"Nora's moving on, Papa," Sayan said tenderly, using the endearment to soften the news.

"The hell you say," Drew sputtered. Sayan squared her shoulders and returned to the house.

Drew stared at me, his eyes like black fire. He spat on the ground. "Fool!" he yelled, then stomped back inside.

I collapsed into the chair again. "That went well," I said, wishing I had just sneaked out of town. I sat there, watching the stars, listening to that lonesome bird, until sunrise.

CHAPTER THIRTY-ONE

I left that day, in the late afternoon. I packed my trusty Wagoneer and got a thermos of strong chicory coffee and a huge shrimp po' boy from Sayan.

"If it's a girl, I'll name her Nora," Sayan said, smoothing her shirt over her stomach.

"Stop it, Sayan; you're killing me. Whatever you do, don't name her Nora." I bent and put my cheek against Sayan's belly.

I wrung Drew in a hard hug. He only glared at me. Ellis walked me to my car. "Take care," he said, shrugging.

"You too." I smiled. My throat hurt. I was saying good-bye to the sweetest time I had ever known. And I could yet have it. I could still change my mind and stay. I could keep everything and just settle into this happy place. I was leaving a ready-made life with a built-in family and loving community. Why? I didn't know and knew it didn't matter why. I just understood and accepted that I had to do this.

"Don't be a stranger."

"I won't."

"I'll be practicing my game. I'll kick your ass yet, nigga." Ellis smiled, his eyes shining.

"Then you better quit your job and practice."

We hugged. When it was over, Ellis gripped my shoulder. "Don't do anything foolish," he said, willing me to comprehend.

"Not me," I answered, both of us knowing I was on my way to New Orleans to find Julia.

"Need this?" Ellis presented a .38 from his pocket.

"Yeah, maybe." I slipped it into my back pack. "The mosquitoes down here are fierce."

"Well, I'll see ya." Ellis slowly walked back to his home.

"See ya, Hambone," I said. I drove away, willing myself not to look back. I drove to the cemetery where Cleo was laid out in his aboveground tomb. The stone was obscene with new shine. I got out and stared at the stone until my eyes watered. I sat on the ground and stayed there until sunset. I got in my car, put it in gear, and as I saw Bayou La Belle D'eau receding in my rearview mirror, I was in shock and heartsick at making this move, scared about what lay ahead, and clueless about where to go after New Orleans, but I had to move on. All the emotions were only that. The truth of my needing to leave was incontrovertible. I breathed deeply as I drove, forgetting to smoke or drink.

CHAPTER THIRTY-TWO

Once in New Orleans, I didn't bother with a hotel, but I drove straight to the cemetery where I had fucked Julia, and parked on the street. I locked my vehicle and took off toward the Quarter on foot, following my instincts about where to find what I was looking for. Finally, a chord struck my memory and I slowed to a walk, discovering, at last, the bar where I had met Julia before our last date.

Dumbfounded, I stared in, seeing Julia perched on that same stool, drinking and chatting up some poor stupid bastard next to her.

I entered, walked up to her, and wedged in between Julia and the slob. "'Scuse me, dog," I said to him, then to Julia, "Where have you been, baby? I've been at the boneyard with my knife all night. Don't do me this way."

"Say, the lady and I were talking," the man started.

"Pipe down. She's a friend of mine and we need to talk," Julia snapped.

"She?" The man looked me up and down. His lip curled with distaste. "Oh."

"Shove off, man. She needs me," I said as I took the man's bar stool.

"Well, well, well, little Nora, come to call. What brings you here?" Julia was cool and flirtatious.

"I hear you're long gone."

"Nobody but you looks for me here. Ever think of becoming an investigator?" Julia winked.

I signaled the bartender and ordered a Guinness. "Just missed you, darlin'," I replied after taking a big swig and grimacing.

Julia grinned. "Of that, I have no doubt. I am frankly surprised I haven't seen you sooner."

"Well, you know." I licked my lips. "Been busy."

"Mmm-hmm." Julia batted her crossed eyes. "Me too."

Rage sent a thin tendril of red vapor up my throat. I touched Ellis's gun, warmed by my body and feeling good and solid. "Nice jewelry."

"Ha, ha, these old things?"

"What's a nice girl like you doing in a place like this?"

Julia held up her glass to signal for a refill. "Let's get to the point, shall we?"

"Why don't you tell me what that is?"

"Payne did it. She did it because I told her to."

"She shot him?" I thought of Payne's swivelly hips, her loopy grin, and the gun in her glove box. "Payne did not do it. You think I'm a moron?"

"Shot? Are you mad? I thought you were talking about the jewel switch."

"Why would she do anything at all for you?"

"Oh, she owes me."

"Why?"

"I can't imagine why you're interested in all this. What a bore." Julia tapped my tobacco pouch, indicating she wanted me to roll her one. I rolled two. I reflected on the version Payne had given me when she visited me at the New Orleans Hotel Royale.

Payne sat, straddling a chair, while I spread out like an X on the hotel's dingy, broken-down bed.

Before Payne arrived, I had been lying down, studying Julia's business card, thinking of revenge, and Payne's unexpected visit did not surprise me as I was persistently drunk. When Payne appeared in the open doorway, I dropped the card to the floor, sat up, and invited Payne to sit. I took a huge gulp of gin straight from my bottle and didn't offer Payne any until she wrested it from my grip and tipped the bottom to the ceiling.

She wiped her mouth with her arm, handed back the bottle, and sighed. "What are you doing holed up in this dump, you loser?"

"You want to lecture me? Get in line." I gestured to the hallway.

"Why? Who else?"

"Nobody, just get in line and outta here."

"Funny. Listen, Nora…"

"Quit with that mess. You can stay and drink, but nothing else."

Payne held up her hands. "Fine. You are grown. Hey, what's this?" She picked up the card.

The sounds of an argument on the street drifted up through the windows. Boat-tailed grackles mocked and laughed from the trees.

I stared at my fingers that were moving lazily like seaweed underwater. "Just some strange I met one night."

"You mean you had sex?" Payne grinned, handing the card back to me.

"Sho 'nuff. Or should I say, sho muff?"

Payne laughed. "Oh, man, oh, man."

I rolled to my side, facing Payne. "What?"

"That woman's like a randy poodle looking for a table leg."

"You know her too?"

"Know her? She brought me out."

I laughed. I cocked a bleary eye on Payne. "How many days ago?"

"Four thousand four hundred fifty-five," Payne replied. "I met her when I was working my way through college. She came in, everyone knew who she was. She was rich and bitchy. She was garish, like a Las Vegas showgirl gone crazy with Home Shopping Network jewelry that she put on every available surface."

"She hasn't changed."

"But we struck up a friendship and she seduced me. Kissing her is like kissing the devil. But I love it."

"You still date?"

"Sure. When I'm between engagements."

"Scuzz."

"Julia is what you call rapacious. So I stepped up and took care of it. Or tried. Damn, she was a sexual bottomless pit."

"So to speak."

"Ha ha. She was dependent on me. She was like a clinging vine, strangling me every minute my mouth wasn't actually between her legs."

"You treated her badly?" I knew the answer.

"Of course. What else could I do? She was needy and she took it and begged for more. I treated her as well as she deserved."

"You're a prince."

"You would've done the same." Payne punched my leg. "You probably have."

I grimaced and drank.

Payne stood. "Well, I came to get you outta your little rat hole. What say we go out and get our tongues pierced?" She stuck out her tongue and laughed.

I ran my tongue around the inside of my mouth, imagining a heavy silver stud there. "Shit, that would slow me down."

"How about a tattoo, then?"

"Not drunk enough," I replied, tipping the bottle to my lips again.

"We'll take care of that. Come on, brown sugar."

That's when I pierced my ears and got my tattoos. Payne had been so drunk she had her clit pierced and then passed out on my floor, snoring ripely.

My memory receded and I was back in the fern bar with Julia. "Tell me why she owes you," I said, holding the cigarette like a reward a few inches from Julia's lips. Julia shrugged, closing her juicy, lacquered mouth around the cigarette.

"I met Payne long, long ago..." Julia began.

"Why don't we move to a booth?" I smiled, picking up both of our drinks. "Cozier."

Julia shrugged and followed.

When we settled, I prompted, "You met Payne long ago." I puffed hard on my cigarette.

"Ah, yes. I've known her for a hundred years. She was just a puppy. She was in college and working her way through LSU. What a dear. She was such a cute young thing, as delectable as dessert and twice as sweet. We struck up a friendship and it got so she would just do anything for me." Julia grinned, sipping her drink.

"So you met her when she was a dealer in a casino while you gambled your husband's money. You blinded her with your voracious cunt," I amended. "Continue."

Julia giggled, squeezing my thigh. "You do understand me, Nora. I like that."

"Get on with it," I snarled, not wanting to agree with how well I comprehended crazy women. They were, with all their unpredictability, volatile personalities, danger and lust, as clean and easy as a road map to me.

"Well, we were associates for several years."

"Pussy partners."

"And when she graduated a full-fledged engineer, I gave her a rec and she began working for one of my husband's companies."

"You bullied him into giving her a job she didn't deserve and you two continued your nasty affair."

Julia tittered. "Oh, how you do prattle. I taught her all I know."

"That should've taken about, what," I said, rolling a cigarette. "Fifteen minutes?"

"Step lightly," Julia said, and although she was pleasant, her teeth showed. Her cigarette had gone out because she had merely played with it. She held it out to me and pulled a pouty face so I would relight it. As I was doing so, Julia continued. "Payne attends all the company functions, so I make sure I'm there too. The Christmas party is the best. To this day, I soak my drawers just smelling a pine tree."

I laughed in spite of myself. "The sweetest panty pudding ever, I'm sure. Is that a yeast infection or are you just glad to see me?"

"You know it," Julia said and then her voice went silken. "You remember." She stroked my arm.

"Get your demon hands off me. I don't even know why I'm here. I must be insane."

"You're here because you want to know *why*. And because you're angry," Julia said, hanging on my shoulder and blowing into my ear. "The eternal downfall of the weak and the good. Pursuit of *why*." She chuckled. "Well, I can't help you understand, but I can help you with your big, black cock."

"Back off, skank. My cigarette comes closer to getting me off than you would."

"Even hell doesn't have as much fire as I do when I'm refused."

I faced her, utterly unimpressed. "I fuck who and when I want. And that's a short list right now and you ain't even a runner-up."

Julia ignored this and caressed my shoulder with the new tattoos. "Who's Max?"

"Someone long dead," I lied to keep Julia's dirty fingers off the topic.

"And she broke your heart, so now you wear her name as a scar of honor. How precious." Julia clapped.

"Shut up, bitch." Julia threw the rest of her drink in my face. I stared at her, exasperated. "You ruined a perfectly good smoke. Now what do you want?"

"You know what," Julia said, her eyes blazing.

"No." I grinned. "Suppose you tell me?"

"Suppose you take a wet and wild guess?"

I dropped her soggy cigarette to the table. "I won't."

"Fuck me," Julia breathed, her hips wriggling in her seat and her bosom heaving.

I looked her over and let my mind wonder about it. First, I would refuse to kiss her. I would grab a fist full of Julia's hair, force her to stand and then push her down to all fours.

"Get down there on the bar floor like the dog you are and lick my boots," I would tell her.

Julia, panting, eyes sparkling and round rump high in the air, would bend to comply.

"No." I would step away. "First take off your skirt and panties. Not your blouse and bra, just expose your bitch parts. And lick me clean. I've been in the Quarter."

Julia, scowling, would hesitate. I would cup my own crotch and wag my finger. Julia would whip off her clothes and put her mouth on my boots. I, in spite of my grief and rage, always enjoyed seeing eager ass wagging in the air, aching, waiting…

While Julia licked hard and fast, I would bend over her soft big butt and slap as hard as I could. Julia would cry out, but would keep working. I would continue to hit her, enjoying the sight and the sound. "You finish too fast, you won't get any." Julia whimpered and slowed her bobbing head. "No. I'm not going to. Not this time," I said almost to myself. "I'm different now." I dropped my hands and stepped over the whimpering figure of Julia. "Get up. Dress your sorry ass. I never want to smell you again." I strode away, my head high, my heart thumping. My fantasy dissolved. I was in the booth with Julia.

Julia still stared at me, waiting for my inevitable assent. I had to unstick my tongue from the roof of my mouth. "Nope, hot pants, you've gotta find another damn fool to mess with you." I swallowed the damp washcloth lodged in my throat. I felt Julia's drink dripping from my jaw and drying sticky around my eyes. "I'll never be that desperate again." The images of Cleo, Ellis, Sayan, and Drew gave my lustful jellybones strength. "You're pure poison. You're garbage and I'll never dabble with a trashy slut like you again." Just then I knew I wouldn't kill Julia or even hurt her. The last time I hugged Ellis before I left, I could smell the clean scent of healing on him already. I wanted that too. I was tired of dirt and squalor and filth and games and bad decisions.

Julia's face blanched and tightened. Her crossed cat's eyes smoldered with scorned shame. She left the booth and the bar without another word.

"Guess I'm buying the drinks," I said to myself and shrugged, ignoring my trembling hands. I sat for another half an hour, lost in a tipsy trance, finishing my own Guinness. Finally, I dabbed my face with the tiny, sodden bar napkin. I paid and left, walking quickly to my car, still with no idea what I was doing or where I was going.

Three men stepped out of the mouth of an alley, blocking my way. I could just see my car less than a block away.

"Hey, guys. I don't want any trouble." I held up my hands and tried to sprint away. They grabbed me and dragged me deep into the alley without a sound. One took my gun.

"You want money? Credit cards? I'll give you my wallet and my watch. C'mon now, this ain't cool."

One punched me in the stomach, causing me to double over the sudden knot of agony. All my Guinness came up and splashed on the man's shoes.

"Quiet," the man said, impervious to the vomit.

Heels echoed in a slow staccato. I turned and saw Julia. She was grinning and smug. She leaned against the wall and very slowly and deliberately removed a cigarette from her purse, lit it, and exhaled.

"Oh, my God, you filthy cooze! All this because I wouldn't fuck you? Come on!"

"I warned you, Nora. You're a worthless, uppity nigger and you need to be brought down a few notches." Julia dropped the partly smoked cigarette and ground it beneath her expensive shoes. "I'm going to have pleasure tonight one way or another. And this way will be just fine." Julia shrugged, smiling.

"You're gonna kill me too? Just like you did Cleo?"

One thug clopped my ear, hard. I dropped to the ground, hearing the ocean and shaking my head. I remained on my knees, knowing if I stood, I would only be knocked down again.

"Cleo?" Who the hell is Cleo?" Julia demanded. The sacred name should've burned her infidel tongue.

"My uncle. You went to the pawn the night of the storm and shot him because you thought he was Ellis. Don't you read the papers?"

"I don't *read* the papers, I am *in* the papers."

"So you did it, didn't you? Tell me before I get the shit kicked out of me."

"No, I didn't."

"That's a damn lie."

Julia dismissed me. "Okay, boys. Beat her ass. Make it good. I am urgent hungry tonight." She crossed her legs at the ankle and her arms at her bosom as if waiting for the theatre.

I remembered curling into a comma, feeling the first blows, but not much after that. I realized when I felt a boot smashing into my mouth that evil is faster and quicker than good.

CHAPTER THIRTY-THREE

I tried to move but it was too great an effort. I opened one eye. The other was gummed shut. Blurry streetlights shone in the dark distance. Sirens wailed over someone else's problems. Traffic noise told me that I was flat on my stomach in an alley.

"Jesus," I muttered through my swollen lips. I tasted the dark iron of my own blood. The asphalt was wet and gritty under my cheek. Garbage smells: rotten bananas, dog shit, bad fish assaulted me further. For a second, I thought I would vomit again, but willed it back. I tried breathing deeply and decided I had at least one broken rib. A large shadow darted. A cat or a cockroach, I grimly tried to smile.

Little by little, I turned myself on to my back. "Aaaahhh!" I groaned as I lay there, staring up through the buildings at the stars, so far away and indifferent.

Remaining on my back, I fumbled in my pockets until I found my cigarettes and a wooden match. After my adventure in Tulsa, I had resigned myself to buying cigarettes on the regular. All foolishness of quitting was gone. I flicked my thumbnail across the head of the match and it exploded into tiny fire. I lit my cigarette and inhaled shallow. My crotch felt cold and wet so I touched my pants.

"Lord God, I done pissed myself!" I whispered, shaking my head, my shaven skull rolling back and forth on the ground. Cleo murdered, me, unemployed and homeless. Life was right on track.

And there, laid out on my back in the French Quarter, I started laughing. It started out small and grew to a ripe richness, floating out to mix with the traffic noise.

I eventually stood, and shaking, bleeding, my breathing short and ragged, I limped out of the alley. I unbuckled my wet slacks and left them at the entrance. I found the .38 on the lid of a trash barrel and I tucked it into the waistband of my boxers. My underwear was wet too, but not as heavy as pants, and I had long since stopped caring what I looked like or who saw me. I got to my car and drove to the pawn. I had to find some answers. Not knowing was the snag that kept me from being free. I would give my life for the answer to this one and I didn't give a flying shit what happened to me anymore. Let the killer come for me too. I tore through the crime scene tape and let myself inside. No one had been here since it happened; the awful scene was frozen in time. I stopped by the fridge and got a beer as fortification. I tried to light a cigarette but my hands shook so badly and my eyes swelled so that I couldn't smoke. I got a battery lantern from the storm supply closet because even if the power was hot, I didn't want the lights on, and carrying my bottle, I held my breath and averted my eyes as I carefully stopped over the blood stain to get to the back room. In that mountain of dirt Ellis collected, there had to be something.

I set the lamp on one of the filing cabinets and looked around. There were eviscerated envelopes everywhere and no blood, so there had been no struggle in here. How would I ever find anything in this wild mess?

I wouldn't. I went to the safe. It was securely locked. Damn! I tried to guess the combination. Ellis's birthday, Sayan's, mine, their anniversary, the pawn street number. I tried Cleo's birthday and heard a deeply satisfying click. I swung the thick door open and pawed randomly through the envelopes, willing the right one to catch my eye. My hand stopped on one marked PP. I tore it open and poured the papers on the floor. There she was in all her glory—Payne Phillips. Crooked undercover New Orleans police officer. Drug busts and "lost" evidence and missing property and a very healthy gambling debt. Jesus Christ. And Johnny Fallana gave Ellis all the info. So was Johnny dead now too? I held my head in my hands. Mother Mary, I thought this shit happened only in the movies. Well, nothing left to do but go see Payne for the coup de grâce. I patted the gun and drove by Johnny's house, since it was close to the pawn, to see what was up. Attached to the trees were pieces of crime scene tape fluttering and flapping in the wind. His house was dark and looked deserted. I called Ellis. "Do you have Payne's address? Give it to me."

"Why?"

"Don't do this, Ellis. Gimme her address."

"Nora, don't do anything foolish, hear? The police are all over this thing."

"Fuck that! Gimme her goddamn address!"

"I can't. I won't. I gave you that gun to defend yourself, not to kill. Nora, for real, you don't want to do anything you'll—"

I hung up. I drove to Filly's house and pounded on her front door until she answered.

"Nora," Carol said coldly. "What do you want?"

"We're going for a ride." I grabbed her and dragged her to my car.

"Wait, I'm in my nightgown. I need to lock up."

I shoved her in, locked and slammed the door. She stayed put. When I got in, I demanded, "Where does Payne live?"

"What?"

I almost slapped her. "Something wrong with your hearing? *Where does Payne live?*"

"Is that all you want?" Carol turned red. "I can write it down for you."

I drove away with a jerk. "No, you're coming with me." Following Carol's directions, we crossed the bridge from Orleans Parish into Jefferson Parish and Gretna, with Carol needling me for info the entire time.

"Listen, we're not playing whiny questions, so just cool it," I said, pulling up my shirt to reveal the gun butt. Carol fell silent.

At last, she said, "There it is."

I parked and put the pistol to Carol's head. "All I need you to do is go in there with me. Everything is okay, but you need to do as I say." Carol nodded.

We rang Payne's bell and she opened the door without a word and without surprise. My blood turned to poison at the sight of her. She closed the door behind us and we all sat in the living room. I held Carol close, the gun barrel poking her kidney. I flung the envelope at Payne's feet. "There's what you killed Cleo for."

"Huh?" Payne sipped from a cocktail.

"Does everyone have a motherfucking hearing problem?" I brought out the gun. "Admit it to my face."

Payne raised her chin to Carol. "Why is she here?"

"Insurance." I cocked the pistol.

"Don't do it!" Carol cried.

"Shut up," Payne said. "Nora, I didn't kill Cleo and I already got what I need." She reached under a couch cushion and withdrew an identical envelope. "So you're all wrong."

"Open it. Ellis outsmarted you."

Payne tore open her envelope and moaned as she rifled through the thick sheaf of blank pages. Payne started to grab the envelope at her feet.

"Do it and you're dead." I said.

Carol whispered, "Come on, Nora, use your head."

"Confess," I ordered Payne.

"Fuck you." she replied. Then Payne drained her glass. "Why should I tell you anything?"

"Because I said so. And you know you want to."

"Payne, did you?" Carol said.

"Fuck both of y'all." Payne dove for the envelope and I shot a bullet into her couch. Carol screamed and covered her face.

"You think I'm playin'?" I shouted.

Payne met my stare. "No, I don't think you're playing. But I'm not either."

"Then it looks like there are some hard decisions to be made." I grabbed Carol by the hair, pulled her into my lap, and put the pistol against her temple. "Your move."

Carol began crying. "Payne, tell her what she wants to know. Please, Nora, don't do this. Payne, help me! Nora, don't, please."

Payne calmly put a cigarette in her mouth, lit it, took a drag, and on her exhale said, "All right, I did it. Satisfied?"

"Oh, yeah," I replied. "That makes everything better." I released Carol and shoved her to sitting up again. "Why?"

Payne shrugged. "Ellis was being a hard-nosed, tough-assed bastard and everything was beginning to crumble. I just needed a little more time, a little more scratch..." She shook her head at the near miss of her fortunes. "So I went to get what's mine and he got in the way." Payne spread her hands apologetically. "I thought he was Ellis, I swear."

"That's sweet." I snapped. Carol continued to weep softly. "Shut the fuck up!" I bellowed at her. "You kill Johnny too?"

"Nope. He set me up, so he's taking the fall for all of this. I made sure his house was loaded and *lousy* with evidence so that even a rookie beat cop could find it. Hell will freeze before he sees daylight." Payne chuckled.

"Okay, thanks." I stood and held out my hand for the envelope that Payne still held. She shook her head. I raised the gun and hit her across the mouth so hard, I felt a jolt of pain in my shoulder. I saw a white Chiclet tooth go flying. I removed the envelope from Payne's loose grasp. Then, with an eagle scream, I emptied my gun into the couch cushion next to Payne. God, that felt good! Then I jerked Carol off the couch and jogged to my car. Carol balked at getting in.

"Oh, relax. I'll give you a ride home." I was twitching with adrenaline.

Carol got in and I heard Payne's front door open.

"Shut the door!" I yelled at Carol and then jumped in the driver's side and took off as I heard Payne start shooting at us. "Stay low!" I swerved crazily, hoping Payne wouldn't hit a tire. As a police officer, she should have excellent marksmanship, but who knew how drunk and sloppy she would be tonight. We escaped with only auto body damage. I shoved Carol out of the car at her house and sped away without comment.

I drove straight to Ellis's. I called ahead, waking him up. In a whisper, he agreed to meet me outside in the street.

"There's your killer." I handed him the envelope. "And you better do something about it or you'll be dead before sunrise." I gave him the gun back. "I killed her couch, so I will ditch this for you if you want me to."

Ellis shook his head and pocketed the gun in his dressing gown.

EPILOGUE

I was thirty-six when I left the big city for the Big Easy. They say New Orleans is like a woman—beautiful, deceitful, and deadly. All I know is, I had to leave Los Angeles on the run and the Crescent City beckoned like a broad on her back. To me, Louisiana remained a country all its own. Half water, half land, half light, half shadow, half evil, half good, half beautiful, half frightening. But mostly I remembered the food and laughter.

About the Author

Clara Nipper is a writer living in Tulsa, Oklahoma. Her book *Femme Noir* was released in September 2009 from Bold Strokes Books. She is currently working on a new murder mystery involving a horndog homicide detective, tentatively titled *Murder on the Rocks*. Clara's hobbies include fanatical gardening, candy-making for her artisan company, Andy's Candies (www.andyscandies.org), and skating as a jammer assassin under the name Catnip for Tulsa Derby Brigade (www.derbystrong.com). Clara also enjoys wrestling plot lines into reluctant submission and collecting particularly creative rejection letters. Contact Clara at www.claranipper.com.

Books Available From Bold Strokes Books

The Devil be Damned by Ali Vali. The fourth book in the best-selling Cain Casey Devil series. (978-1-60282-159-0)

Descent by Julie Cannon. Shannon Roberts and Caroline Davis compete in the world of world-class bike racing and pretend that the fire between them is just professional rivalry, not desire. (978-1-60282-160-6)

Kiss of Noir by Clara Nipper. Nora Delany is a hard-living, sweet-talking woman who can't say no to a beautiful babe or a friend in danger—a darkly humorous homage to a bygone era of tough broads and murder in steamy New Orleans. (978-1-60282-161-3)

Under Her Skin by Lea Santos. Supermodel Lilly Lujan hasn't a care in the world, except life is lonely in the spotlight—until Mexican gardener Torien Pacias sees through Lilly's facade and offers gentle understanding and friendship when Lilly most needs it. (978-1-60282-162-0)

Fierce Overture by Gun Brooke. Helena Forsythe is a hard-hitting CEO who gets what she wants by taking no prisoners when negotiating—until she meets a woman who convinces her that charm may be the way to win a battle, and a heart. (978-1-60282-156-9)

Trauma Alert by Radclyffe. Dr. Ali Torveau has no trouble saying no to romance until the day firefighter Beau Cross shows up in her ER and sets her carefully ordered world aflame. (978-1-60282-157-6)

Wolfsbane Winter by Jane Fletcher. Iron Wolf mercenary Deryn faces down demon magic and otherworldly foes with a smile, but she's defenseless when healer Alana wages war on her heart. (978-1-60282-158-3)

Little White Lie by Lea Santos. Emie Jaramillo knows relationships are for other people, and beautiful women like Gia Mendez don't belong anywhere near her boring world of academia—until Gia sets out to convince Emie she has not only brains, but beauty...and that she's the only woman Gia wants in her life. (978-1-60282-163-7)

Witch Wolf by Winter Pennington. In a world where vampires have charmed their way into modern society, where werewolves walk the streets with their beasts disguised by human skin, Investigator Kassandra Lyall has a secret of her own to protect. She's one of them. (978-1-60282-177-4)

Do Not Disturb by Carsen Taite. Ainsley Faraday, a high-powered executive, and rock music celebrity Greer Davis couldn't be less well suited for one another, and yet they soon discover passion has a way of designing its own future. (978-1-60282-153-8)

From This Moment On by PJ Trebelhorn. Devon Conway and Katherine Hunter both lost love and neither believes they will ever find it again—until the moment they meet and everything changes. (978-1-60282-154-5)

Vapor by Larkin Rose. When erotic romance writer Ashley Vaughn decides to take her research into the bedroom for a night of passion with Victoria Hadley, she discovers that fact is hotter than fiction. (978-1-60282-155-2)

Wind and Bones by Kristin Marra. Jill O'Hara, award-winning journalist, just wants to settle her deceased father's affairs and leave Prairie View, Montana, far, far behind—but an old girlfriend, a sexy sheriff, and a dangerous secret keep her down on the ranch. (978-1-60282-150-7)

Nightshade by Shea Godfrey. The story of a princess, betrothed as a political pawn, who falls for her intended husband's soldier sister, is a modern-day fairy tale to capture the heart. (978-1-60282-151-4)

Vieux Carré Voodoo by Greg Herren. Popular New Orleans detective Scotty Bradley just can't stay out of trouble—especially when an old flame turns up asking for help. (978-1-60282-152-1)

The Pleasure Set by Lisa Girolami. Laney DeGraff, a successful president of a family-owned bank on Rodeo Drive, finds her comfortable life taking a turn toward danger when Theresa Aguilar, a sleek, sexy lawyer, invites her to join an exclusive, secret group of powerful, alluring women. (978-1-60282-144-6)

A Perfect Match by Erin Dutton. The exciting world of pro golf forms the backdrop for a fast-paced, sexy romance. (978-1-60282-145-3)

Father Knows Best by Lynda Sandoval. High school juniors and best friends Lila Moreno, Meryl Morganstern, and Caressa Thibodoux plan to make the most of the summer before senior year. What they discover that amazing summer about girl power, growing up, and trusting friends and family more than prepares them to tackle that all-important senior year! (978-1-60282-147-7)

The Midnight Hunt by L.L. Raand. Medic Drake McKennan takes a chance and loses, and her life will never be the same—because when she wakes up after surviving a life-threatening illness, she is no longer human. (978-1-60282-140-8)

Long Shot by D. Jackson Leigh. Love isn't safe, which is exactly why equine veterinarian Tory Greyson wants no part of it—until Leah Montgomery and a horse that won't give up convince her otherwise. (978-1-60282-141-5)

In Medias Res by Yolanda Wallace. Sydney has forgotten her entire life, and the one woman who holds the key to her memory, and her heart, doesn't want to be found. (978-1-60282-142-2)

Awakening to Sunlight by Lindsey Stone. Neither Judith or Lizzy is looking for companionship, and certainly not love—but when their lives become entangled, they discover both. (978-1-60282-143-9)

Fever by VK Powell. Hired gun Zakaria Chambers is hired to provide a simple escort service to philanthropist Sara Ambrosini, but nothing is as simple as it seems, especially love. (978-1-60282-135-4)

Truths by Rebecca S. Buck. Two women separated by two hundred years are connected by fate and love. (978-1-60282-146-0)

High Risk by JLee Meyer. Can actress Kate Hoffman really risk all she's worked for to take a chance on love? Or is it already too late? (978-1-60282-136-1)

Spanking New by Clifford Henderson. A poignant, hilarious, unforgettable look at life, love, gender, and the essence of what makes us who we are. (978-1-60282-138-5)

Missing Lynx by Kim Baldwin and Xenia Alexiou. On the trail of a notorious serial killer, Elite Operative Lynx's growing attraction to a mysterious mercenary could be her path to love—or to death. (978-1-60282-137-8)

Magic of the Heart by C.J. Harte. CEO Susan Hettinger and wild, impulsive rock star M.J. Carson couldn't be more different if they tried—but opposites attract in ways neither woman can resist. (978-1-60282-131-6)

Ambereye by Gill McKnight. Jolie Garoul is falling in love with her assistant. The big problem is, Jolie is a werewolf. (978-1-60282-132-3)

Collision Course by C.P. Rowlands. Tragedy leaves Brie O'Malley and Jordan Carter fearful and alone. Can they find the courage to take a second chance on love? (978-1-60282-133-0)

Mephisto Aria by Justine Saracen. Opera singer Katherina Marov's destiny may be to repeat the mistakes of her father when she becomes involved in a dangerous love affair. (978-1-60282-134-7)

Battle Scars by Meghan O'Brien. Returning Iraq war veteran Ray McKenna struggles with the battle scars that can only be healed by love. (978-1-60282-129-3)

Chaps by Jove Belle. Eden Metcalf wants nothing more than to flee from her troubled past and travel the open road—until she runs into rancher Brandi Cornwell. (978-1-60282-127-9)

Lightbearer by John Caruso. Lucifer dares to question the premise of creation itself and reveals that sin may be all that stands between us and living hell. (978-1-60282-130-9)

The Seeker by Ronica Black. FBI profiler Kennedy Scott battles ghosts from her past, deadly obsession, and the evil that haunts her. (978-1-60282-128-6)

Power Play by Julie Cannon. Businesswomen Tate Monroe and Victoria Sosa are at odds in the boardroom, but not in the bedroom. (978-1-60282-125-5)

The Remarkable Journey of Miss Tranby Quirke by Elizabeth Ridley. When love enters Tranby's life in the form of a beautiful nineteen-year-old student, Lysette McDonald, she embarks on the most remarkable journey of all. (978-1-60282-126-2)

Returning Tides by Radclyffe. Insurance investigator Ashley Walker faces more than a dangerous opponent when she returns to the town, and the woman, she left behind. (978-1-60282-123-1)

Veritas by Anne Laughlin. When the hallowed halls of academia become the stage for murder, newly appointed Dean Beth Ellis's search for the truth leads her to unexpected discoveries about her own heart. (978-1-60282-124-8)

The Pleasure Planner by Larkin Rose. Pleasure purveyor Bree Hendricks treats love like a commodity until Logan Delaney makes Bree the client in her own game. (978-1-60282-121-7)

everafter by Nell Stark and Trinity Tam. Valentine Darrow is bitten by a vampire on her way to propose to her lover Alexa Newland, and their lives and love are placed in mortal jeopardy. (978-1-60282-119-4)

Summer Winds by Andrews & Austin. When Maggie Turner hires a ranch hand to help work her thousand acres, she never expects to be attracted to the very young, very female Cash Tate. (978-1-60282-120-0)

Beggar of Love by Lee Lynch. Jefferson is the lover every woman wants to be—or to have. A revealing saga of lesbian sexuality. (978-1-60282-122-4)

The Seduction of Moxie by Colette Moody. When 1930s Broadway actress Violet London meets speakeasy singer Moxie Valette, she is instantly attracted and her Hollywood trip takes an unexpected turn. (978-1-60282-114-9)

Goldenseal by Gill McKnight. When Amy Fortune returns to her childhood home, she discovers something sinister in the air—but is former lover Leone Garoul stalking her or protecting her? (978-1-60282-115-6)

Romantic Interludes 2: Secrets edited by Radclyffe and Stacia Seaman. An anthology of sensual lesbian love stories: passion, surprises, and secret desires. (978-1-60282-116-3)

Femme Noir by Clara Nipper. Nora Delaney meets her match in Max Abbott, a sex-crazed dame who may or may not have the information Nora needs to solve a murder—but can she contain her lust for Max long enough to find out? (978-1-60282-117-0)

The Reluctant Daughter by Lesléa Newman. Heartwarming, heartbreaking, and ultimately triumphant—the story every daughter recognizes of the lifelong struggle for our mothers to really see us. (978-1-60282-118-7)

Erosistible by Gill McKnight. When Win Martin arrives at a luxurious Greek hotel for a much-anticipated week of sun and sex with her new girlfriend, she is stunned to find her ex-girlfriend, Benny, is the proprietor. Aeros Ebook. (978-1-60282-134-7)

Looking Glass Lives by Felice Picano. Cousins Roger and Alistair become lifelong friends and discover their sexuality amidst the backdrop of twentieth-century gay culture. (978-1-60282-089-0)

Breaking the Ice by Kim Baldwin. Nothing is easy about life above the Arctic Circle—except, perhaps, falling in love. At least that's what pilot Bryson Faulkner hopes when she meets Karla Edwards. (978-1-60282-087-6)

It Should Be a Crime by Carsen Taite. Two women fulfill their mutual desire with a night of passion, neither expecting more until law professor Morgan Bradley and student Parker Casey meet again…in the classroom. (978-1-60282-086-9)

Rough Trade edited by Todd Gregory. Top male erotica writers pen their own hot, sexy versions of the term "rough trade," producing some of the hottest, nastiest, and most dangerous fiction ever published. (978-1-60282-092-0)

The High Priest and the Idol by Jane Fletcher. Jemeryl and Tevi's relationship is put to the test when the Guardian sends Jemeryl on a mission that puts her not only in harm's way, but back into the sights of a previous lover. (978-1-60282-085-2)